A Young Macedonian in the Army of Alexander the Great

A Historical Fiction of Ancient Greece

By Alfred John Church

PANTIANOS
CLASSICS

Published by Pantianos Classics

ISBN-13: 978-1-78987-009-1

First published in 1912

Contents

A Wrong...5

A Revenge 8

Preparations 14

At Troy 20

At the Granicus 23

Halicarnassus 28

Memnon...33

At Sea 37

In Greece Again 44

At Athens...50

A Perilous Voyage..54

On the Wrong Side 60

Damascus 65

Manasseh The Jew...70

Andromaché 75

To Jerusalem...78

Tyre 82

The Escape..88

The High Priest...92

From Tyre to The Tigris...97

Arbela 101

At Babylon 107

A Glimpse into The Future..112

Vengeance...117

Darius 121

Invalided 125

News from The East 128

The End..134

THE visit of Alexander to Jerusalem is recorded by Josephus only. The fact that it is not mentioned by Arrian, who had contemporary diaries before him, by Quintus Curtius, or by Diodorus Siculus, certainly throws some doubt upon it. But it must be remembered that Jerusalem was not more interesting than any other Syrian town to these writers. Bishop Westcott thinks that Josephus's narrative may be true, and I am content to make this opinion my defence for introducing the incident into my story.

A.C.

A Wrong

THE "Boys' Foot-race" at the great games of Olympia, celebrated now for the one hundred and eleventh time since the epoch of Corœbus, has just been run, and the victor is about to receive his crown of wild olive. The herald proclaims with a loud voice, "Charidemus, son of Callicles of Argos, come forward, and receive your prize!" A lad, who might have been thought to number seventeen or eighteen summers, so tall and well grown was he, but who had really only just completed his fifteenth year, stepped forward. His face was less regularly handsome than those of the very finest Greek type, for the nose was more arched, the chin more strongly marked, and the forehead more square, than a sculptor would have made them in moulding a boy Apollo; still the young Charidemus had a singularly winning appearance, especially now that a smile shone out of his frank blue eyes and parted lips, lips that were neither so full as to be sensual, nor so thin as to be cruel. The dark chestnut curls fell clustering about his neck, for the Greek boy was not cropped in the terrier fashion of his English successor, and the ruddy brown of his clear complexion showed a health nurtured by clean living and exercise. A hum of applause greeted the young athlete, for he had many friends among the young and old of Argos, and he was remarkable for the worth that—

"appears with brighter shine
When lodged within a worthy shrine"

—a charm which commends itself greatly to the multitude. As Charidemus approached the judges a lad stepped forward from the throng that surrounded the tribunal, and exclaimed, "I object."

All eyes were turned upon the speaker. He was immediately recognized as the competitor who had won the second place, a good runner, who might have hoped for victory in ordinary years, but who had had no chance against the extraordinary fleetness of the young Argive. He was of a well-set, sturdy figure; his face, without being at all handsome, was sufficiently pleasing, though just at the moment it had a look which might have meant either sullenness or shame.

"Who is it that speaks?" said the presiding judge. "Charondas, son of Megasthenes, of Thebes," was the answer.

"And what is your objection?" asked the judge.

"I object to Charidemus, alleged to be of Argos, because he is a barbarian."

The sensation produced by these words was great, even startling. There could scarcely be a greater insult than to say to any one who claimed to be a Greek that he was a barbarian. Greeks, according to a creed that no one

5

ght of questioning, were the born rulers and masters of the world, for
m everything had been made, and to whom everything belonged; bar-
arians were inferior creatures, without human rights, who might be permitted to exist if they were content to minister to the well-being of their masters, but otherwise were to be dealt with as so many noxious beasts.

An angry flush mounted to the young runner's face. A fierce light flashed
from his eyes, lately so smiling, and the red lips were set firmly together. He
had now the look of one who could make himself feared as well as loved. His
friends were loud in their expressions of wrath. With an emphatic gesture of
his hand the judge commanded silence. "Justify your words," he said to the
Theban lad.

For a few moments Charondas stood silent. Then he turned to the crowd,
as if looking for inspiration or help. A man of middle age stepped forward
and addressed the judge.

"Permit me, sir, on behalf of my son, whose youth and modesty hinder him
from speaking freely in your august presence, to make a statement of facts."

"Speak on," said the judge, "but say nothing that you cannot prove. Such
charges as that which we have just heard may not be lightly brought."

"I allege that Charidemus, said to be of Argos, is not in truth the son of Callicles, but is by birth a Macedonian."

The word "Macedonian" produced almost as much sensation as had been
made by the word "barbarian." The Macedonians were more than suspected
of compassing the overthrow of Greek liberties.

"Where is your proof?" asked the judge.

"There will be proof sufficient if your august tribunal will summon Callicles himself to appear before it and make confession of what he knows."

The judge accordingly commanded that Callicles should be called. The
summons was immediately obeyed. A man who was approaching old age,
and whose stooping form and shrunken limbs certainly showed a striking
contrast to the blooming vigour of Charidemus, stood before the judges. The
president spoke.

"I adjure you, by the name of Zeus of Olympia, that you tell the truth. Is
Charidemus indeed your son?"

The man hesitated a moment. "I adopted Charidemus in his infancy."

"That proves your affection, but not his race," said the judge in a stern
voice. "Tell us the truth, and prevaricate no more."

"He was the son of my sister."

"And his father?"

"His father was Caranus of Pella."

"A Macedonian, therefore."

"Yes, a Macedonian."

"Why then did you enter him as your son for the foot-race?"

"Because I had adopted him with all due formalities, and in the eye of the
law he is my son."

"But that did not make him a Greek of pure descent, such as by the imme-
morial custom of these games he is bound to be."

A hum of approval went round the circle of spectators, whilst angry glanc-
es were cast at the Argive and his adopted son. Only the sanctity of the spot
prevented a show of open violence, so hateful had the name of Macedonian
become.

Callicles began to gather courage now that the secret was out. He addressed the judges again.

"You forget, gentlemen, that in the time of the war with the Persians Alexander of Macedon was permitted to compete in the chariot-race."

"True," replied the judge, "but then he showed an unbroken descent from
the hero Achilles."

"Just so," rejoined Callicles, "and Caranus was of the royal kindred."

"The blood may easily have become mixed during the hundred and forty
years which have passed since the days of Alexander. Besides, that which
may be accepted as a matter of notoriety in the case of a king must be duly
proved when a private person is concerned. Have you such proof at hand in
regard to this youth?"

Callicles was obliged to confess that he had not. The presiding judge then
intimated that he would consider the matter with his colleagues, and give the
decision of the court probably in less than an hour. As a matter of fact, the
consultation was a mere formality. After a few minutes the judges reap-
peared, and the president announced their decision.

"We pronounce Charidemus to be disqualified as having failed to prove
that he is of Hellenic descent, and adjudge the prize to Charondas the Theban. We fine Callicles of Argos five minas for having made a false representation."

Loud applause greeted this judgment. Such was the feeling in force at that
time that any affront that could be offered to a Macedonian was eagerly welcomed by a Greek audience. Very likely there were some in the crowd who
had felt the touch of Philip's "silver spears." If so, they were even louder than
their fellows in their expressions of delight.

It would be difficult to describe the feelings of dismay and rage which
filled the heart of the young Charidemus as he walked away from the tribunal. As soon as he found himself alone he broke out into a violent expression
of them. "A curse on these cowardly Greeks," he cried; "I am heartily glad
that I am not one of them. By Zeus, if I could let out the half of my blood that
comes from them I would. They dare not meet us in the field, and they revenge themselves for their defeats by insults such as these. By Ares, they
shall pay me for it some day; especially that clumsy lout, who filches by craft
what he could not win by speed."

If he had seen the way in which the young Theban received the prize that
had been adjudged to him in this unsatisfactory way, he would have thought
less hardly of him. Charondas had been driven into claiming the crown; but

he hated himself for doing it. Gladly would he have refused to receive it; glad-ly, even—but such an act would have been regarded as an unpardonable im-piety—would he have thrown the chaplet upon the ground. As it was, he was compelled to take and wear it, and, shortly afterwards, to sit out the banquet given by his father in his honour. But he was gloomy and dissatisfied, as little like as possible to a successful competitor for one of the most coveted dis-tinctions in Greek life. As soon as he found himself at liberty he hastened to the quarters of Charidemus and his father, but found that they were gone. Perhaps it was as well that the two should not meet just then. It was not long before an occasion arose which brought them together.

A Revenge

FOUR years later Charidemus found the opportunity of revenge for which he had longed in the bitterness of his disappointment. It was the even-ing of the day which had seen the fall of Thebes. He had joined the army, and, though still full young to be an officer, had received the command of a com-pany from Alexander, who had heard the story of his young kinsman, and had been greatly impressed by his extraordinary strength and agility. He had fought with conspicuous courage in the battle before the walls, and in the assault by which the town had been carried. When the savage sentence which Alexander permitted his Greek allies to pass on the captured city, had been pronounced, the king called the young man to him. "Thebes," he said, "is to be destroyed; but there is one house which I should be a barbarian indeed if I did not respect, that is the house of Pindar the poet. Take this order to Perdiccas. It directs him to supply you with a guard of ten men. I charge you with the duty of keeping the house of Pindar and all its inmates from harm."

Charidemus saluted, and withdrew. He found no great difficulty in per-forming his duty. The exception made by the Macedonian king to the general order of destruction was commonly known throughout the army, and the most lawless plunderer in it knew that it would be as much as his life was worth not to respect the king's command. Accordingly the flag, which, with the word "Sacred" upon it, floated on the roof of the house, was sufficient protection, and the guard had nothing to do.

The young officer's first care had been to ascertain who were the inmates of the house that were to have the benefit of the conqueror's exemption. He found that they were an old man, two women of middle age who were his daughters, and a bright little boy of some six years, the child of another daughter now deceased. He assured them of their safety, and was a little sur-prised to find that even after two or three days had passed in absolute secu-rity, no one attempting to enter the house, the women continued to show lively signs of apprehension. Every sound seemed to make them start and tremble; and their terror seemed to come from some nearer cause than the thought of the dreadful fate which had overtaken their country.

On the fifth day the secret came out. For some reason or other Charidemus was unusually wakeful during the night. The weather was hot, more than commonly so for the time of year, for it was now about the middle of September, and, being unable to sleep, he felt that a stroll in the garden would be a pleasant way of beguiling the time. It wanted still two hours of sunrise, and the moon, which was some days past the full, had only just risen. He sat down on a bench which had been conveniently placed under a drooping plane, and began to meditate on the future, a prospect full of interest, since it was well known that the young king was preparing for war against Persia. His thoughts had begun to grow indistinct and unconnected, for the sleep which had seemed impossible in the heated bed-chamber began to steal over him in the cool of the garden, when he was suddenly roused by the sound of a footstep. Himself unseen, for he was entirely sheltered from view by the boughs of the plane-tree, he commanded a full view of the garden. It was not a little to his surprise that in a figure which moved silently and swiftly down one of the side paths he recognized the elder of the two daughters of the house. She had with her, he could perceive, an elderly woman, belonging to the small establishment of slaves, who carried a basket on her arm. The lower end of the garden was bounded by a wall; beyond this wall the ground rose abruptly, forming indeed part of one of the lower slopes of the Acropolis. It puzzled him entirely when he tried to conjecture whither the women were going. That they should have left the house at such an hour was a little strange, and there was, he knew, no outlet at that end of the garden; for, having, as may be supposed, plenty of time on his hands, he had thoroughly explored the whole place. Watching the two women as far as the dim light permitted, he lost sight of them when they reached the laurel hedge which served as an ornamental shelter for the wall. His instincts as a gentleman forbade him to follow them; nor did he consider it part of his military duty to do so. Nevertheless, he could not help feeling a strong curiosity when about an hour afterwards the two women returned. With the quick eye of a born soldier, he observed that the basket which the attendant carried swung lightly on her arm. It was evident that it had been brought there full, and was being carried back empty. He watched the two women into the house, and then proceeded to investigate the mystery. At first sight it seemed insoluble. Everything looked absolutely undisturbed. That the women could have clambered over the wall was manifestly impossible. Yet where could they have been? If, as he supposed, the basket had been emptied between their going and their returning, what had been done with its contents? They were certainly not above ground, and they had not been buried—in itself an unlikely idea—for the soil was undisturbed. He had walked up and down the length of the wall some half-dozen times, when he happened to stumble over the stump of an old laurel tree which was hidden in the long grass. In the effort

9

to save himself from falling he struck his hand against the brick wall with some smartness, and fancied that a somewhat hollow sound was returned. An idea struck him, and he wondered that it had not occurred to him before. Might there not be some hidden exit in the wall? There was too little light for him to see anything of the kind, but touch might reveal what the sight could not discover. He felt the surface carefully, and after about half-an-hour's diligent search, his patience was rewarded by finding a slight indentation which ran perpendicularly from about a foot off the top to the same distance from the bottom. Two similar horizontal indentations were more easily discovered. There was, it was evident, a door in the wall, but it had been skillfully concealed by a thin layer of brick-work, so that to the eye, and even to the touch, unless very carefully used, it suggested no difference from the rest of the surface. This discovery made, another soon followed, though it was due more to accident than to any other cause. The door opened with a spring, the place of which was marked by a slight hollow in the surface. Charidemus stumbled, so to speak, upon it, and the door opened to his touch. It led into an underground passage about five or six yards long, and this passage ended in a chamber which was closed by a door of the ordinary kind. Opening this, the young soldier found himself in a room that was about ten feet square. In the dim light of a lamp that hung from the vaulted ceiling, he could see a couch occupied by the figure of a sleeper, a table on which stood a pitcher and some provisions, a chair, and some apparatus for washing. So deep were the slumbers of the occupant of the room that the entrance of the stranger did not rouse him from them, and it was only when Charidemus laid his hand upon his shoulder that he woke. His first impulse was to stretch out his hand for the sword which lay under his pillow; but the young Macedonian had been beforehand with him. Unarmed himself, for he had not dreamt of any adventure when his sleeplessness drove him into the garden, he had promptly possessed himself of the weapon, and was consequently master of the situation.

The next moment the two men recognized each other. The occupant of this mysterious chamber was Charondas, the Theban, and Charidemus saw the lad who had, as he thought, filched away his prize, lying unarmed and helpless before him.

The young Theban struggled into a sitting posture. Charidemus saw at once that his left arm was disabled. His face, too, was pale and bloodless, his eyes dim and sunken, and his whole appearance suggestive of weakness and depression.

"What are you doing here?" he asked, though the question was needless; it was clear that the young man had taken part in the recent fighting, and was now in hiding.

"I scarcely know; but I suppose life is sweet even to one who has lost everything; and I am too young," he added with a faint smile, "to relish the idea of Charon and his ferry-boat."

10

"Are you of the lineage of Pindar?"

"I cannot claim that honour. The husband of old Eurytion's sister, and father of the little Creon, whom you have seen doubtless, was my kinsman; but I am not related to the house of Pindar by blood. No; I have no more claim to the clemency of Alexander than the rest of my countrymen."

The young Macedonian stood lost in thought. He had often imagined the meeting that would take place some day, he was sure, between Charondas and himself. But he had never dreamt of it under such circumstances as these. He was to encounter him on the battle-field and vanquish him, perhaps overtake him in the pursuit, and then, perhaps, spare his life, perhaps kill him—he had never been quite able to make up his mind which it should be. But now killing him was out of the question; the man could not defend himself. And yet to give him up to death or slavery—how inexpressibly mean it seemed to him!

"I have no right," said the young Theban, "to ask a favour of you. I wronged you once——"

"Stop," interrupted Charidemus, "how came you to think of doing such a thing? It was shameful to win the prize in such a way."

"It is true," said the other; "but it was not of my own will that I came forward to object. Another urged me to it, and he is dead. You know that our cities give a handsome reward in money to those who win these prizes at the games; and we were very poor. But I could have trampled the crown in the dust, so hateful was it to win by craft what you had won by speed."

"Well, well," said Charidemus, who now had greater prizes than Olympia could give before his eyes, "it was no such great matter after all;" and he held out his hand to the wounded lad.

"Ah!" said the other, "I have no right to ask you favours. Yet one thing I may venture on. Kill me here. I could not bear to be a slave. Those poor women, who have risked their lives to save me, will be sorry when they hear of it, and little Creon will cry; but a child's tears are soon dried. But a slave— that would be too dreadful. I remember a poor Phocian my father had—sold to him after the taking of Crissa, of which, I suppose, you have heard—as well bred a man as any of us, and better educated, for we Thebans, in spite of our Pindar, are not very clever. What a life he led! I would die a hundred times over sooner than bear it for a day! No, kill me, I beseech you. So may the gods above and below be good to you when your need comes! Have you ever killed a man?" he went on. "Hardly, I suppose, in cold blood. Well, then, I will show you where to strike." And he pointed to a place on his breast, from which, at the same time, he withdrew his tunic. "My old trainer," he went on, "taught me that. Or, if you would sooner have it so, give me the sword, and I dare say that I can make shift to deal as straight a blow as will suffice."

The young Macedonian's heart was fairly touched. "Nay," he said, after a brief time given to thought, "I know something that will be better than that. If it fail, I will do what you will. Meanwhile here is your sword; but swear by

Zeus and Dionysus, who is, I think, your special god at Thebes, that you will not lift it against yourself, till I give you leave. And now, for three or four hours, farewell."

That morning, as Alexander was sitting with his intimate friend Hephaestion, at a frugal meal of barley cakes and fruit, washed down with wine that had been diluted, sweetened, and warmed, the guard who kept the door of the chamber, a huge Illyrian, who must have measured nearly seven feet in height, announced that a young man, who gave the name of Charidemus, craved a few minutes' speech with the king.

A more splendid specimen of humanity than the Macedonian monarch has seldom, perhaps never, been seen. In stature he did not much surpass the middle height, but his limbs were admirably proportioned, the very ideal of manly strength and beauty. His face, with well-cut features and brilliantly clear complexion, showed such a model as a sculptor would choose for hero or demigod. In fact, he seemed a very Achilles, born again in the later days, the handsomest of men, the strongest, the swiftest of foot.

"Ah!" said the king, "that is our young friend to whom I gave the charge of Pindar's house. I hope no harm has happened to it or him. To tell you the truth, this Theban affair has been a bad business. I would give a thousand talents that it had not happened. Show him in," he cried out, turning to the Illyrian.

"Hail, sire," said Charidemus, saluting.

"Is all well?"

"All is well, sire. No one has offered to harm the house or its inmates. But, if you will please to hear me, I have a favour to ask."

"What is it? Speak on."

"I beg the life of a friend."

"The life of a friend! What friend of yours can be in danger of his life?"

Charidemus told his story. Alexander listened with attention, and certainly without displeasure. He had already, as has been seen, begun to feel some repentance and even shame for the fate of Thebes he was not sorry to show clemency in a particular case.

"What," he cried, when he heard the name of the lad for whom Charidemus was making intercession. "What? was it not Charondas of Thebes who filtched from you the crown at Olympia? And you have forgiven him? What did the wise Aristotle," he went on, turning to Hephaestion, "say about forgiveness?"

"Sire," said Hephaestion, "you doubtless know better than I. You profited by his teaching far more than I—so the philosopher has told me a thousand times."

"Well," rejoined the king, "as far as I remember, he always seemed a little doubtful. To forgive showed, he thought, a certain weakness of will; yet it might be profitable, for it was an exercise of self-restraint. Was it not so, my friend?"

"Just so," said Hephaestion. "And did not the wise man say that if one were ever in doubt which to choose of two things, one should take the less pleasant. I don't know that I have ever had any experiences of forgiveness, but I certainly know the pleasure of revenge."

"Admirably said," cried the king. "Your request is granted," he went on, speaking to Charidemus. "But what will you do with your friend?"

"He shall follow you, sire, when you go to conquer the great enemy of Hellas."

"So be it. Mind that I never repent this day's clemency. And now farewell!"

The young man again saluted, and withdrew.

But when he unfolded his plan to the Theban, he found an obstacle which he might indeed have foreseen, but on which, nevertheless, he had not reckoned. Charondas was profoundly grateful to his deliverer, and deeply touched by his generosity. But to follow the man who had laid his country in the dust—that seemed impossible.

"What!" he cried, "take service with the son of Philip, the hereditary enemy of Hellas!"

"Listen!" said Charidemus; "there is but one hereditary perpetual enemy of Hellas, and that is the Persian. Since the days of Darius, the Great King has never ceased to scheme against her liberty. Do you know the story of the wrongs that these Persians, the most insolent and cruel of barbarians, have done to the children of Hellas?"

"Something of it," replied Charondas; "but in Thebes we are not great readers; and besides, that is a part of history which we commonly pass over."

"Well, it is a story of nearly two hundred years of wrong. Since Salamis and Platæa, indeed, the claws of the Persian have been clipped; but before that— it makes my blood boil to think of the things that they did to freeborn men. You know they passed through Macedonia, and left it a wilderness. There are traditions in my family of their misdeeds and cruelties which make me fairly grind my teeth with rage. And then the way in which they treated the islands! Swept them as men sweep fish out of a pond! Their soldiers would join hand to hand, and drag the place, as if they were dragging with a net."

"They suffered for it afterwards," said Charondas.

"Yes, they suffered for it, but not in their own country. Twice they have invaded Hellas itself; and they hold in slavery some of the sons of Hellas to this day. But they have never had any proper punishment."

"But what do you think would be proper punishment?" asked the Theban.

"That Hellas should conquer Persia, as Persia dreamt of conquering Hellas."

"But the work is too vast."

"Not so. Did you never hear how ten thousand men marched from the Ægean to the Euxine without meeting an enemy who could stand against them? And these were mere mercenaries, who thought of nothing but their pay. Yes, Persia ought to have been conquered long ago, if your cities had

13

only been united; but you were too busy quarrelling—first Sparta against Athens, and then Thebes against Sparta, and Corinth and Argos and the rest of them backing first one side, and then the other."

"It is too true."

"And then, when there seemed to be a chance of something being done, luck came in and helped the Persians. Alexander of Pheræ had laid his plans for a great expedition against the King, and just at the moment when they were complete, the dagger of an assassin—hired, some said, with Persian gold—struck him down. Then Philip took up the scheme, and worked it out with infinite patience and skill; and lo! the knife again! Well, 'all these things lie upon the knees of the gods.' Alexander of Pheræ was certainly not strong enough for the work, nor, perhaps, Philip himself. And besides, Philip had spent the best years of life in preparing for it, and was scarcely young enough. But now the time has come and the man. You must see our glorious Alexander, best of soldiers, best of generals. Before a year is over, he will be well on his way to the Persians' capital. Come with me, and help him to do the work for which Hellas has been waiting so long. Your true country is not here, among these petty states worn out with incessant strifes, but in the new empire which this darling of the gods will establish in the East."

"Well," said the Theban, with a melancholy smile, "anyhow my country is not any longer here. And what you tell me seems true enough. To you, my friend, I can refuse nothing. The life which you have saved is yours. I will follow you wherever you go, and, perhaps, some day you will teach me to love even this Alexander. At present, you must allow, I have scarcely cause."

Thus began a friendship which was only to be dissolved by death.

Preparations

ABOUT six months have passed since the events recorded in my last chapter. Charidemus had reported to Alexander so much of the young Theban's answer as it seemed to him expedient to communicate; and the king had been pleased to receive it very graciously. "I am glad," he said, "that you will have a friend in your campaigns. I should like to have such friendships all through my army. Two men watching over each other, helping each other, are worth more than double two who fight each for his own hand. You shall be a captain in the Guards. I can't give your friend the same rank. It would give great offence. My Macedonians would be terribly annoyed to see a young untried Greek put over them. He must make his way. I promise you that as soon as my men see that he is fit to lead, they will be perfectly willing to be led by him. Meanwhile let him join your company as a volunteer. He can thus be with you. And I will give orders that he shall draw the same pay and rations as you do. And now that is settled," the king went on, "I shall want

14

you with me for a little time. Your friend shall go to Pella, and learn his drill, and make himself useful."

This accordingly had been done. Charondas had spent the winter in Pella. In this place (which Alexander's father had made the capital of his kingdom) the army was gathering for the great expedition. A gayer or more bustling scene could not well be imagined, or, except the vast array which Xerxes had swept all Asia to bring against Greece a century and a half before, a stranger collection of specimens of humanity. Savage mountaineers from the Thracian Highlands, and fishermen from the primitive lake-villages of Pćonia, jostled in the streets with representatives of almost every city of Greece, the Lesser Greece which was the home of the race, and the Greater Greece which had spread its borders over the shores of the Mediterranean and the Black Sea, which had almost touched with its outposts the Caspian on the east and the Pillars of Hercules on the west. The prospect of a booty such as passed all the dreams of avarice, the hope of ransacking the treasuries into which all Asia had poured its wealth for generations, had drawn adventurers from all points of the compass. The only difficulty that the recruiting officers had was in choosing. The king was determined that the strength of his army should be his own Macedonians. A sturdy race, untouched by the luxury which had corrupted the vigour of more civilized Greece, they supplied a material of the most solid value. Nor was it now the rough, untempered metal that it had been a generation before. Philip had wrought it by years of patient care into a most serviceable weapon, and it only remained for his son to give its final polish and to wield it.

So complete was the organization left behind him by the great king, that such recruits as were needed to make up the necessary numbers of the army of Asia—and none but tried soldiers were recruited—easily fell into their proper places. The preparation of siege trains, of such machines as battering-rams and the like, of the artillery of the time, catapults, small and great, some used for throwing darts and some for hurling stones, was a more laborious business. The equipment of the army was far from complete. Every anvil in Macedonia was hard at work. Of provisions no great store was prepared. The king counted for supplying his needs in this direction in the country which he was about to overrun. The military chest was empty, or worse than empty; for Philip, who always preferred the spear of silver to the spear of steel, had left little but debt behind him. The personal baggage of the army was on the most moderate scale. Never was there a force which gave a better promise of being able to "march anywhere," and more amply fulfilled it.

Charondas, as it may easily be imagined, did not find the time hang heavily on his hands. His drill was easily learnt; he had served in the Theban infantry, the best in the world till it was dispossessed of its pride of place by the admirable force created by the military genius of Philip. But after this there was no lack of employment. Being a clever young fellow, who quite belied the common character of his countrymen for stupidity, and as modest as he was clever, he soon became a great favourite, and found himself set to any employment that required a little more tact and management than usual. When business permitted, there was always amusement in plenty. The lakes and marshes round Pella swarmed with wild geese and swans; and there were woods which might always be reckoned upon as holding a wild boar, and in which a bear might sometimes be found.

Such had been the employment of the last six months.

When I take up again the thread of my story the two friends had met at Sestos, from which place the army was preparing to cross into the Troad. They had much to tell each other. Charidemus, who had joined the army only the night before, was anxious to learn many military details which Charondas had had the opportunity of acquainting himself with. His own story was interesting, for he had been with Alexander and had also had a mission of his own, and had some notable experiences to relate. This is an outline of his narrative:

"After we parted, I went with the king to Megara. Hephaestion was urgent with him to go to Athens; but he refused. He would give no reasons; in fact, I never saw him so abrupt and positive; but I think that I know the cause. It is certain that there would have been trouble, if he had gone. The Athenians are the freest-spoken people in the world, and the king felt, I am sure, that it would be more than he could do to command himself, if he should hear himself, and still more hear his father, insulted. And besides, he had something very unpleasant to say, the sort of thing which any one would sooner say by another man's mouth than by his own. He was going to demand that the ten men who had been his worst enemies among the statesmen and soldiers of Athens should be given up to him. I was at table with him when the envoys from the city came back with their answer. He had them brought into the room where we were. No one could have been more polite than was the king. 'Be seated, gentlemen,' he said; and he ordered the pages to carry round cups of wine. Then he poured a libation from his own goblet. 'To Athené,' he cried, 'Athené the Counsellor, Athené the Champion,' and took a deep draught at each title. The envoys stood up, and followed his example. 'And now, gentlemen, to business,' he went on. 'You have brought the prisoners, of course. I mean no harm to them; but I don't care to have them plotting against me while I am away.' 'My lord,' said the chief of the embassy—and I could see him tremble as he spoke, though his bearing was brave enough—'my lord, the Athenian people, having met in a lawful assembly, and duly deliberated on this matter, has resolved that it cannot consent to your demand. The ten citizens whom you named in your letter have not been convicted of any crime; and it would not be lawful to arrest them.' I saw the king's face flush when he heard this answer; and he half started up from his seat. But he mastered himself by a great effort. 'Is that so?' he said in a low voice; 'then I shall have to come and take them. You hear that, gentlemen? Tell those who sent you what they must look for.' And he took up the talk with us just at the point at which it had been broken off when the envoys were announced. But he was not as calm as he looked. One of his pages told me that he did not lie down to sleep till it wanted only two hours of dawn. All night the lad heard the king pacing up and down in his chamber. The wall of partition was very thin, and he could not help hearing much that he said. 'A set of scribblers and word-splitters, to dare to set themselves up against me! I'll fetch the villains, if I have to go for them myself; and if I go, it will be the worse for all of them!' Then his mood changed. 'I can't have another business like the last! Thebes was bad enough, but Athens—no it is impossible. Even the Spartans would not put out the "eye of Greece"; and I must not be more brutal than a Spartan. And then to make another enemy among the Immortals! It is not to be thought of. The wrath of Bacchus is bad enough; and I have sinned against him beyond all pardon. But the wrath of Athené!—that would be a curse indeed for it would be the ruin both of valour and counsel.' So he went on talking to himself till the best part of the night was spent. Well, two days afterwards there came another embassy from Athens. This time they had a man of sense with them, one who knew how to make the best of things, and who, besides, was a special favourite of the king. This was Phocion, who, as I daresay you know, had the sense to accept the inevitable, and counseled peace with us, when the so-called patriots were raving for war. The king was as gracious as possible to him. 'Ah! my dear friend,' he cried, as soon as he saw him, 'I am indeed glad to see you. Now I know that I have an intelligent person to deal with, and I am quite sure that we shall have no difficulty in settling matters on a satisfactory footing. Well, what have you got to tell me? What proposition do you make? You may be sure that I will accept anything in reason.' 'Sir,' said Phocion—a singularly venerable-looking man, by the way—'the Athenians beg you not to take it ill if they are unwilling to break their laws even to win your favour; at the same time they are ready to do anything to satisfy you!' 'Ah! I see,' said the king; 'anything but what I want. But hearken: I have thought the matter over, and have come to this conclusion: I won't ask your people to give anybody up. It is a thing that has an evil look; and, upon my word, I think the better of them for refusing. At the same time, I can't have my enemies plotting against me when my back is turned. You may keep your speakers, and they may talk against me as much as they please. They did not hurt my father much, and I do not suppose that they will hurt me. But as to the soldiers, that is another matter. They must go. I don't want to have them myself; but they must not stop at Athens. If you can promise so much for those who sent you, then I shall be satisfied.' 'You are as moderate,' said Phocion, 'as I always expected you would be. I can promise what you demand. Indeed, the two soldiers are gone already.' 'That is well,' said the king. 'Perhaps it is all that I ought to have asked for at the first. Yes; tell your countrymen that I honour them for their courage, and that I don't forget what they have done for Greece. If it had not been for them we should be slaves beneath the heel of the Persian this day. And tell them that if anything happens to me, it is they who are to take my place, and be the leaders of Greece. They were so once, and it may be the pleasure of the gods that they should be so again.' "

"Ah!" interrupted Charondas, smiling, "your king knows how to use his tongue as well as he knows how to use his sword. That will flatter the Athenians to the top of their bent. After that they are Alexander's firm friends for ever. But to take his place—what an idea! If they only knew it, it was the cruellest satire. They have orators, I allow. I heard two of them when I was a boy. I thought that nothing could beat the first Ćschines, I think they called him—till the second got up. Good gods! that man could have persuaded me of anything. Demosthenes, they told me, was his name. But as for a general, they haven't such a thing, except it be this same Phocion, and he must be close upon seventy. They have no soldiers even, except such as they hire. They used to be able to fight, though they were never a match for us. You shrug your shoulders, I see, but it is a fact; but now they can do nothing but quarrel. But I am interrupting you. Go on."

"Well," continued Charidemus, "from Megara we went on to Corinth. There the king held a great reception of envoys from all the states. I acted, you must know, as one of his secretaries, and had to listen to the eloquence of all these gentlemen. How they prevaricated, and lied, and flattered! and the king listening all the while with a gentle smile, as if he were taking it all in, but now and then throwing in a word or putting a question that struck them dumb. These were the public audiences. And then there were the private interviews, when the envoys came one by one to see what they could get for themselves. What a set of greedy, cringing beggars they were, to be sure. Some put a better face on it than others; but it was the same with all—gold; gold, or office, which of course, means gold sooner or later. I used to want to be thought a Greek, but I never——"

He stopped abruptly, for he had forgotten to whom he was talking. Charondas smiled. "Speak your mind," he said, "you will not offend me."

"Well," continued the Macedonian, "there was at least one man at Corinth whom I could honestly admire. I had gone with the king and Hephaestion to dine with a rich Corinthian. What a splendid banquet it was! The king has no gold and silver plate to match what Xeniades—for that was our host's name—produced. The conversation happened to turn on the sights of Corinth, and Xeniades said that, after all, there was not one of them could match what he had to show. 'Can we see it?' asked Alexander. 'Not to-day, I am afraid,' said our host, 'but come to-morrow about noon, and I can promise you a good view.' Accordingly the next day we went. Xeniades took us into the open court inside his house, and showed us a curious little figure of a man asleep in the sunshine. 'That,' said he, 'is the one man I know, or ever have known, who never wanted anything more than what he had. Let me tell you how I came to know him. About thirty years ago I was travelling in Crete, and happened to stroll into the slave-market at Gnossus. There was a lot of

18

prisoners on sale who had been taken by pirates out of an Athenian ship. Every man had a little paper hanging round his neck, on which were written his age, height, and accomplishments. There were cooks, tailors, tent-makers, cobblers, and half-a-dozen other trades, one poor wretch who called himself a sculptor, the raggedest of the lot, and another, who looked deplorably ill, by the way, who called himself a physician. They were poor creatures, all of them. Indeed, the only one that struck my fancy was a man of about fifty— too old, of course, in a general way, for a slave that one is going to buy. He certainly was not strong or handsome, but he looked clever. I noticed that no occupation was mentioned in his description; so I asked him what he could do. "I can rule men," he said. That seemed such a whimsical answer, for certainly such a thing was never said in the slave-market before, that I could do nothing less than buy the man. "You are just what I have been wanting," I said. Well, to make a long story short, I brought him home and made him tutor to my children, for I found that he was a learned man. He did his work admirably. But of late he has grown very odd. He might have any room in my house, but you see the place in which he prefers to live,' and he pointed to a huge earthenware vat that had been rolled up against the side of the house. 'But let us go and hear what he has to say.' Well, we went, and our coming woke the old man. He was a curious, withered, bent creature, nearly eighty years old, our host said, with matted white hair, eyes as keen as a hawk's, and the queerest wrinkles round his mouth. 'Who are you?' he said. 'I am Alexander, King of Macedonia,' said the king. 'I am Diogenes the Cynic,' said the old man. 'Is there anything that I can do for you,' asked the king. 'Yes; you can stand out of the sunshine.' So the king stood aside, whereupon the old man curled himself up and went to sleep again. 'Well,' said the king, 'if I were not Alexander, I would gladly be Diogenes,' ' You may well say so, my lord,' said Xeniades; 'that strange old creature has been a good genius in my house.' "

"And what became of you after the king came back to Pella?" asked Charondas.

"I stayed behind to do some business which he put into my hands. Most of the time I spent in Argos, where I was brought up, and where I have many friends, but I paid visits to every town of importance in the Peloponnesus. I may say so much without breaking any confidence, that it was my business to commend the Macedonian alliance to any people of note that I might come into contact with. I was very well received everywhere except in Sparta. The Spartans were as sulky as possible; in fact, I was told to leave the city within a day."

At this point the conversation of the two friends was interrupted by the entrance of one of Alexander's pages. The lad—he was about sixteen years of age, —saluted, and said "a message from the king." The two friends rose from their seats and stood "at attention" to receive the communication. "The king commands your attendance to-morrow at sunrise, when he goes to Troy." His errand done, the lad relaxed the extreme dignity of his manner, and greeted the two young men in a very friendly way. "Have you heard the news," he asked, "that has set all the world wondering? The statue of Orpheus that stands in Pieria has taken to sweating incessantly. The priest thought it important enough to send a special messenger announcing the prodigy. Some of the old generals were very much troubled at the affair," went on the young man, who was by way of being an esprit fort, "but luckily the soothsayer was equal to the occasion. 'Let no one be troubled,' he said, 'it is an omen of the very best. Much labour is in store for the poets, who will have to celebrate the labours of our king.' "

"Well," said Charidemus, who was a well-educated young man, and had a certain taste in verse, "our friend Chŝrilus, with all that I have seen of him and his works, will have to sweat very hard before he can produce a decent verse."

"Very true," said the page, "but why Orpheus should trouble himself about such a fool as Chœrilus passes my comprehension. Now, if you want a really good omen, my dear Charidemus, you have one in the king's sending for you. That means good luck if anything does. There are very few going. Perdiccas, Hephaestion, half-a-dozen of us pages (of whom I have not the luck to be one), the soothsayer, of course, with the priests and attendants, and a small escort make up the company."

"And where is he going?" asked the two friends together.

"To the ruins of Troy. And now farewell."

At Troy

EARLY as it was when our hero passed through the camp on his way to the point from which the king's galley was to start, everything was in a great bustle of preparation. More than a hundred and fifty vessels of war and a huge array of trading ships of every kind and size were standing as near the shore as their draught would permit, ready to receive the army and to transport it to the Asiatic shore. The munitions of war and the artillery had been already embarked, relays of men having been engaged on this part of the work for some days past. The pier was crowded with horses and their attendants, this being the only spot from which the animals could be conveniently put on ship-board. Alexander, however, contemplated mounting some part of his cavalry with chargers to be purchased on the soil of Asia, and, with that extraordinary faculty for organization and management that was as marked in him as was his personal courage, had provided that there should be no delay in procuring a proper supply. The soldiers themselves were not to go on board till everything else had been arranged. The king's galley, which was the admiral's own ship, presented a striking appearance. At the stern stood Alexander, a splendid figure, tall and stately, and clad in gilded armour. The pages, wearing purple tunics with short cloaks richly embroidered with gold thread, were clustered about him on the after deck, while, close at hand, conspicuous in their sacrificial white garments, stood the priest and his attendants. All the crew wore holiday attire, and every part of the vessel was crowned with garlands.

At a signal from the king the galley pushed off from the shore; the fugleman struck up a lively strain of martial Dorian music; the rowers, oarsmen picked for strength and endurance from the whole fleet, struck the water with their oars in faultless time, while Alexander himself held the rudder. At first he steered along the shore, for he was bound for the southern extremity of the peninsula, on which stood the chapel of Protesilaüs, the hero who, whether from self-sacrifice or ill-luck, had expiated by his death the doom pronounced on his people. Reaching the place he went ashore, followed by his companions and attendants, and, after duly performing sacrifice to the hero, returned to his ship. The prow was then turned straight to the opposite coast. In mid-channel the music of the fugleman's flute ceased, and the rowers rested on their oars. Leaving the rudder in the charge of Hephaestion, the king advanced to sacrifice the milk-white bull, which, with richly gilded horns and garlands of flowers hanging about its neck, stood ready for the rite. He plucked some hair from between the horns, and duly burned them on the coals of a brasier, and then sprinkled some salted meal and poured a few drops of wine on the animal's forehead. The attendants meanwhile plunged knives into its throat, and caught the streaming blood in broad shallow dishes. The entrails were then duly examined by the soothsayer, who, after an apparently scrupulous investigation, declared that they presented a singularly favourable appearance. This done, the king took a golden cup from the hand of an attendant, and after filling it with the choicest Chian wine, poured out libations to Poseidon, the sea-god, and to the sisterhood of the nymphs, imploring that they would continue to him and to his companions the favour which they had shown to the Greek heroes of old times. His prayer ended, he flung the goblet, as that which should never be profaned by any meaner function, into the dream of the Hellespont.

These ceremonies ended, a very brief space of time sufficed to bring the galley to the "Harbour of the Achæans," the very spot which tradition asserted to have been the landing-place of the host of Agamemnon. The king was the first to leap ashore. For a moment he stood with his spear poised, as if awaiting an enemy who might dispute his landing; then, no one appearing, stuck the weapon in the ground, and implored the favour of Zeus and the whole company of the dwellers in Olympus on the undertaking of which that day's work was the beginning. Then followed a number of remarkable acts. They were partly, one cannot doubt, intended for effect, the performances of a man who desired above all things to pose as the representative of Greek feeling, to show himself to the world as the successor of the heroes who had championed Greece against the lawless insolence of Asia. But they were also in a great degree the expression of a genuine feeling. Alexander had a roman-

21

tic love for the whole cycle of Homeric song and Homeric legend. A copy of the Iliad was the companion of all his campaigns; he even slept with it under his pillow. It was his proudest boast that he was descended from Achilles; and now he was actually performing in person the drama which had been the romance of his life. His first visit was to the temple of Athené that crowned the hill, identified at least by the inhabitants of the place with the Pergama of ancient Troy. The walls of the temple were adorned with suits of armour, worn, it was said, by the guardians of the place, by heroes who had fought against Troy. The king had several of these taken down, not intending to wear them himself, but meaning to have them carried with him during his campaigns, a purpose which was afterwards fulfilled. He left instead his own gilded armour, and added other valuable offerings to the temple. From Athené's shrine he went to the palace of Priam, where his guides showed him the very altar of Zeus at which the old king was slaughtered by the savage son of Achilles. But this son was an ancestor of his own, and he felt himself bound to expiate by offering sacrifice the wrath which the murdered man might feel against the descendant of the murderer. The sight which crowned the glories of the day was the tomb and monumental column of Achilles. It was the practice of pilgrims to this sacred spot to strip off their garments, anoint themselves, and run naked round the mound under which the great hero reposed.

"Happy Achilles," he cried, when the ceremony was finished; "who didst find a faithful friend to love thee during life, and a great poet to celebrate thee after death. The friend is here," he went on, turning with an affectionate gesture to Hephaestion, "but the poet——" and he was thinking, it may be possible, of the unlucky Chœrilus.

Nothing adverse had occurred from morning to evening, but those who were responsible for the success of the operation had been profoundly anxious. Sentinels stood on the highest ground at the western end of the Hellespont, to watch the seas both toward the south and the west for the first signs of the approach of a hostile squadron, but not a sail was to be seen; and the tedious and dangerous operation of transferring the army from one continent to the other had been executed in safety. A squadron of agile Phœnician galleys, driven by resolute captains on that helpless crowd of transports, might have wrought irreparable damage, and even crushed the undertaking in its first stage. This would have been done if the Persian king had listened to his wisest counsellors; but it was not to be. Then, as ever, it was true, "Whom the gods will ruin they first strike with madness."

The army bivouacked that night, as it best could, on or near the shore. Next morning it marched past the king in battle array. A more perfect instrument of war the world had never seen. Skirmishers, light infantry, cavalry, all were as highly disciplined and as admirably equipped as the lavish expenditure of trouble and money could make them. But the irresistible strength of the force was in its famous phalanx. Each division—there were six of them that passed that day under their general's eyes—had a front file of 128 men, while the files were sixteen deep. Every soldier in this compact body of more than two thousand men carried the huge Macedonian pike. It was twenty-two feet in length, being so weighted that the fifteen feet which projected beyond the bearer were fairly balanced by the six behind him. The pikes of the second rank, which stood three feet behind the first, projected twelve feet before the line, those of the third nine, of the fourth six, of the fifth three. The other ranks sloped their pikes upward, over the shoulders of their comrades, to form a sort of protection against missiles that might be discharged against them. The whole presented a most formidable appearance; and its appearance was not more formidable than its actual strength. It was cumbrous; it could not manœuvre with ease; it could not accommodate itself to difficult ground. But on ground of its own, and when it could bring its strength to bear, it was irresistible. The best infantry of Greece, though led by skilful generals, and fighting with desperate courage, had been crushed by it. Long afterwards, when the Macedonian army was but the shadow of its former self, the sight of the phalanx could still strike terror into the conquerors of the world.

Alexander's eyes were lighted up with pride as the massive columns marched past him. "Nothing can resist them," he cried; "with these I shall conquer the world."

At the Granicus

THE army now marched slowly eastward, covering scarcely eight miles a day. Alexander was not commonly a general who spared his troops; but he was, for the present, almost timidly careful of them. A large Persian force had, as he knew from his spies, been massed for several weeks within striking distance of his point of disembarkation. Thanks to the supineness or pride of the Persian leaders, he had been allowed to make good his footing on Asian soil without opposition; but he would not be suffered, he knew perfectly well, to advance without having to force his way. He wanted to fight his first battle with every advantage on his side; a victory would produce an immense impression in Western Asia, a check on the other hand would be almost fatal. To bring his army into the field perfectly fresh and unimpaired in numbers was, for the present, his chief object. About noon on the fourth day his scouts came racing back with the intelligence that the Persians were posted on the right or eastern bank of the Granicus, a torrent-like stream which came down from the slopes of Ida. A halt was immediately called, and a hasty council of war held. The general opinion of the officers summoned, as expressed by Parmenio, was to delay the attack till the following day. The king, who was as ready to overrule his advisers as great generals commonly are, decided to fight at once. His men were flushed with high spirits and confidence. Their strength had been so carefully husbanded that they would be still perfectly fresh after a few more miles marching. The king's only fear was lest the enemy should decamp before he came up with them. "I thanked the gods," he said, in announcing his decision to the council, "that the enemy did not offer me battle when I was landing my army. I shall thank them not less fervently, if the enemy do offer it now when I am better prepared to meet them than I shall ever be again."

It was about an hour from sunset when Alexander, who was riding in advance with a small staff, came in sight of the Persian army. It was, indeed, but a single mile distant; and through the clear air, unencumbered by the smoke of modern artillery, every detail of its formation could be distinctly seen. The bank was lined with cavalry. On the right were the Medes and Bactrians, wearing the round-topped cap, the gaily-coloured tunic, and the scale armour which were distinguishing parts of their national dress; the Paphlagonians and Hyrcanians, equipped in much the same way, occupied the centre. Memnon the Rhodian, the ablest of the counsellors of Darius, of whom we shall hear more hereafter, shared with a Persian satrap the command of the right. He had a few Greek troopers with him, but most of his men were Asiatics. These were, however, the best horsemen that the vast empire of Darius could send into the field. The descendants of the Seven Deliverers, with the flower of the Persian youth, in all the pride of a caste that claimed to rule more than a hundred provinces, stood in all the splendour of their gilded arms, to dispute the passage of the river. The stream, greatly diminished indeed from its volume in early spring, when it is swollen by the melting snows of Mount Ida, but not yet dwindled to the slender proportions of summer, was flowing with considerable volume. The ford was many hundred yards in length, and for all this distance the right bank opened out into level ground. The whole of this was occupied by the cavalry. On the rising ground behind, marking the extreme limit reached by the floods of water, or, rather, of early spring, the infantry, both Greek and Asiatic, were posted in reserve. Mounted on his famous steed Bucephalus, the king rode along the line, addressing a few words of encouragement to each squadron and company as he passed it, and finally placed himself at the head of the right division of the army. (There were, it should be remembered, but two divisions.) For some minutes the two armies stood watching each other in silence. Then, as the Persian leaders recognized the presence of Alexander on the right wing of his own force— and it was easy to distinguish him by his gilded arms, his splendid charger, and the movement of the line as he rode along it—they began to reinforce their own left. The fame of his personal prowess had not failed to reach them; and they knew that the fiercest struggle would be where he might be in immediate command. Alexander saw the movement, and it hastened his own action. If he could catch his antagonists in the confusion of a change he would have them at a disadvantage. The word to advance was given, and the whole army moved forward towards the river, the right wing being somewhat in advance. Here was the famous corps d'élite, a heavy cavalry regiment that went under the name of the "Royal Companions." This was the first to enter the river. A number of javelin-throwers and archers covered them on either flank; and they were followed by some light horse, and by one of the regiments of light infantry. This happened to be Charidemus's own; he had begged and obtained permission to return to his place in its ranks.

The van of the attacking force made its way in fair order through the stream. The bottom was rough and uneven, full of large stones brought down by winter floods, with now and then a hole of some depth, but there was no mud or treacherous sand. The first onset on the defenders of the further bank was not successful. A line of dismounted troopers stood actually in the water, wherever it was shallow enough to allow it; on the bank above them (the summer bank, as it may be called, in distinction from that mentioned before as the limit of the winter floods) was ranged a dense line of horsemen, two or three files deep. The combatants below plied their swords, or thrust with their short spears; those above them showered their javelins upon the advancing enemy, and these, not only finding their footing insecure, but having to struggle up a somewhat steep ascent, failed to get any permanent hold on the coveted bank. The few who contrived to make their way up were either slain or disabled, and the rest were thrust back upon the troops that followed them. These were of course checked in their advance, and it was not till the king himself at the head of the main body of his army took up the attack that there appeared a prospect of success. Then indeed the tide of battle began to turn. For the first of many times throughout these marvellous campaigns the personal strength, the courage, the dexterity in arms of Alexander, a matchless soldier as well as a matchless general, changed the fortune of the day. He sprang forward, rallying after him his disheartened troops, struck down adversary after adversary, and climbed the bank with an agility as well as a daring which seemed to inspire his companions with an irresistible courage. What a few minutes before had seemed impossible was done; the first bank of the Granicus was gained. But the battle was not yet won. The Persians had been beaten back from their first line of defence, but they still held the greater part of the level ground in what seemed overwhelming force. And now they could deliver charges which with the superior weight of horses and men might be expected to overthrow a far less numerous foe. Again Alexander was in the very front of the conflict. His pike had been broken in the struggle for the bank. He called to one of the bodyguards, a man whose special office it was to hold his horse when he mounted or dismounted, and asked for another. The man, without speaking, showed him his own broken weapon. Then the king looked round on his followers, holding high the splintered shaft. The appeal was answered in an instant. This time it was a Greek, Demaratus of Corinth, who answered his call, and supplied him with a fresh lance. It was not a moment too soon. A heavy column of Persian horse was advancing against him, its leader, Mithradates, son-in-law of Darius, riding a long way in advance of his men. Alexander spurred his horse, charged at Mithradates with levelled pike, struck him on the face, and hurled him dying to the ground. Meanwhile another Persian noble had come up. He struck a fierce blow at the king with his scymetar, but in his excitement almost missed his aim, doing no further damage than shearing off the crest of the helmet. Alexander replied with a thrust which broke through his breastplate, and inflicted a mortal wound. There was a third antagonist behind, but his arm was severed by a sword-cut from a Macedonian officer just as it was in the act of delivering a blow. The mêlée, however, still continued with unabated fury. The Persian nobles pressed forward with a reckless courage; and it was not till almost every leader had fallen that the cavalry gave way.

In other parts of the field the resistance had been less obstinate. The élite of the Persian army had been brought together to oppose Alexander, and the remainder did not hold their ground with the same tenacity. When the phalanx, after meeting no opposition in making the passage of the river, formed again on the other shore, and made its way over the level ground, it encountered no resistance. All the defending force either had perished or was scattered in a wild flight over the plain.

A force, however, still remained unbroken, which, had it been properly handled, might have been found a serious difficulty for the conquerors. The infantry had remained, during the conflict just described, in absolute inaction on the rising ground, watching without attempting to share in the battle that was being fought on the plain below. They had no responsible leader; no orders had been issued to them. The Persian nobles had felt, in fact, so blind a confidence in the strength of their own special arm, the cavalry, that they had treated this important part of their resources with absolute neglect. And yet, not to speak of the native troops, there were not less than ten thousand Greek mercenaries, resolute, well-armed men, got together and supported at a vast expense, who were never utilized in the struggle, but simply left to be slaughtered. These now remained to be dealt with. The king had recalled his cavalry from their pursuit of the flying Persians, and had launched them against the unprotected flanks of the Greek infantry. Not content with what he had already done in the way of personal exertion—and it was, perhaps, his one defect that he was incontrollably eager in his passion for "drinking the delight of battle," he charged at the head of the troopers, and had a horse killed under him by a thrust from a mercenary's lance. This horse was not the famous Bucephalus, which, as it had fallen slightly lame in the course of the battle, he had exchanged for another charger. While he was waiting for another horse to be brought to him, the light infantry came up, and with it Charidemus and his Theban friend. "Ah!" cried the king, recognizing the two comrades, with whom indeed he had exchanged a few words several times on the march from the place of landing, "the crowns of victory have fallen so far to the horsemen; now it is your turn." He had scarcely spoken when he remembered that one at least of the two might find former friends or even kinsmen in the hostile ranks, for many Thebans, he knew, had, after the fall of their city, taken service with Persia. With the thoughtful kindness that distinguished him till his temper had been spoilt by success and by absolute power, he devised for the young man an escape from so painful a dilemma. Hastily improvising a reason for sending him away from the scene of action he said, "You must be content to help me just now as an aide-de-camp: run to Parmenio with all the speed you can command and deliver to him this tablet. It contains some instructions which I should like him to receive at once." As a matter of fact the instructions contained nothing more than this, "Keep the messenger with you till the battle is over."

The final struggle of the day, from which the young Theban thus unconsciously received his dismissal, was fierce, but not protracted. The light-armed infantry, following the charges of the cavalry, acquitted themselves well, and Charidemus especially had the good luck to attract the notice of Alexander by the skilful way in which he disposed of a huge Arcadian. But the mercenaries continued to hold their own till the phalanx came up. The native levies which supported them broke in terror at the sight of that formidable array of steel; and even the hardy Greeks felt an unaccustomed fear. Some indeed, having served all their time in Asia, had never seen it in action before. With slow resistless advance it bore down upon the doomed survivors of the infantry. The front ranks fell before it; the rest stood for a few moments, wavered, and then broke up in hopeless confusion. Two thousand were admitted to quarter; some escaped by feigning death as they lay amidst the piles of their comrades' corpses; but more than half of the ten thousand perished on the field.

After this nothing was left but to collect the spoils and to bury the dead. This latter duty Alexander caused to be performed with special care. The enemy received the same decent rites of sepulture as were accorded to his own men.

Late that night, for it was already dark before the battle was over, the two friends sat talking in the tent which they shared over the events of the day.

"What think you of our king now?" said the young Macedonian. "Was there ever such a warrior?"

"No," returned the Theban. "I compared him in my mind with our own Epaminondas. Epaminondas was as brave; but he was less possessed with the passion for fighting. Our great general felt it his duty to do everything that a common soldier could be asked to do; he thought it a part of a general's work; and, consequently, he was lost to his country when he was most needed. The life for which ten thousand talents would have been but a poor equivalent was expended in doing something for which one that would have been dear at a score of drachmas would have sufficed. It has always been a puzzle to me, but doubtless so wise a man must have known what was best. But to your king the fighting is not a duty but a pleasure. He is greedy of it. He grudges it to others. He would like to do all of it himself. Yes; you are right, he is an incomparable warrior. He is a veritable Achilles. But I tell you he won my heart in quite another way to-day. I have been thinking over his sending me on that message, and I can see what he meant. I did in fact see more than one face that I knew opposite to me, and though I should have done my duty, I hope, it was a terrible dilemma. The general who can think of such a thing on a battlefield, the king who can remember a humble man like myself, is one to be honoured and loved. Yes, after to-day I can follow your Alexander everywhere."

Charidemus grasped his hand, "The gods send us good fortune and a prosperous issue!" he exclaimed.

Halicarnassus

IT is no part of my purpose to tell again in detail what has been so often told before, the story of the campaigns of Alexander. The victory of the Granicus had far-reaching results. It is scarcely too much to say that it gave all Lesser Asia to the conqueror. The details of the battle had been of a singularly impressive kind. It was a veritable hero, men said, a manifest favourite of heaven, who had come to overthrow the kingdom of Cyrus. He was incomparably skilful in counsel; he was irresistible in fight. And then, as a matter of fact, so totally had the beaten army disappeared, the Great King had no force on the western side of the Taurus range that could pretend to meet the invaders in the field. Here and there a city or a fortress might be held for him, but the country, with all its resources, was at the mercy of the invaders; and the fortresses, for the most part, did not hold out. The terror of this astonishing success was upon their governors and garrisons, and there were few of the commanders who did not hasten to make terms for themselves. The capital of the satrapy of Phrygia, with all its treasures, was surrendered without a struggle. But a more surprising success, a success which astonished Alexander himself, was the capitulation of Sardis. He had not hoped to take it without a long blockade, for an assault was impossible except the garrison should be utterly negligent or faithless, and yet he got it without losing a single soldier or wasting a single day. The Persian governor, accompanied by the notables of the city, met him as he was advancing towards the walls, and surrendered everything to him.

What he felt himself he expressed when the next day he inspected the capabilities of the city, notoriously the strongest place in Lesser Asia, which had fallen so unexpectedly into his hands. The town, he said, might have been held for a long time by a resolute garrison; but the citadel, with its sheer descent on every side and its triple wall was absolutely impregnable. "Well," he went on, turning to Hephaestion, "well might old Meles have neglected to carry his lion's cub round such a place as this!"

A garrison of Argive soldiers was left to hold the place. Alexander, who, like all generals of the very first ability, possessed a gift for remembering everything, had not forgotten that Charidemus had many friends and connections in Argos, and offered the young man the post of second in command, but was not at all displeased when he refused it. "You are right," he said, "though I thought it well to give you the choice. But a young man like you is fit for something better than garrison duty. You wish to follow me then? to see Susa and Babylon, and Tyre and Jerusalem, and Egypt, perhaps India." As he said this last word a cloud passed over his face. It brought back what to his dying day was the great remorse and terror of his life, the fate of Thebes and the dreaded anger of Bacchus, that city's patron god. For was not Bacchus the conqueror of India, and who could hope to be under his ban, and yet safely tread in his footsteps?

"Young man," he said, "thank the gods that they have not made you a king, or given you the power to kill and to keep alive."

Ephesus was won as easily as Sardis had been; Miletus refused to surrender, but was taken by storm a few days after it had been invested. The only place of any real importance that remained in the west of Lesser Asia was Halicarnassus. But the capture of this town would, it was evident, be a task of difficulty. Memnon, now Commander-in-chief of the Persian forces in the west, had thrown himself into it. It was strongly placed and strongly fortified, Memnon himself, who was a skilful engineer, having personally superintended the improvement of the defences; and it could not be attacked by sea, for the Persian fleet, which had been prevented from helping Miletus by being shut out from the harbour, held the port of Halicarnassus in great force. Under these circumstances, the fall of the town would be nearly as great a blow to the Great King, as had been the signal defeat of his army at the Granicus.

Alexander's first experience was encouraging. He had scarcely crossed the borders of Caria when he was met by the Carian princess, Ada. The army had just halted for the midday meal, and Alexander with his staff was sitting under a tree when the approach of the visitor was announced by one of his outriders. Shortly afterwards she arrived, and, alighting from her litter, advanced to salute the king.

The princess was a majestic figure, worthy, at least in look, of the noble race from which she sprang. She was nearly seventy years of age, and her hair was white; but her face was unwrinkled, her form erect, and her step light and vigorous. Alexander, who had not forgotten to make himself acquainted with Carian politics, advanced to meet her, and kissed her hand. "Welcome, my son, to my land," she said, as she kissed him on the cheek. She then seated herself on a chair which a page had set for her, and told her story. Briefly, it was a complaint against her brother and the Persian king who had dispossessed her of her throne. "My brother took it; the Great King has supported him in his wrong. My ancestors fought for his house at Salamis, and was faithful to it when others failed; and this is his gratitude. It is enough; we Carians have never been slaves, and, if he will not have us for friends, we will be enemies. One fortress the robber has not been able to filch from me. That is yours, and all that it contains. My people love not these Persian tyrants, and they will help you for my sake. One favour I ask. The gods have not given me the blessing of children; will you be my son? I shall be more than content, for the gods could scarcely have allowed me an offspring so noble."

Alexander kneeled before her; "Mother," he said, "give me your blessing. I have now another wrong to avenge on these insolent Persians. And remember that Caria, when I shall have wrested it from the hand of these usurpers, is yours."

The siege of Halicarnassus was a formidable undertaking. A wall of unusual height and strength surrounded the town, and the wall was protected by the outer defence of a moat, more than forty feet wide and twenty deep. Two citadels overlooked the town; and the besieged, besides being well provided with food and ammunition, had the command of the sea. The harbour, itself strongly fortified, was occupied by the Persian fleet.

The first efforts of the besiegers failed. An attack on the north-east of the town was repulsed with loss; and an attempt to take the neighbouring town of Myndos, from which Alexander hoped to operate with advantage against Halicarnassus, was equally unsuccessful. The king then moved his army to the west side of the town, and commenced the siege in regular form. The soldiers working under the protection of pent-houses, which could be moved from place to place, filled up the ditch for a distance of seven hundred yards, so that their engines could be brought up close to the walls.

But these operations took time, and the army, intoxicated by its rapid success–in the course of a few weeks it had conquered the north-western provinces of Lesser Asia—loudly murmured at the delay which was keeping it so long before the walls of a single town.

About a month after the commencement of the siege, Parmenio, who was in chief command of the infantry, gave a great banquet to the officers of the light division, at which Charidemus, in virtue of his commission, and his Theban friend, by special invitation, were present. The occasion was the king's birthday, and Alexander himself honoured the entertainment with his company for a short time in the earlier part of the evening. He was received, of course, with enthusiastic cheers, which were renewed again and again when he thanked the guests for their good will, and ended by pledging them in a cup of wine. Still a certain disappointment was felt when he withdrew without uttering a word about the prospects of the siege. There had been a general hope that he would have held out hopes of an immediate assault. The fact was that the battering rams had levelled to the ground a considerable distance of the wall, including two of the towers, and that a third tower was evidently tottering to its fall. If many of the older soldiers would have preferred to wait till the breach should have been made more practicable, the common opinion amongst the younger men was that the place might be stormed at once.

When the king had left the banqueting tent, there was a general loosening of tongues among the guests. The senior officers, sitting near Parmenio at the upper end of the table, were sufficiently discreet in the expression of their opinions, but the juniors were less prudent and self-restrained.

"What ails our Achilles?" cried one of them, Meleager by name, who had been applying himself with more than common diligence to the wine-flask. "Is he going to play the part of Ulysses? If so, we shall have to wait long enough before we find our way into Troy. And if a single town is to keep us for months, how many years must we reckon before we can get to Susa? The breach, in my judgment, is practicable enough; and unless we are quick in trying it, the townsmen will have finished their new wall behind it, and we shall have all our labour over again."

A hum of applause greeted the speaker as he sat down. A noisy discussion followed as to the point where the assault might be most advantageously delivered. When it was concluded—and this was not till a polite message had come down from the head of the table that a little more quiet would be desirable—it was discovered that Meleager and his inseparable friend Amyntas had left the tent. This was sufficiently surprising, for they were both deep drinkers, and were commonly found among the latest lingering guests wherever the wine was good and plentiful.

"What has come to the Inseparables?" asked one of the company. "Has the wine been too much for them? Meleager seemed a little heated when he spoke, but certainly not more advanced than he usually is at this hour."

The next speaker treated the suggestion with contempt. "Meleager," he said, "and Amyntas, too, for that matter, could drink a cask of this Myndian stuff without its turning their brains or tying their tongues. It may be as good as they say for a man's stomach, but there is not much body in it. No; they are up to some mischief, you may depend upon it."

"Run to the tent of Meleager," said the officer who sat at the lower end of the table to one of the attendants, " and say that we are waiting for him."

The lad went on the errand and returned in a few minutes. He brought back the news that neither of the occupants of the tent were there; and he added an interesting piece of information which, being an intelligent young fellow, he had gathered on his way, that they had been seen to come back, and to go out again with their weapons and armour.

"It was odd," said Charidemus, who had his own idea about the matter, "that Meleager had nothing to say about the place where the breach might be best stormed, when we consider the speech he made."

Some one here remarked that he had observed the two Inseparables whispering together while the discussion was going on.

"Then," cried Charidemus, "depend upon it, they have gone to make a try for themselves."

"Impossible!" said one of the guests. "What, these two! They cannot have been such mad-men!"

"If they have," laughed another, "this Myndian vintage must be more potent, or our friends' brains weaker, than Pausanias thinks."

But the incredulity with which this astonishing suggestion was at first received soon gave way to the belief that it was not only possibly, but even probably, true. The two friends were notorious dare-devils and the fact that they had taken their arms with them was, considering that they were neither of them on duty for the night, almost conclusive.

"Run to Parmenio's tent," said Charidemus' superior officer to him, "and tell him what we suppose."

The young man overtook the general before he had reached his quarters, and told his story. Parmenio, as may be supposed, was greatly annoyed at having his hand forced in this way. "The Furies seize the hot-headed young fools! Are they in command or am I—not to speak of the king? They have made their pudding; let them eat of it. I shall not risk any man's life on such hare-brained follies."

As he was speaking, the king himself, who was making a nightly round among the men's quarters, came up. Parmenio told him the story, and was not a little surprised at the way in which he took it.

"Ah," said the king, "perhaps they are right. After all, we must be audacious, if we are to succeed. Life is short, and the world is large; and if we are to conquer it, we cannot afford to wait. It is madness, as you say; but sometimes madness is an inspiration of the gods. Perhaps, after all, they will have shown us the way. Anyhow, they must be supported. Go," he went on, addressing himself to Charidemus, "and get all the volunteers you can to follow at once. And you, Parmenio, get three companies under arms at once."

The young officer found that the king's commands had been anticipated. The volunteers were ready, and hurrying up at the double, found that they had just come in time. Meleager and Amyntas had been at first astonishingly successful. So absolutely unlooked-for was their attack, that the party told off by the commander of the garrison to defend the weak point in the defences of the city was taken completely by surprise. Man after man was cut down almost without resistance, and the survivors, who did not realize that the assailants were but a simple pair, began to retire in confusion. But such a panic naturally did not last long. The clash of swords attracted other defenders from the neighbouring parts of the walls, and the Inseparables found themselves hard pressed. They had indeed been parted by the rush of the enemy. Amyntas had set his back against a broken piece of wall, and was defending himself with desperate courage against some half-dozen assailants; Meleager had been forced about twenty yards backwards, and at the moment of the arrival of the Macedonian volunteers, had been brought to his knees by a blow from the sword of a Theban refugee. A furious conflict ensued. Reinforcements hurried up from within the walls, and for a time the besiegers were forced back. But when the regular Macedonian infantry appeared upon the scene, the aspect of affairs was changed, and the garrison could no longer hold their own. Indeed, it became evident that if proper preparations had been made, the town might have been taken there and then.

"You see that the madmen were inspired after all," said Alexander to Parmenio.

Meanwhile one of the two original assailants was in serious danger. The tide of battle had left him stranded, so to speak, and alone, and a disabling wound on the right knee prevented him from regaining the line of his friends. His companion saw his predicament, and rushed to his help, followed by a score of Macedonians, among whom were Charidemus and Charondas. The rescue was successfully effected, but not without loss. By this time the sky had become overcast, and the darkness was so thick that it was necessary to suspend the attack. The signal for retreat was accordingly sounded, and the besiegers hastened to retire within their lines. At this moment a missile discharged at random from the walls struck Charidemus on the head with a force that at once prostrated him on the ground. Charondas, who was close by him when he fell, lifted him on to his shoulders, and carried him as well as he could. But the burden of a full-grown man—and the young Macedonian was unusually tall and broad—was considerable, not to speak of the additional weight of his armour, and Charondas, who had been slightly wounded in the course of the struggle, fainted under the exertion. Partially recovering consciousness, he struggled on for a few paces in the hope of getting help. Then he lost his senses again. When he came to himself he was in the camp, but about his friend nothing was known. The soldier who had carried the Theban off had supposed him to be alone, and had unwittingly left his companion to his fate.

Memnon

CHARIDEMUS was partially stunned by the blow. He retained, however, a dim consciousness of what followed, and found afterwards, from such information as he was able to obtain from friends and enemies, that his impressions had not deceived him. First, then, he was aware of being carried for a certain distance in the direction of the besiegers' lines; and, secondly, of this motion ceasing, not a little to his immediate relief, and of his being left, as he felt, in peace. It was a fact, we know, that his companion endeavoured to carry him off, and did succeed in doing so for a few yards; we know also how he was compelled to abandon his burden. The Macedonian's next impression was of being carried exactly the opposite way. He had even an indistinct remembrance of having passed through a gateway, and of a debate being held over him and about him, a debate which he guessed but with a very languid interest indeed—so spent were all his forces of mind and body—

might be to settle the question of his life or death. After this, he was conscious of being carried up a steep incline, not without joltings which caused him acute pain; sometimes so overpowering as to make him, as he was afterwards told, lose consciousness altogether. Finally came a feeling of rest, uneasy indeed, but still most welcome after the almost agonizing sensations which had preceded it. This condition lasted, as he subsequently learnt, for nearly three days and nights, causing by its persistence, unbroken as it was by any hopeful symptoms, no small fears for his life. Relief was given by the skill of a local physician, possibly the Diopeithes whose name and praise still survive among the monuments of Halicarnassëan worthies which time has spared and modern research disinterred.

This experienced observer discovered that a minute splinter of bone was pressing on the brain, and removed it by a dexterous operation. The patient was instantaneously restored to the full possession of his senses. Diopeithes (so we will call him) thought it best, however, to administer a sleeping draught, and it was late in the morning of the following day before the young man could satisfy his curiosity as to the events which had befallen him.

One thing indeed became evident to him at almost the very moment of his waking. He knew that he must be in one of the two citadels of the town, for he could see from his bed, and that in a way which showed it to be slightly below him, the splendid building which, under the name of the Mausoleum, was known as one of the "Seven Wonders of the World." It was then in all the freshness of its first splendour, for little more than ten years had passed since its completion. The marble steps which rose in a pyramid of exquisite proportions shone with a dazzling whiteness. The graceful columns with their elaborately sculptured capitals, the finely proportioned figures of Carian and Greek heroes of the past, the majestic lions that seemed, after the Greek fashion, to watch the repose of the dead king, and, crowning all, Mausolus himself in his chariot reining in the "breathing bronze" of his four fiery steeds—these combined to form a marvel of richness and beauty. After nature and man had wrought their worst upon it for fifteen hundred years, a traveller of the twelfth century could still say, "It was and is a wonder." What it was as it came fresh from the hand of sculptor and architect it would be difficult to imagine.

Charidemus was busy contemplating the beauties of the great monument when a slave entered bringing with him the requisites for the toilet. After a short interval another presented himself with the materials of a meal, a piece of roast flesh, a loaf of bread, cheese, a bunch of dried grapes, a small flagon of wine, and another of water, freshly drawn from the well, and deliciously cool.

By the time the prisoner had done justice to his fare, a visitor entered the apartment. In the newcomer he recognized no less important a personage than the great Memnon himself. Charidemus had seen him at the Granicus, making desperate efforts to stem the tide of defeat; and he knew him well by reputation as the one man who might be expected to hold his own in a battle against Alexander himself. Memnon was a man of about fifty, of a tall and commanding figure, with bright and penetrating eyes, and a nose that, without wholly departing from the Greek type, had something of the curve which we are accustomed to associate with the capacity of a leader of men. But he had a decided appearance of ill-health; his cheeks were pale and wasted, with a spot of hectic colour, and his frame was painfully attenuated. He acknowledged the presence of his prisoner with a very slight salutation, and after beckoning to the secretary who accompanied him to take a seat and make preparations for writing, proceeded to put some questions through an interpreter. He spoke in Greek, and the interpreter, in whom Charidemus recognized a soldier of his own company, translated what he said into the Macedonian dialect.

The first question naturally concerned his name and rank in Alexander's army. Charidemus, who indeed spoke Macedonian with much less fluency than he spoke Greek, ventured to address his answer directly to the great man himself. The effect was magical. The cold and stern expression disappeared from the commander's face, and was replaced by a pleasant and genial smile.

"What!" he cried, "you are a Greek, and, if I do not mistake the accent—though, indeed, an Athenian could not speak better—you are a Dorian."

Charidemus explained that his mother was an Argive woman, and that he had spent all his early years in the Peloponnese.

"Then I was right about the Dorian," said the Memnon, in a still more friendly tone. "My heart always warms to hear the broad 'a' of our common race; for we are kinsmen. I came, as I daresay you know, from Rhodes. But come, let us have a chat together; we can do without our friends here."

He dismissed the secretary and the interpreter. When they were gone, he turned to Charidemus. "Now tell me who you are. But, first, are you quite sure that you are strong enough for a talk? Diopeithes tells me that he has found out and removed the cause of your trouble; and he knows his business as well as any man upon earth; but I should like to hear it from your own lips."

The young man assured him that he was perfectly recovered, and then proceeded to give him an outline of the story with which my readers are already acquainted.

"Well," said Memnon, when the end was reached, "I have nothing to reproach you with. For the matter of that, you might, with much more reason, reproach me. Why should I, a Greek of the Greeks, for I claim descent from Hercules himself," he added, with a smile, "why should I be found fighting for the Persians, for the very people who would have turned us into bondmen if they could? Ask me that question, and I must confess that I cannot answer it. All I can say is that I have found the Great King an excellent master, a generous man who can listen to the truth, and take good advice, which is more, by the way, than I can say for some of his lieutenants. And then his subjects are tolerably well off; I don't think that they improve their condition by coming under the rule of Spartan warriors or Athenian generals, so far as I have had an opportunity of seeing anything of these gentlemen. What your Alexander may do for them, if he gets the chance, is more than I can say. But I am quite sure that if he manages to climb into the throne of the Great King, he will not find it a comfortable seat."

After a short pause, during which he seemed buried in thought, the commander began again. "I won't ask you any questions which you might think it inconsistent with your duty to your master to answer. In fact, there is no need for me to do so. I fancy that I know pretty nearly everything that you could tell me. Thanks to my spies I can reckon to a few hundreds how many men your king can bring into the field; I have a shrewd idea of how much money he has in his military chest, and of how much he owes—the first, I am quite sure, is a very small sum, and the second a very big one. As for his plans, I wish that I knew more about them; but then you could not help me, if you would. But that he has great plans, I am sure; and it will take all that we can do, and more too, unless I am much mistaken, to baffle them."

He paused, and walked half-a-dozen times up and down the room, meditating deeply, and sometimes talking in a low voice to himself.

"Perhaps you may wonder," he began again, "why, if I don't expect to get any information out of you, I don't let you go. To tell you the plain truth, I cannot afford it. You are worth something to me, and we are not so well off that I can make any present to my adversaries. Macedonian or Greek, you are a person of importance, and I shall have to make use of you—always," the speaker went on, laying his hand affectionately on the young man's shoulder, "always in as agreeable and advantageous a way to yourself as I can possibly manage. Perhaps I may be able to exchange you; but for the present you must be content to be my guest, if you will allow me to call myself your host. I only wish I could entertain you better. I can't recommend a walk, for your friends outside keep the place a little too lively with their catapults. Books, I fear, are somewhat scarce. Halicarnassus, you know, was never a literary place. It produced one great writer, and appreciated him so little as positively to drive him away. As for myself, I have not had the opportunity or the taste for collecting books. Still there are a few rolls, Homer and our Aristophanes among them, I know, with which you may while away a few hours; there is a slave-boy who can play a very good game of draughts, if you choose to send for him; and you can go over the Mausoleum there, which is certainly worth looking at. And now farewell for the present! We shall meet at dinner. I, as you may suppose, have got not a few things to look after."

With this farewell Memnon left the room, but came back in a few moments. "I am half-ashamed," he said, in an apologetic tone, "to mention the matter to a gentleman like yourself; still it is a matter of business, and you will excuse it. I took it for granted that you give me your word not to escape."

Charidemus gave the required promise, and his host then left him, but not till he had repeated in the most friendly fashion his invitation to dinner. "We dine at sunset," he said, "but a slave will give you warning when the time approaches."

Charidemus found the literary resources of his quarters more extensive than he had been led to expect. By the help of these, and of a long and careful inspection of the Mausoleum, he found no difficulty in passing the day.

Dinner was a very cheerful meal. The party consisted of four—the two to whom my readers have not yet been introduced being Barsiné, a lady of singular beauty, and as accomplished as she was fair; and Nicon, an Athenian of middle age, who was acting as tutor to Memnon's son. Nicon was a brilliant talker. He had lived many years in Athens, and had heard all the great orators, whose manner he could imitate with extraordinary skill. Plato, too, he had known well; indeed, he had been his disciple, one of the twenty-eight who had constituted the inner circle, all of them duly fortified with the knowledge of geometry, to whom the philosopher imparted his most intimate instructions. Aristotle, not to mention less distinguished names, had been one of his class-fellows. But if Nicon's conversation was extraordinarily varied and interesting, it was not more than a match for Barsiné's. Charidemus listened with amazement to the wit and learning which she betrayed in her talk—betrayed rather than displayed—for she had no kind of ostentation or vanity about her. Her intelligence and knowledge was all the more amazing because she was a Persian by birth, had the somewhat languid beauty characteristic of her race, and spoke Greek with an accent, delicate indeed, but noticeably Persian. Memnon seemed glad to play the part of listener rather than a talker; though he would now and then interpose a shrewd observation which showed that he was thoroughly competent to appreciate the conversation. As for the young Macedonian, he would have been perfectly content to spend the whole evening in silent attention to such talk as he had never heard before; but Nicon skilfully drew him out, and as he was a clever and well-informed young man, he acquitted himself sufficiently well.

At Sea

IT was not for long, however, that Charidemus was destined to enjoy these somewhat lonely days, and evenings that seemed only too short. About a week after the day on which he made his first acquaintance with Memnon and his wife, he was roused from his sleep about an hour before dawn by a visit from the governor himself.

"Dress yourself at once," said Memnon, "I will wait for you."

"We can hold the place no longer," the governor explained to his prisoner, as they hurried down the steep path that led from the citadel to the harbour.

"I am leaving a garrison in the citadels, but the town is lost. Luckily for me, though not, perhaps, for you, I have still command of the sea."

The harbour was soon reached. Memnon's ship was waiting for him, and put off the moment the gangway was withdrawn; the rest of the squadron had already gained the open sea.

"You must make yourself as comfortable as you can on deck; the ladies have the cabin. Happily the night is fine, and our voyages hereabouts are not very long. The Ægean is the very Elysium of fair-weather sailors."

Charidemus rolled himself up in the cloak with which, at Memnon's bidding, a sailor had furnished him, and slept soundly, under one of the bulwarks, till he was awakened by the increasing heat of the sun. When he had performed as much of a toilet as the means at his disposal would permit, he was joined by Memnon, and conducted to the after-deck, where the breakfast table had been spread under an awning of canvas.

Presently the ladies appeared. Barsiné was one of them; the other was a very beautiful girl, who may have numbered thirteen or fourteen summers. "My niece, Clearista," said Memnon, "daughter," he added in a whisper, "of my brother Mentor;" and then aloud, "The most troublesome charge that a poor uncle was ever plagued with." The damsel shook her chestnut locks at him, and turned away with a pout, which was about as sincere as her uncle's complaint. The next moment a lad of ten, who had been trailing a baited hook over the stern, made his appearance. This was Memnon's son, another Mentor. His tutor, the Nicon, whose acquaintance we have already made, followed him, and the party was now complete.

It was Clearista's first voyage, and her wonder and delight were beyond expression. The sea, calm as a mirror, and blue as a sapphire, under a cloudless sky; the rhythmic dash of the oars as they rose and fell in time to the monotonous music of the fugleman standing high upon the stern; the skimming flight of the sea-birds as they followed the galley in the hope of some morsels of food; the gambols of a shoal of dolphins, playing about so near that it seemed as if they must be struck by the oars or even run down by the prow—these, and all the sights and sounds of the voyage fairly overpowered her with pleasure. Everything about her seemed to breathe of freedom; and she had scarcely ever been outside the door of the women's apartments, or, at most, the walks of a garden. Who can wonder at her ecstasy? Memnon and Barsiné looked on with indulgent smiles. Young Mentor, who had seen a good deal more of the world than had his cousin, felt slightly superior. As for Charidemus he lost his heart on the spot. Child as she was—and she was young for her years—Clearista seemed to him the most beautiful creature that he had ever beheld.

The day's companionship did not fail to deepen this impression. With a playful imperiousness, which had not a touch of coquetry in it, the girl commanded his services, and he was more than content to fetch and carry for her from morning till night. He brought her pieces of bread when it occurred to her that she should like to feed the gulls; he baited her hook when she conceived the ambition of catching a fish; and he helped her to secure the small sword-fish which she was lucky enough to hook, but was far too frightened to pull up. When the sun grew so hot as to compel her to take shelter under the awning the two told each other their stories. The girl's was very brief and uneventful, little more than the tale of journeys, mostly performed in a closed litter, from one town to another; but the young man thought it profoundly interesting. He, on the other hand, had really something to tell, and she listened with a flattering mixture of wonder, admiration, and terror. Towards evening the unwonted excitement had fairly worn her out, and she was reluctantly compelled to seek her cabin.

Our hero was gazing somewhat disconsolately over the bulwarks when he felt a hand laid upon his shoulder. He turned, and saw Memnon standing behind him with a somewhat sad smile upon his face.

"Melancholy, my young friend?" he said. "Well, I have something to tell you that may cheer you up. I did not forget you yesterday when we left the town. Of course it would not have done to let your people get any inkling of my plans. If they had guessed that we were going to evacuate the place, they might have given us a good deal of trouble in getting off. So instead of sending any message myself, I left one for the commander of the garrison to send as soon as we were safely gone. Briefly, it was to say that I was ready to exchange you for any one of four prisoners-of-war whom I named—I might have said all four without making a particularly good bargain, for, if you will allow a man who is old enough to be your father to say so, I like your looks. If they accepted—and I cannot suppose for a moment that they will hesitate— they were to send out a boat with a flag of truce from Miletus, where we shall be in two hours' time or so, if the weather holds good. Then we shall have to say good-bye."

"I shall never forget your kindness," cried Charidemus.

"Well, my son, some day you may be able to make me or mine a return for it."

"Command me," answered the young man in a tone of unmistakable sincerity; "you shall be heartily welcome to anything that I can do for you or yours."

"Listen then," said Memnon. "First, there is something that you can do for me. Perhaps it is a foolish vanity, but I should like to be set right some day in the eyes of the world. You will keep what I am going to tell you to yourself till you think that the proper time for telling it is come. I shall be gone then, but I should not like those that come after me to think that I was an incompetent fool. Well, then, your king never ought to have been allowed to land in Asia. We could have prevented it. We had the command of the sea. We had only to bring up the Phœnician squadron, which was doing nothing at all, and our force would have been perfectly overwhelming. Look at the state of affairs now! Your king has positively disbanded his fleet. He knew perfectly well

39

that it had not a chance with ours, and that it was merely a useless expense to him. Just as we could now prevent him from returning, so we could have prevented him from coming. For, believe me, we were as strong in ships six months ago as we are now, and I urged this on the king with all my might. He seemed persuaded. But he was overborne. Some headstrong fools, who unfortunately had his ear, could not be content, forsooth, but they must measure their strength with Alexander. So he was allowed to come, to land his army without losing a single man. Still, even then, something might have been done. I knew that we could not bring an army into the field that could stand against him for an hour. The Persians never were a match for the Greeks, man to man; and besides, the Persians are nothing like what they were a hundred and fifty years ago. And the Greek mercenaries could not be relied upon. They were the scum of the cities, and many of them no more Greeks than they are gods. Any man who had a smattering of Greek, and could manage to procure an old suit of armour, could get himself hired; and very likely the only thing Greek about him was his name, and that he had stolen. Well, I knew that such as they were, and without a leader, too—even the best mercenaries without a leader go for very little—they would be worth next to nothing. So I went to Arsites, who was satrap of Phrygia, and in chief command, and said to him, 'Don't fight; we shall most infallibly be beaten. There is nothing in Asia that can stand against the army which we have allowed Alexander to bring over. Fall back before him; waste the country as you go, burn the houses; burn even the towns, if you do not like to detach men enough to hold them. Don't let the enemy find a morsel to eat that he has not brought himself, or a roof to shelter him that he does not himself put up. And then attack him at home. He has brought all the best of his army with him. What he has left behind him to garrison his own dominions is very weak indeed, poor troops, and not many of them. And then he has enemies all round him. The Thracians on the north are always ready for a fight, and in the south there are the Greeks, who hate him most fervently, and have a long score against him and his father, which they would dearly like to wipe out. Half the men that you have with you here, and who will be scattered like clouds before the north-wind, if you try to meet him in battle, will raise such a storm behind him in his own country that he will have no choice but to turn back.' Well, Arsites would not listen to me. 'If you are afraid,' he said, 'you can go, you and your men; we shall be able to do very well without you. As for wasting the country and burning the houses, the idea is monstrous. The king has given it into my sole keeping, and there it shall be. Not a field shall be touched, not a house shall be burnt in my province. As for dividing the army, and sending half of it into Europe, it is madness. What good did Darius and Xerxes get by sending armies thither? No—the man has chosen to dare us on our ground, and we will give him a lesson which he and his people will never forget.' I urged my views again, and then the fellow insulted me. 'Of course,' he said, 'it does not suit you to put an end to the war. The more it is prolonged, the more necessary you will be thought.' After that, of course, there was nothing more to be said. We fought, and everything happened exactly as I had foretold. Then the king made me commander-in-chief; but it was too late. I shall be able to do something with the fleet, of course; I shall get hold of some of the islands; but what good will that do when your Alexander is marching, perhaps, on Susa?"

He paused for a while, and took a few turns upon the deck, then he began again.

"As for myself, the end is very near; I have not many months to live. I should like to have measured my strength with this Alexander of yours without having a pack of incompetent satraps to hamper me. Perhaps it is as well for me and my reputation that I never shall. You know my name is not exactly a good omen. He calls himself the descendant of Achilles, and verily I can believe it. Any one who saw him fighting by the river bank on the day of the Granicus might well have thought that it was Achilles come to life again, just as he was when he drove the Trojans through the Xanthus. How gloriously handsome he was! what blows he dealt! Well, you remember—though I don't think it is in Homer, that there was another Memnon who fought with the son of Peleus, and came off the worse; and I might do the same. Doubtless it was in the fates that all this should happen. I have felt for some time that the end was coming for the Great King; though, as I think I told you the other day, I am not at all sure that the change from Darius to Alexander will be for the better. And now for my present concerns. My wife and child are going to Susa. It is the way with the Persians to take a man's family as hostages when they put him into a place of trust. Under other circumstances I might have refused. If the Persians wanted my services they must have been content to have them on my own terms. As it is, I do not object. My people will be safer there than anywhere else where I can put them. And that sweet child Clearista will go with them. But I feel troubled about them; they have that fatal gift of beauty. Good Gods, why do ye make women so fair? they break men's hearts and their own. And there is little Mentor too. My elder sons—children, you will understand, of my first wife—can take care of themselves; but my wife and my niece and the dear boy are helpless. Now what I want you to promise is that, if you can, you will protect them. Your Alexander may reach Susa; I think he will; I do not see what there is to stop him. If he does, and you are with him, think of me, and do what you can to help them."

The young man felt a great wave of love and pity surge up in his heart as this appeal was made to him.

"By Zeus and all the gods in heaven," he cried, "I will hold them as dear as my own life."

"The gods reward you for it," said Memnon, wringing his young friend's hand, while the unaccustomed tears gathered in his eyes.

Then silence fell between the two. It was interrupted by the approach of a sailor.

"My lord," said the man, addressing himself to Memnon, "there is a boat coming out from Miletus with a flag of truce."

"Ha!" cried Memnon, "they are sending for you. Well, I am sorry to part. But it is for your good, and for mine too, for I trust you as I would trust my own son."

Turning to the man who had brought the message, he said, "I expected the boat. Tell the captain from me to lie to till she boards us."

When the little craft drew near enough for the occupants to be distinguished, Memnon burst into a laugh. "Ah!" he said, "they have put a proper value on you, my young friend. They have positively sent all four. I did not like, as I told you, to ask for more than one; but here they all are. It is not exactly a compliment to them; but they won't mind that, if they get their freedom."

Very shortly afterwards the boat came alongside; and a Macedonian officer climbed up the side of the galley. He made a profoundly respectful salutation to Memnon, and then presented a letter. The document ran thus:

"Alexander, King of the Macedonians, and Commander of the United Armies of the Hellenes to Memnon, Commander of the Armies of the King, greeting.

"I consent to the exchange which you propose. But as I would not be as Diomed, who gave brass in exchange for gold, I send you the four prisoners whom you mention, in exchange for Charidemus the Macedonian. Farewell."

The letter had been written by a secretary, but it had the bold autograph of Alexander, signed across it.

"My thanks to the king your master, who is as generous as he is brave," was the message which Memnon gave to the officer in charge. The four exchanged prisoners now made their way up the side of the ship, were courteously received by Memnon, and bidden to report themselves to the captain.

"Will your lordship please to sign this receipt for the prisoners?" said the Macedonian officer.

This was duly done.

"Will you drink a cup of wine?" asked Memnon.

The officer thanked him for his politeness, but declined. He was under orders to return without delay.

"Then," said Memnon, "your countryman shall accompany you directly. You will give him a few moments to make his adieus."

The Macedonian bowed assent, and the two descended into the cabin. Barsiné was sitting busy with her needle by the side of a couch on which Clearista lay fast asleep.

"Our young friend leaves us immediately," said Memnon to his wife; "I proposed an exchange, as you know, and it has been accepted. The boat is waiting to take him ashore. He is coming to say farewell."

"We are sorry to lose you," said Barsiné, "more sorry, I fancy, than you are to go."

"Lady," said Charidemus, "you put me in a sore strait when you say such a thing. All my future lies elsewhere; but at least I can cherish the recollection of your kindness. Never, surely, had a prisoner less reason to wish for freedom."

"And now," said Memnon, in as light a tone as he could assume, "I should like to give our young friend a keepsake. It is possible that you may meet him at Susa."

"Meet him at Susa," echoed Barsiné, in astonishment, "how can that be?"

"My darling," returned Mentor, "if our people cannot make any better stand against Alexander than they did at the Granicus, there is no reason why he should not get to Susa, or anywhere else for that matter."

Barsiné turned pale, for lightly as her husband spoke, she knew that he meant something very serious indeed.

"Yes," continued her husband, "you may meet him there, and he may be able to be of some use to you. I give him, you see, this ring;" he took, as he spoke, a ring set with a handsome sapphire from a casket that stood near. "If he can help you I know he will come himself, if anything should hinder him from doing that, he will give it to some one whom he can trust. Put yourself and your children in his hands, or in the hands of his deputy."

"Oh! why do you talk like this?" cried Barsiné.

"Darling," replied Memnon, "it is well to be prepared for everything. This invasion may come to nothing. But if it does not, if Alexander does make his way to the capital—well, it is not to me you will have to look for help; by that time I shall—"

The poor woman started up and laid her hand upon the speaker's mouth.

"Good words, good words!" she cried.

He smiled. "You are right, for as your favourite Homer says:

" 'In sooth on the knees of the gods lieth all whereof we speak.'

And now give him something yourself that he may remember you by."

She detached a locket that hung round her neck, and put it into his hand. He raised it respectfully to his lips.

"And Clearista—she might spare something. Artemis bless the child! how soundly she sleeps!" said Memnon, looking affectionately at the slumbering girl. And indeed the voices of the speakers had failed to rouse her. Exquisitely lovely did she look as she slept, her cheek tinged with a delicate flush, her lips parted in a faint smile, her chestnut hair falling loosely over the purple coverlet of the couch.

"The darling won't mind a curl," said Memnon; "put that in my wife's locket, and you will remember both of them together;" and he cut off a little ringlet from the end of a straggling lock.

One of the sailors tapped at the cabin door.

"Yes; we are coming," said Memnon. The young man caught Barsiné's hand and pressed it to his lips; he knelt down and imprinted a gentle kiss on Clearista's right hand. She smiled in her sleep, but still did not wake. A few moments afterwards he was in the boat, Memnon pressing into his hand at the last moment a purse, which he afterwards found to contain a roll of thirty Darics and some valuable jewels. In the course of an hour he stepped on to the quay of Miletus, a free man, but feeling curiously little pleasure in his recovered liberty.

In Greece Again

ON landing at Miletus Charidemus found a letter from the king awaiting him. After expressing his pleasure that he had been able to regain services that were so valuable, and paying him the compliment of saying that he considered the exchange had been very much to his own advantage, Alexander continued, "I desire to see you so soon after you have regained your liberty as you can contrive to come to me. You can journey either by land or sea. In either case you have at your disposal all that you may need. But I should advise that you come by sea, for I expect by the time within which you can probably reach me to be not far from the coast of Syria. The gods preserve you in the future as they have in the past!"

The officer in charge of the garrison of Miletus held very decidedly the same opinion as the king. "You can understand," he said, when Charidemus went to report himself, "that the country is at present very unsettled. When such an army as that we fought with at the Granicus is broken up, a great number of the men naturally become brigands. I do not doubt but that every forest between here and Lycia is full of them. Even without the brigands, the roads would hardly be safe. At present, you see, it is all an enemy's country, except where we have garrisons. No; you could not travel without danger, unless I gave you all my garrison for an escort. Of course there are risks by sea. In the first place, it is very late for a voyage; and then there are Phœnician cruisers about. Still I should strongly recommend this way of going; and, by good luck, I can put the very fastest ship and the very best captain that we have at your disposal. I will send for him, and you shall hear what he says."

In about an hour's time, accordingly, the captain presented himself, a weather-beaten sailor, somewhat advanced in years, if one might judge from his grizzled hair and beard, but as vigorous and alert as a youth. He made light of the difficulty of the time of the year. "Give me a good ship and a good crew, and I will sail at any time you please from one equinox to the other; and let me say that you will not find a better ship than the Centaur between here and the Pillars of Hercules. As for the crew, I can warrant them. I have trained them myself. And I am not much afraid of Phœnician cruisers. Of course accidents may happen; but I know that in a fair fight or a fair chase, the Centaur and its crew can hold their own against anything that ever came out of Tyre or Sidon. And now, my good sir, when can you start? The sooner the better, I say, for the Persians are busy just now in the north, and we may very well get to our journey's end without any trouble at all."

Charidemus said that he had nothing to keep him in Miletus, and that the speedier the start the better he would be pleased. Before sunrise next morning, accordingly, the Centaur was on its way, with a fresh following breeze from the north that spared the rowers all trouble. Halicarnassus was passed towards evening, and Rhodes the next day, brilliant in the sunshine with which its patron, the sun-god, was said always to favour it. The wind here began to fail them somewhat, as their course became more easterly; but the sea was calm, and the rowers, an admirably trained crew, who acknowledged no equals in the Western Mediterranean, got over distances that would have seemed incredible to their passenger had he not been an eye-witness of their accomplishment. Pleusicles, the captain, was in high spirits, and brought out of the store of his memory or his imagination yarn after yarn. He had begun his seafaring life nearly forty years before under the Athenian admiral Iphicrates—he was an Æginetan by birth—and had seen that commander's brilliant victory over the combined fleets of Sparta and Syracuse. He had been in every naval battle that had been fought since then; first in the service of Athens, and then, either from some offence given or from unpunctuality in the matter of payment, going over to Philip of Macedon. Intervals of peace he had employed in commercial enterprises. He knew the Mediterranean from end to end, from Tyre to the Pillars, from Cyrene to Massilia. From Massilia, indeed, he had gone on his most adventurous voyage. A Greek traveler, Pytheas by name, had engaged him for an expedition which was to explore regions altogether unknown. Pleusicles related how they had sailed through the Straits of Calpe into the immeasurable Ocean beyond, how they had with difficulty forced their way through leagues of matted sea-weed, and had come after months of difficult travel to an island in the northern sea, a land of much rain and little sunshine, where on a narrow strip of open ground between vast forests and the sea the natives cultivated some precarious crops of corn. Of so much Pleusicles had been himself an eye-witness: but there were greater marvels of which he knew only by hearsay, a yet remoter island surrounded by what was neither land nor sea nor air, but a mixture of all, one huge jelly-fish, as it were, and a tribe with whom amber, a rare and precious thing among the Greeks, was so abundant that it was used as firewood.

On the third day the Centaur reached Patara on the Lycian coast, and on the next the Greek city of Phaselis. Here Charidemus found the king, who was engaged in one of those literary episodes with which he was wont to relieve his military life. The pride of Phaselis was its famous citizen, Theodectes, poet and orator. He had been the pupil, or rather the friend, of Aristotle. As such Alexander had known him when he himself had sat at the feet of the great philosopher. Indeed, though there was as much as twenty years difference between their ages, the prince and the poet had themselves been friends. Theodectes had died the year before in the very prime of life, and his fellow-citizens had exerted themselves to do him all possible honour. They had given the commission for his statue to Praxiteles, the first sculptor of the time, paying him a heavy fee of two talents, a sum which severely taxed their modest resources. The statue had just then been set up. And now, by a piece of singular good fortune, as they thought it, the townsfolk had the future conqueror of Asia to inaugurate it. The king took a part in the sacrifice, crowned the statue with garlands, was present with some of his principal officers at the representation of a tragedy by the deceased author, and laughed heartily at the concluding farce in which the story of the healing of Cheiron, the Centaur, was ludicrously travestied.

Early the next day Charidemus was summoned to the royal presence. The king greeted him with more than his usual kindness, and proceeded to explain the business in which he proposed to employ him. "I am going to send you," he said, "first to Greece, and then home; I have not the same reason," he went on, with a smile, "that I had with Ptolemy and his detachment, that they were newly married. But for the next three months or so there will be very little doing here, and you can be more profitably employed elsewhere. First, you must go to Athens. You will be in charge of an offering which I am sending to the goddess, three hundred complete suits of armour from the spoils of the Granicus. You should be a persona grata there. You are half an Argive, and the Argives have always been on good terms with the Athenians. And then you speak good Greek. If I were to send one of my worthy Macedonians they would laugh at his accent; he might lose his temper, and all the grace of the affair would be lost. That, then, is your mission, as far as the world sees it; you will take sealed instructions about other matters which you will not open till you have crossed the sea. . . . The offering is all ready; in fact, it was lying shipped at Miletus when you landed there. But I wanted to see you, and to be sure also that you received my instructions. These you shall have at sunset. When you have received them, start back at once."

Punctually at sunset one of the royal pages brought a roll of parchment sealed with the royal seal. Charidemus, who had been waiting on board the Centaur for it, gave a formal receipt for it, and within half an hour was on his way westward. The good ship and her picked crew had better opportunities for showing their mettle than had occurred on the eastward journey. Things were easy enough as long as they were under the lee of the Lycian coast; but at Rhodes a strong head wind encountered them; and it was only after a hard struggle of at least twelve days, during which even the bold Pleusicles thought more than once of turning back, that they reached Miletus. By that time the weather had changed again; and the voyage to Athens, though undertaken with fear and trembling by the captains of the heavily-laden merchantmen that carried the armour, was prosperous and uneventful.

Charidemus spent about a month in Athens, finding, as might have been expected, a vast amount of things to interest, please, and astonish him. Some of the impressions made upon him by what he saw and heard may be gathered from extracts taken from letters which he wrote at this time to his Theban friend.

"... The armour has been presented in the Temple of Athené Polias. A more splendid spectacle I have never seen. They told me that it was almost as fine as the great Panathenæa, the grand triennial festival of which I dare say you have heard. The Peplos was not there nor the Basket-bearers —I missed, you see, the chance of seeing the beauty, though I saw the rank and fashion of Athens. But the magistrates were there, in their robes of office, headed by the King Archon, and, behind them a huge array of soldiers in complete armour, good enough to look at, but poor stuff in a battle, I should fancy—indeed the Athenians have long since done most of their fighting, I am told, by paid deputies. The best of these troops was a battalion, several thousands strong, of the 'youths,' as they called them. Students they are who do a little soldiering by way of change after their books. They can march, and they know their drill; and they are not pursy and fat, as are most of their elders. Their armour and accoutrements are excellent. If their wits are only as bright as their shields and their spear-points, they must be clever fellows in the lecture-room. And the Temple itself! I simply have not words to describe it and its spendours. And then there was the great statue of the goddess outside the Temple; I had never seen it close at hand, though I remember having had the point of the lance which she holds in her hand and the crest of her helmet pointed out to me as I was sailing along the coast. But the effect of the whole when one stands by the pedestal is overpowering. Its magnificent stature—it is more than forty cubits high —its majestic face, its imposing attitude—she is challenging the world, it would seem, on behalf of her favourite city—all these things produce an impression that cannot be described. It is made, you must understand, of bronze, and the simplicity of the material impressed me more than the gorgeous ivory and gold of the Athené Polias, as they call her. While I am talking about statues I must tell you about one which I was allowed to see by special favour; it is made of olive wood, and is of an age past all counting; the rudest shape that can be imagined, but extraordinarily interesting. The keeper of the Temple where it is (not the same as that of which I have been speaking, but called, by way of distinction, the Old Temple) have a story that it fell down from heaven. In the evening there was a great banquet in the Town-hall, a very gorgeous affair, with delicacies brought from all the four winds—pheasants from the Black Sea, and peacocks, and dolphins, and I know not what in flesh, fish, and fowl. Of course the special Attic dishes were prominent—honey, figs, and olives—and there were a great choice of vintages. I was amazed at the abundance and luxury of the entertainment, and could not help thinking that there was a great deal of foolish waste. Far more interesting to me than the dishes and the drinks were the guests. I do not mean the magistrates and generals, for they had nothing particularly distinguished about them; I mean those who have a permanent seat at the table. You must know that the Athenians have an excellent custom of rewarding men who have done conspicuously good service to the state by giving them such a seat. Of course I saw Phocion there. I had seen him before in the king's camp; and he has been very civil and serviceable to me. I sat next to a veteran who was the oldest of the public guests, and must have numbered fully a hundred years. What a storehouse of recollections the old man's mind was! Of recent things and persons he knew nothing. When I was speaking of our king he stared blankly at me. But he remembered the plague—his father and mother and all his family died of it, he told me. His first campaign was in Sicily. He had been taken prisoner and thrust into the stone quarries of Syracuse. He could not bear to think, he told me, even now of the horrors of the place. Then he had fought at Œgos-Potami, and I know not where else. His last service, I remember, was at Mantinea, where he was in command of an Athenian contingent. He was seventy years old then, he told me, but as vigorous, he boasted, as the youngest of them. He saw your Epaminondas struck down, though he was not very near. And he was a disciple of Socrates. 'To think,' he said, 'that I should be dining here at the State's expense, and that he had the hemlock draught! I remember,' he went on, 'when he was put on his trial and had been found guilty, and the president asked him to name his own penalty, he mentioned this very honour that I enjoy. He deserved it much better, he said, for showing his countrymen how foolish and ignorant they were, than if he had won a victory at Olympia. What a stir of rage went through the assembly when he said it! It quite settled the matter for the death penalty. And now here am I and he— well he has his reward elsewhere, if what he always said is true—and that I shall soon know.' A most interesting old man is this, and I must try to see him again."

A week or two afterwards, he wrote again.

"I have seen Demosthenes. A young Athenian with whom I have become acquainted introduced me to him. At first he was cold and distant. It is no passport to his favour to be a Macedonian. Afterwards he became sufficiently friendly, and we had much talk together. He is not as hopeful as I am about the king's undertaking. He thinks, indeed, that it will succeed, though, very likely, in his heart he wishes that it may not. But he does not expect much good from it. 'So Greece, you think,' he said to me one day 'will conquer Persia. I doubt it. I don't doubt indeed that your Alexander will overrun Asia from one end to the other. Philip was a great soldier, and his son is a greater, while your Macedonians are the stuff out of which armies rightly so called are made. Persia, on the other hand, is thoroughly rotten, and will fall almost at a touch. But this is not the same thing as Greece conquering Persia. No; Persia will conquer Greece; we shall be overwhelmed with a flood of eastern vices and servilities. True Greece will perish, just as surely as she would have perished had the bow triumphed over the spear at Marathon or Platæa. But this will scarce be welcome to you,' and he broke off. Still what he said has set me thinking. Only I do believe that our king is too thorough a Greek to be spoilt. But we shall see.

"I hoped to hear the great man speak, but was disappointed. He very seldom speaks now. The fact is there are no politics in Athens; and for the plaintiffs and defendants in civil causes the orators write speeches, but do not deliver them. That the parties concerned have to do themselves. I heard, it is true, a speech of Demosthenes, but it was spoken by a very commonplace person, and, you will understand, was made commonplace to suit him. Of course it would not do to put a piece of eloquence into the mouth of some ordinary farmer or shipbuilder. Everybody knows that the suitors do not write the speeches, but still the proprieties have to be observed.

"The plaintiff in this case—his name was Ariston—had a very strange and piteous story to tell. Unfortunately there was something about the man that moved the court irresistibly to laughter. (The court, you must know, is the strangest that the wit or folly of man ever devised—a regular mob of thousands of men who shout and groan if anything displeases them, and chatter or fall asleep if they are pleased to find the proceedings dull.) Well, Ariston was an eminently respectable man; his hair and beard carefully arranged without being in the least foppish, and his cloak and tunic quite glossy; and the indignities of which he had to complain were so out of keeping with all that he looked that it was almost impossible not to be amused. His story was this, put briefly:

"Three years before (i.e., just before King Philip's death) he had been sent on outpost duty to the frontier. The sons of a certain Conon were his neighbours in the bivouac, wild young fellows who began drinking after the midday meal, and kept it up to nightfall. 'Whereas,' said he in a dignified tone which raised a roar of laughter, 'I conducted myself there just as I do here.' The young men played all sorts of drunken tricks on Ariston and his messmates, till at last the latter complained to the officer in command. The officer administered a severe reprimand, which did, however, no manner of good, for that very night the ruffians made an attack on Ariston's tent, gave him and his friends a beating, and indeed, but for the timely arrival of the officer in command, might have killed them. Of course when the camp broke up there was not a little bad blood between the parties to the quarrel. Still, Ariston did nothing more than try his best to steer clear of these troublesome acquaintances. One evening, however, as he was walking in the market-place with a friend, one of Conon's sons caught sight of him. The young fellow, who was tipsy, ran and fetched his father, who was drinking with a number of friends in a fuller's shop. The party rushed out; one of them seized Ariston's friend and held him fast, while Conon, his son, and another man, caught hold of Ariston himself, tore his cloak off his back, tripped him up, and jumped upon him, as he lay in the mud, cutting his lip through, and closing up both his eyes. So much hurt was he that he could not get up or even speak. But he heard Conon crowing like a cock to celebrate his victory, while his compan-

49

ions suggested that he should flap his wings, by which they meant his elbows, which he was to strike against his sides. Other things he heard, but they were so bad that he was positively ashamed to repeat them to the court. At last some passers-by carried him home, where there was a terrible outcry, his mother and her domestics making as much ado as if he had been carried home dead. After this came a long illness in which his life was despaired of. When he had told his story he gravely controverted what he supposed would be Conon's defence, that this was a quarrel of hot-headed deep-drinking young men; that both parties were gay young fellows who found a pleasure in roaming the streets at night, and playing all kinds of pranks on passers-by, and that the plaintiff had no business to complain, if he happened to get the worst of it. He was no roisterer, Ariston said, with a solemnity which convulsed the court. Indeed, the idea that such a paragon of respectability should be anything of the kind was sufficiently amusing. However, he won his cause, and got thirty minas damages, or will get them if he can manage to make Conon pay, a thing which, the friend who took me into court tells me, is more than doubtful.

"You see, my dear Charondas, that there are other people besides philosophers in Athens. Indeed, from all that I could make out, though clever and learned men come to the city from all parts, the Athenians themselves seldom show any genius. As for those noisy, roistering young fellows, there are numbers of them in the streets at night. I have seen them myself, again and again, though they have never molested me. Indeed, they keep far enough away from any one who is likely to give them a warm reception. I cannot help thinking that, whatever Demosthenes may say, they would be better employed if they were following our king."

At Athens

IN addition to his formal duties as commissioner in charge of the offering to the goddess, Charidemus was entrusted with special messages from Alexander to his old teacher, Aristotle, who had been a resident at Athens for now about two years. He found the philosopher in his favourite haunt of the Lyceum just after he had dismissed his morning class of hearers. Aristotle was somewhat slight and insignificant in person, but he had a singularly keen and intelligent face. His appearance, as far as dress was concerned, was rather that of a man of the world than of a thinker. In fact, it was almost foppish. His hair was arranged with the greatest care. His dress was new and fashionable in cut; and his fingers were adorned with several costly rings. Charidemus could not help thinking what a remarkable contrast he presented to the eccentric being whom he had seen in his tub at Corinth. But in the great man's talk there was not a vestige of affectation or weakness. Charidemus was struck with the wide range of subjects which it embraced. There was nothing in the world in which he did not seem to feel the keenest interest. He cross-examined the young man as to the features of the countries which he had traversed, the products of their soil, the habits of the natives, in a word, as to all his experiences. He expressed a great delight at hearing of the rich collection of curious objects which the king was making for him, and exhorted his young visitor never to let either the duties or the pleasures of a military life interfere with his persistent observation of nature. "If the king's designs are carried out," he said, "if the gods permit him to go as far as I know he purposes to go, he and those who go with him will have the chance of solving many problems which at present are beyond all explanation. This is a world in which every one may do something; and I implore you not to miss your chance. Mind that no fact, however insignificant it may seem, is unworthy of attention. Once the followers after wisdom began with theories; I begin with facts, and I take it that I cannot have too many of them."

Charidemus then put to the philosopher a question on Greek politics, which he had been specially instructed to ask. It was, in effect, whether Alexander had any reason to dread a coalition of the Greek states taking advantage of his occupation in his schemes of conquest to assail him in the rear. "I stand aloof from politics," was the answer of Aristotle. "No one, either now, or when I was in this city before, ever heard me express an opinion on any political subject; no one ever ventured to put me down as a Macedonian or an anti-Macedonian partisan. But though I stand aloof, I observe, and observe, perhaps, all the better. Tell the king that he need have no fear of a coalition against him. Here in Athens there will be no movement in that direction. The parties are too equally balanced; and the patriots, even if they were stronger than they are, would not stir. As for Sparta, it is sullen and angry; but the Spartans have long since lost their vigour. No; tell the king that his danger is at home. His mother and his regent are deadly foes. He must be friendly to both, and this it will require all his practical wisdom to do. And let him beware of plots. Plots are a poisonous weed that grows apace in an Eastern soil. And he has theories about men which may be a source of peril to him. I have often told him that there are two races, the free by nature and the slave by nature, races which are pretty well equivalent, I take it, to Greeks and barbarians. He thinks that he can treat them both as equal. I fear that if he tries the experiment he will alienate the one and not conciliate the other. But it is useless to talk on this subject. If I have not been able to persuade him, I do not suppose that you can. But you can at least tell him from me to beware."

From Athens Charidemus went to Pella. Alexander was perfectly well aware of the state of affairs at home. The letters of his mother, Olympias, had been full of the bitterest complaints against Antipater the regent, and the ill-feeling between the two was a source of serious danger, especially in view of the concealed disaffection of some of his own kinsmen. Charidemus, whose sagacity and aptitude for affairs the king's penetration had noticed, came to observe these facts for himself. This was, in fact, the secret errand which Alexander had entrusted to him. No one would suspect that a serious political mission had been confided to one so young; the fact that he had been brought up in Greece had detached him from native parties; in fact, he would have especially favourable opportunities of observing the set of feeling in Macedonia, while he was engaged in his ostensible occupation of looking after the reinforcements and stores which were to be sent out to Alexander in the spring.

Whilst he was thus employed he found the winter pass rapidly away. At the same time he had no particular reason for regretting his absence from the army. It was engaged in the important but tedious work of establishing a perfectly solid base of operations. Alexander felt that he must have Lesser Asia thoroughly safe behind him, and he employed the earlier part of the year in bringing about this result. But the romantic part of the expedition was yet to come. The great battle or battles which the Persian king was sure to fight for his throne were yet in the future. The treasures of Persepolis and Ecbatana, Babylon, and Susa, were yet to be ransacked; and all the wonders of the further East were yet to be explored. A letter from Charondas, which was put by a courier into the young man's hand on the very eve of his departure from Pella, will tell us something about the doings of the army during this interval. It ran thus—

"You have missed little or nothing by being at home during our winter campaign. For my part I have not so much as once crossed swords with an enemy since I saw you last. Our experiences repeat themselves with a curious monotony. There are strongholds in the country which might give us an infinitude of trouble; but, after a mere pretence of resistance, they yield themselves without a blow. Hear what happened at Celenæ as a specimen of all. The town itself was unwalled—I cannot help thinking, by the way, that walls often do a town more harm than good—but the citadel was impregnable. I never saw a place which it would be more absolutely hopeless to attack. The garrison was ample; they were provisioned, as we have afterwards discovered, for two years, and there was a never-failing spring within the walls. Yet the king had a message the very next day after he occupied the town, offering to surrender the place if within sixty days no succour should come from Darius. And surrendered it was. Here was one of the strongest positions in Asia, and it did not cost us a single arrow, much less a single life. The fact is these people have no country to fight for. The natives have changed masters again and again; and the mercenaries would quite as soon receive pay from one side as the other, and naturally prefer to be with that which gives the hardest knocks.

"At Gordium we had a very interesting experience. There is a strange story connected with the place which an old Greek merchant who had lived there for many years told me. It was something of this kind:

52

"There was once—some four hundred years ago, as nearly as I could make out—a certain Gordius in this country. He was a poor peasant, cultivating a few acres of his own land. One day as he was guiding his plough with two oxen before him, an eagle settled on it, and kept its place till the evening. The man went to Telmissus, a town famous for its soothsayers, to find out, if he could, what this marvel might mean. Outside the gate of Telmissus he met a girl; and finding that she, too, practised the soothsaying art, he told her his story. 'Offer a sacrifice to King Zeus of Telmissus,' she said. This he did, the girl showing him how he should proceed, and afterwards becoming his wife. For many years nothing happened, not indeed till Gordius' son by this marriage had grown up to manhood. At this time there were great troubles in Phrygia, and the people, inquiring of an oracle how they might get relief, received this answer:

"Phrygians, hear: a cart shall bring
To your gates your fated king.
He, 'tis writ, shall give you peace;
Then shall Phrygia's troubles cease."

The people had just heard this answer when Gordius, who had come into the town on some ordinary business of his farm, appeared in the market-place riding on his cart with his wife and son. He was recognized at once as the person pointed out by the oracle, and named with acclamations as the new king of Phrygia. The first thing that he did was to take the cart with its yoke to the temple of Zeus the King, and tie the two to the altar. Whoever should untie the knot of this fastening, a later oracle declared, should be king of all Asia.

"This was the story which I heard, and which, of course, reached the king's ears. The rumour ran through the army that the king was going to try his fortune, and the next day the temple was crowded with chiefs of the country and with officers of our own army. The Phrygians, we could see, believed the whole story implicitly; our people did not know what to think. There is not much faith now-a-days in such things. Still there was a general feeling that the king had better have left the matter alone. Well, it was as ugly a knot as ever was seen. No one could possibly discover where the cord began or where it left off. For a time the king manfully struggled with the puzzle. Then as it defied all his efforts, one could see the angry colour rising in his cheeks, for he is not used to be baffled by difficulties. At last he cried, 'The oracle says nothing about the way in which the knot is to be undone. If I cannot untie it, why should I not cut it?' And in a moment he had his sword out, dealt the great tangle a blow such as he might have delivered at a Persian's head, and cleft it in two as cleanly as if it had been a single cord—there was not a shred left hanging on either side. Did he fulfill the decree of fate, or cheat it? Who can say? This, however, must be pretty clear to every one by now, that there

53

is no knot of man's tying which that sword will not sever. But there are knots, you know, dearest of friends, that are not of man's tying. May he and we have safe deliverance out of them!"

A Perilous Voyage

IT had been originally arranged that Charidemus should rejoin the army at Gordium, where Alexander was giving his men a few days' rest after their winter's campaign, while he waited for the reinforcements from Macedonia, the fresh levies, that is, and the newly-married men who had been allowed to spend the winter at home. But circumstances occurred which made a change of plan necessary. Some heavy siege engines which were to have gone with the troops were not finished in time. The men could not wait till they were ready, for the very good reason that they were being themselves waited for. Nor could they be sent after the army, for means of transport were wanting. The only alternative was to send them by water, a very convenient arrangement as far as easiness of carriage was concerned, but, seeing that the Persians were decidedly superior at sea, not a little hazardous. However they had to go somehow, and by sea it was determined to send them, Tarsus being the port of destination, as being a city which Alexander had good reasons for believing would easily fall into his hands.

Ten merchantmen had been chartered by the regent to convey the machines. All were provided with a certain armament. This, however, was to be used only in case of extreme necessity; for protection against ordinary attacks the fleet had to rely upon its convoy, two ships of war, the Dolphin and the Lark. Charidemus was second in command of the Dolphin.

Everything seemed to conspire against the unlucky enterprise. First, the workmen were intolerably slow. Then, when everything had at last been finished, some of the machinery was seriously damaged in the process of shipping. And, finally, when at last the squadron got under weigh, the Lark was run by a drunken steersman on a rock that was at least ten feet above the water, and that in broad daylight. Happily she was only a few hundred yards from the mouth of the harbour when the disaster occurred, and the crew by desperate exertions were able to get her into shallow water before she went down. But the diver who inspected the damage reported that at least a month would be wanted before the necessary repairs could be completed. To wait a month was a sheer impossibility, and there was not another war-ship at hand, so bare had the harbours been stripped to supply transport for the army of Asia. There was, therefore, nothing for it but for the Dolphin to undertake the whole duty of the convoy. But the chapter of accidents was not yet finished. On the fourth night of the outward voyage Chærephon, the Dolphin's captain, had been talking to his second-in-command. The latter had just left him to go below when he heard a cry and a splash. He ran to the vessel's side, and was just in time to see the captain's white head above the water in perilous proximity to the oars, which the rowers were plying at the time at full speed. The signal to back water was immediately given, and obeyed without loss of time; but the captain was never seen again. He was known to have been an excellent swimmer, and it is very probable that he had been struck by one of the oars.

Charidemus found himself in command of the fleet, a promotion that was as unwelcome as it was unexpected. As soon as it was light the next day, he signalled to the captains of the merchantmen that he wished for a conference. The captains accordingly came on board; he laid the situation before them, and asked their advice. The consultation ended in his choosing the most experienced among them as his sailing master. What may be called the military command he was compelled to retain in his own hands. It was evident that they were both unfit and unwilling to exercise it.

For some days the voyage was continued under favourable conditions. A brisk breeze by day spared the rowers all labour, and this daily rest enabled them to utilize the calm moonlight nights. To the war-ship, with its superior speed, progress was easy enough; and the crews of the merchantmen, under the stimulus of a promised reward if Tarsus was reached within a certain time, exerted themselves to the utmost to keep up with her.

The squadron touched at Patara, where Charidemus found some much desired intelligence about the movements of the Persian fleet. The main body, he heard, was still in the Northern Ægean; but there was a small detachment cruising about Rhodes, with the object, it was supposed, of intercepting any eastward-bound ships. It was quite possible, the Persians having an highly organized spy system, that the voyage of the Dolphin was known to them. The enemy was, of course, to be avoided if possible, as an engagement would be sure to end in loss. The old sailor whom Charidemus had taken as his prime minister, had intervened with some sagacious advice. "The Phœnicians," he said, "will be sure to watch the channel between Rhodes and the mainland. The best way, therefore, of giving them the slip, will be to turn your ships' heads due south. I think, sir," he went on, "that we sailors are far too fond of hugging the shore. The shore, it seems to me, is often more dangerous than the open sea. For us, sir, under present circumstances, it is so most certainly." The signal to sail south was accordingly hoisted on board the Dolphin, and obeyed, though not, it may be supposed, without much surprise by the merchant vessels. The result was a complete success. The Phœnicians, as Charidemus afterwards learnt, must have been encountered had he followed the usual route. As it was, he saw nothing of them.

After sailing about thirty miles on a southerly tack the course of the squadron was changed to the eastward. Before long Cyprus was sighted, and, by the old sailor's advice, passed on the left hand. They had just rounded the eastern extremity of the island (now called Cape Andrea), and had Tarsus almost straight before them to the north, and not more than ninety miles distant, when they found that their adventures were not yet over. Two craft hove in sight which the experienced eye of the sailing master at once recognized as Cilician pirates. Charidemus immediately resolved on his plan of action, a plan which he had indeed already worked out in his mind in preparation for the emergency that had actually occurred. He signalled to the merchantmen to scatter, and then make the best of their way to their destination. This done he ordered his own steersman to steer straight for the enemy. The pirates had not anticipated any such bold manœuvre, and in their anxiety to prevent the escape of the merchantmen had parted company. The distance between the two Cilician galleys was now so great that Charidemus was sure that he could get at close quarters with the nearest of the two before the more remote could come up to help her consort. He had the advantage of the wind behind him, and putting up all his sails, while he bade his fugleman strike up his liveliest and quickest tune, he bore down with all the speed that he could make on the enemy. The issue of the engagement was scarcely doubtful. The pirate was a long craft, very low in the water, and crowded with men. Able to row and sail with unusual speed, it could always count on overtaking the cumbrous and slow-moving traders, who, when overtaken, could be boarded with irresistible force. But the pirates were not prepared to meet an attack from a strongly built and well equipped man-of-war. Indeed, they were obviously paralyzed by the surprise of so bold a movement. In any case they would not have been a match for the Dolphin, a vessel of much superior weight, and furnished with a powerful ram. As it was, the pirate captain acted with a vacillation that ensured his destruction. When it was too late, he resolved to fly, and, if possible, to join his consort. The resolve might have been judicious had it been taken earlier; as it was, it had a fatal result. The crew were flurried by finding themselves in circumstances so unusual— for they were not accustomed to stand on the defensive—and were slow and clumsy in executing the captain's order. The consequence was that the Dolphin struck the pirate craft, and cut it down to the water's edge. No sooner had the blow been delivered than Charidemus gave the signal to back-water. The pirates, if they were only given a chance to board, might well change the fortunes of the day, so numerous were they, so well armed, and so experienced in boarding attacks. All such chance was gone when the Dolphin had got fifty yards away. With mainmast broken, and the oars of one side shattered to pieces, the pirate ship could not attempt to pursue. So damaging indeed had been the blow that all the efforts of the crew, and of the consort ship which hurried up to give help, were wanted to keep the vessel afloat.

Late in the evening of the following day, and without meeting with any further adventure, Charidemus reached the mouth of the Cydnus. That night he anchored with his charges inside the bar, and the next day made his way up to the city of Tarsus, which was situated, I may remind my readers, some seven or eight miles from the mouth of the river.

The new-comers found the city in a state of consternation. The king was dangerously ill. Some said that he was dying. Now and then it was whispered that he was dead. The cause of his malady was simple enough. After a long march under a burning sun—for Alexander had a passion for sharing all the fatigues as well as all the dangers of his men—he had plunged into the Cydnus, an ice-cold stream, fed by the melting snows from the Cilician Highlands. But the maladies of great men are not so easily accounted for. There were mysterious rumours of poison, nor could Charidemus forget the sinister hints which he had heard from Aristotle. It was possible, he could not help thinking, that Persian drugs, aided by Persian gold, might have had something to do in bringing about this most untoward event.

After reporting his arrival, and the safe conveyance of the munitions of war which had been under his charge, Charidemus made his way to the quarters of his regiment, and was heartily welcomed by his comrades. He had, of course, much to tell, but it was impossible at that time to discuss any topic but the one absorbing subject of the king's illness.

"The king's doctors have refused to prescribe for him," said Charondas, "nor am I surprised. A couple or so of gold pieces if you succeed, and to lose your head if you fail, is not a fair bargain."

"Is there any news, Polemon?" was the general cry, as a young officer entered the room.

"Yes," said the new-corner, "but whether it is good or bad is more than I can say. Philip the Acarnanian has consented to prescribe for the king."

"Philip is an honest man," cried the young Theban. "He and his father before him were great friends of ours."

"Apollo and Æsculapius prosper him!" said one of the company, and the prayer was heartily echoed by all who were present.

Hour after hour bulletins of the king's condition were issued. They were cautiously worded, as such documents commonly are, but there was nothing encouraging about them. The general fear grew deeper and deeper as the day wore slowly on.

"Let us go and see Philip," said Charondas to his friend, as they were sitting together in gloomy silence after their evening meal. "I think that he will admit us when he hears my name, and we shall at least know all that is to be known."

The friends found the physician's house strongly guarded. So excited were the soldiers that there was no knowing what they might not do. Were a fatal result to follow, the guard itself would hardly be able to protect the unfortunate man. Charondas obtained, as he had expected, admission for himself and his companion by the mention of his name. The first sight of the physician was curiously reassuring. He was perfectly calm and confident. "What about the king;" was the question eagerly put to him. "Do not fear," was the quiet reply, "he will recover." Just as he spoke a slave entered the room with a communication from the attendants of the king. The physician read it with unmoved face, and after taking a small phial from a case of medicines, prepared to follow the messenger.

"Wait for me here," he said, "I shall be back shortly, and shall have something to tell you."

The friends sat down, and waited for an hour, an hour as anxious as any that they had ever spent in their lives. At the end of that time Philip came back. In answer to the inquiries which they looked rather than put into words, he said—

"He goes on well; it is just as it should be. He had to be worse before he could be better. And he is young, and strong, and the best of patients. He deserves to get well, for he trusts his physician. Such patients I very seldom lose. When I gave him the medicine that I had mixed, he took it, and drank it without a word. Afterwards—mark you, afterwards—he handed me a letter which some one had sent him. 'I had been bribed by Darius'—that was the substance of it—'to poison him.' Now, if I had had that letter before I prescribed, I should have hesitated. I do not think I should have ventured on the very potent remedy which I administered. And yet there was nothing else, I felt sure, that could save his life. Yes, as I said, he deserves to live, and so he will. He has been very near the gates; but I left him in a healthy sleep, and, unless something untoward happens, from which Apollo defend us, he will be well before the new moon."

The physician's prophecy was fulfilled. The king, when the crisis of the fever was once successfully passed, recovered his strength with amazing quickness. The solemn thanksgiving for his recovery actually was fixed, so accurate had been the Acarnanian's foresight, for the day of the new moon.

The thanksgiving was a great festival, kept with greater heartiness than such celebrations commonly are. That the army was delighted to recover their heroic leader need not be said; but their joy was equalled by that of the townsfolk of Tarsus. This city, though Assyrian in origin, had become thoroughly Greek in sentiment and manners, and was already acquiring something of the culture which afterwards made it the eastern rival of Athens. It was proportionately impatient of Persian rule, and hailed the Macedonian king as a genuine deliverer. The festivities of the day were crowned by a splendid banquet, at which Alexander entertained the chief citizens of Tarsus and the principal officers of the army. He was in the act of pledging his guests when an attendant informed him that a stranger, who was apparently a deserter from the Persian army, had urgently demanded to see him, declaring that he had information of the greatest importance to communicate.

"Bring him," cried the king. "Something tells me that this is a lucky day, and that the gods have not yet exhausted their favours."

The stranger was brought in between two soldiers. A more remarkable contrast to the brilliant assemblage assemblage of the royal guests could hardly have been imagined. His face was pale and haggard, his eyes bloodshot, his hair unkempt, his dress—the one sleeved tunic of a slave—worn and travel-stained. The splendour of the scene into which he had been brought seemed to overpower him. He reeled and would have fallen, but that the soldiers on either side held him up.

"Give him a draught of wine," cried the king.

A page handed him a brimming goblet of Chian. He drained it, and the draught brought back the light to his eyes and the colour to his cheek.

"And now," said the king, "tell us your story. But first, who are you, and whence do you come?"

"My name is Narses," said the man, "I am a Carian by birth. I was the slave of Charidemus the Athenian."

"And you have run away from your master," interrupted the king, who began to think that the man was only a common deserter, hoping to get a reward for information that was probably of very little value.

"The gods forbid!" said the man. "There was never a better master, and I had been a thankless knave to leave him. No, my lord, Charidemus the Athenian is no more."

"How so?" asked the king. "Tell us what you know."

"The Persian king held a great review of his army in the plain of Babylon. First he numbered them, sending them into a sort of camp, surrounded by a ditch and rampart, that was reckoned to hold ten thousand men. I watched them march in and out, my lord, for I was then with my master, for the whole of a day from sunrise to sunset. As they came out they took their places on the plain, stretching as far as I could see and further too. 'What think you of that?' said King Darius to my master, when the last detachment had marched out, 'what think you of that? are there not enough there to trample these insolent Greeks under foot?' My master was silent; at last he said, 'Does my lord wish me to speak what is in my heart?' 'Speak on,' said the king. Then my master spoke out: 'This is a splendid sight, I confess. No one could have believed that there could have been gathered together so great, so splendid a host. And I can well believe that there is no people in Asia but would see it with fear and a very just fear too. But the Macedonians and the Greeks are a very different race. You have nothing here that can be matched for a moment with the solidity of their array, with their discipline, with the speed and order of their movements. If you want my advice, my lord king, it is this: It is only in Greece that you can find men who can stand against Greeks. Send these useless crowds away. Take the silver and gold with which they make all this useless display, and use it to hire men who can really fight.' There was a perfect howl of rage from all the Persian nobles who were standing by, when my master said this. Some of them shook their fists at him; some drew their scymetars. As for the king himself he was as furious as any of them. He jumped up from his seat, and caught my master by the throat. 'Take him away,' he shouted to the guards who stood behind his throne, 'take him away, and behead him.' My master's face did not change one whit. 'You asked for the truth, my lord,' he said, 'but it does not please you. When it comes to

59

you, not in word but in deed, it will please you less. Some day you will re-member what has been said to-day, and Charidemus will be avenged.' After that the executioners led him away, and I saw him no more."

"And about yourself," said the king, "how came you hither?" There was a fierce light in the man's eyes as he answered this question. "My lord," he said, "the king divided all that belonged to my master between the executioners. I watched my time, and the day after his death I plunged my dagger into the heart of one of the ruffians; I wish that I could have plunged it into the king's. Then I escaped."

"To-morrow," said the king, "you shall tell me in what way you came, and what you saw on the road. Just now you are only fit for rest. Treat him well, and take care of him," he went on to the attendants. "And now, gentlemen," he said to his guests, "said I not well that the gods had good tidings for me on this day? What could be better than this? If the choice had been given me, I could have chosen nothing more to be desired—Darius means to give battle."

On the Wrong Side

THE good fortune of Alexander was not yet exhausted; indeed, if it was to be called good fortune at all, it remained with him in a remarkable way up to the very end of his career. It was a distinct gain that the Persian king had abandoned the waiting policy of Memnon, and, in a haughty self-confidence that, as has been seen, brooked no contradiction, resolved to give battle to the invader; but there was a yet greater gain remaining behind. Not only was he going to give battle, but he was going to give it exactly in the place which would be the least advantageous to himself and the most advantageous to his antagonist. How this came about will now be explained.

Alexander called a hurried council of war after the banquet to consider the intelligence which had been just brought to him. He expounded to his lieu-tenants at length the views which he had briefly expressed at the banqueting hall. If Darius was in the mind to fight, their policy was to give him the oppor-tunity that he desired as soon as possible. The suggestion was received with enthusiasm by the majority of the officers present; but there was a small mi-nority, led by Parmenio, that ventured to dissent. Parmenio was the oldest and most experienced general in the army, numbering nearly fifty cam-paigns. He had often been extraordinarily successful, and Philip had trusted him implicitly. "I have never been able to find more than one general," the king had been wont to remark, "and that general is Parmenio." Accordingly his voice had no little weight. Even Alexander had at least to listen. The sub-stance of his counsel on the present occasion was this: "Let us fight by all means; but let us fight on our own ground. If we march to attack Darius on the plains where he has pitched his camp, we shall be giving him all the advantage of place; if we wait here till he comes to attack us here, this advantage will be ours."

Alexander listened with respectful attention, but was not convinced. "We cannot afford to wait," he said, "an invader must attack, not be attacked. But perhaps we shall be able to combine your policy, which I allow to be admirable, and mine, which I hold to be necessary."

The event justified the hope. We may attribute the result to good fortune; but it was probably due to the extraordinary power of guessing the probable action of an antagonist, which was one of Alexander's most characteristic merits as a general.

To put the thing very briefly, the king's idea was this. Let Darius once get the impression that the invaders were hanging back, and in his overweening confidence in his own superior strength, he would abandon his favourable position, and precipitate an attack. And this is exactly what happened.

The Macedonian army was formed into two divisions. With one of them Parmenio hurried on to occupy the passes from Cilicia into Syria. There were strong places which might have been easily defended; but it was not Darius's policy to hinder the advance of an enemy whom he felt sure of being able to crush; and the garrisons retired according to order when the Macedonian force came in sight.

Some little time after, Alexander himself followed with the rest of his army, taking the same route, and overtaking Parmenio's force at a place that was about two days' march beyond the passes.

And now came the extraordinary change of policy on the part of Darius which Alexander, with a sagacity that seemed almost more than human, had divined. The delay of the Macedonian king in advancing from Cilicia had produced just the impression which apparently it had been intended to produce. Darius imagined, and the imagination was encouraged by the flatterers who surrounded him, that his enemy was losing confidence, that though he had routed the king's lieutenants, he shrank from meeting the king himself. And now the one prevailing idea in his mind was that the invader must not be permitted to escape. Accordingly, though his ablest counsellors sought to dissuade him, he broke up his encampment on the level ground which suited so admirably the operations of his huge army, and hurried to get into the rear of Alexander. He blindly missed the opportunity that was almost in his hands of cutting Alexander's army in two, and took up a position wholly unsuited to the character of his forces, but which had the advantage, as he thought, of cutting off the enemy's retreat.

And now that I have explained the antecedent circumstances of the great struggle that followed, I must return to the fortunes of Charidemus and his friend. A rapid march performed under a burning sky had caused not a little sickness in the army, and Alexander had left his invalids at Issus, a delightful little town which had the advantage of enjoying both sea and mountain air. A detachment was told off to protect the place, and as Charondas was among the sick, Charidemus, though always anxious to be with the front, was not altogether displeased to be left in command.

But the change in the Persian plan brought terrible disaster on the occupants of Issus. It was an unwalled town, and, even had it been strongly fortified, it could not have been defended by the couple of hundred men under Charidemus's command. When the Persians appeared, for it was naturally in their line of march, there was nothing for it but to capitulate and to trust to the mercy of the conquerors. Unhappily the Persian temper, always pitiless when the vanquished were concerned, had been worked up into furious rage by recent disasters. Many of the prisoners were massacred at once; those whose lives were spared were cruelly mutilated, to be sent back, when the occasion served, to the camp of Alexander, as examples of the vengeance which the audacious invaders of Asia might expect.

Charidemus and his Theban friend, with such other officers as had been captured, were brought before the king himself. Charondas, happily for himself, was recognized by a Theban exile, who had attached himself to the fortunes of Darius, and who happened to be a distant relative of his own. The man made an effort to save him. "O king," he said, "this is a kinsman and a fellow-citizen. I saw him last fighting against the Macedonians. How he came hither I know not, but I beseech you that you will at least reserve him for future inquiry. Meanwhile I will answer for his safe custody."

Darius, whose naturally mild temper had been overborne by the savage insistence of the Persian nobles, signified assent; and Charondas, who had not been asked to renounce his allegiance, or indeed questioned in any way, did not feel himself constrained in honour to reject the chance of escape.

No one now remained to be dealt with but Charidemus himself, who as the chief in command had been reserved to the last.

"Of what city are you?" asked the king.

"Of Argos," replied the prisoner, who was certainly glad to be able to make this answer without departing from the truth. To have avowed that he was a Macedonian would probably have sealed his fate at once.

"And your name?"

"Charidemus."

The king was evidently struck by this answer. Though he had given the order for the execution of the unhappy Athenian whose death has been already related, and, indeed, had been the first to lay hands upon him, the deed had been out of keeping with his character, and he had already repented of it.

"Knew you your namesake of Athens?" he went on.

"I knew him well, my lord. He was the guest-friend of my mother's father."

Darius turned round to the Persian noble, a scion of one of the great Seven Houses, who stood behind his seat, and said, "Keep this man safe as you value your own head."

The Persian took him by the hand, and led him to the king's quarters, where he committed him to the safe keeping of his own personal attendants.

The next morning the army resumed its march, following the same route that had been taken a few days before, but in an opposite direction, by Alexander, crossed the Pinarus, a small stream which here runs a short course, from the mountains to the sea, and encamped on its further or northern shore.

Though the young Macedonian's life had been saved for the moment, he was still in imminent danger. The clemency of the king had not approved itself to his courtiers, though the habit of obedience had prevented them from questioning his orders. Indeed all the Greeks about the royal person were regarded by the Persian nobles with jealousy and suspicion. So strong were these feelings that Darius, though himself retaining full confidence in their attachment and fidelity, thought it best to send them all away before the anticipated battle should take place. They were accordingly despatched under the protection of a strong detachment of troops of their own nation to Damascus, whither a great portion of the royal treasure and of the large retinue which was accustomed to follow the Persian king had been already sent. Charondas of course accompanied his Theban kinsman, while Charidemus remained under the immediate protection of the king.

Alexander, when his scouts brought in the intelligence of the Persian movement in his own rear, had hardly been able to believe that his anticipations had been so speedily and so completely fulfilled. That Darius would leave his position on the plain he had hoped; that he would crowd his enormous forces into a place where not a third of them could possibly be used, seemed almost beyond belief. Yet it was undoubtedly true. A light galley was sent out from the shore to reconnoitre, and what the sailors saw fully confirmed the news. Across the bay of Issus was a distance of little more than ten miles, though the way by land between the two armies may have been nearly double as much, and it was easy to descry the thronging multitudes of the Persian host, crowding, as far as could be seen, the whole space between the mountain and the sea. The day was now far advanced. But Alexander would not lose an hour in seizing the great opportunity thrown in his way. The soldiers were ordered to take their evening meal at once, and to be ready to march afterwards.

It is, however, with the preparations of the Persians that we are now concerned. Informed of the approach of Alexander, and perhaps somewhat shaken in his confidence by the news, Darius resolved to await the attack where he was, that is, behind the stream of the Pinarus. His main line was formed of ninety thousand heavy-armed infantry. A third of these were Greek mercenaries, and occupied the centre; the rest were Asiatics armed in Greek fashion. Darius himself took his place in the centre behind his Greek troops. It was in them, after all, notwithstanding the jealousy of his nobles, that he put his chief confidence. The cavalry were massed on the right wing, that end of the line which was nearest to the sea, for there alone was there any ground suitable for their action. On the left wing, reaching far up the mountain side, were twenty thousand light-armed troops who were to throw themselves on the flank of the Macedonians when they should attempt to cross the stream. Of these, indeed, nothing more need be said. They did not attempt to make the movement which had been assigned to them; but remained inactive, easily held in check by a handful of cavalry which was detached to watch them. Behind this line of battle, numbering, it will have been seen, somewhat more than a hundred thousand men, stood a mixed multitude, swept together from all the provinces of the vast Persian Empire. This mass of combatants, if they may be so called, already unwieldy, received the addition of fifty thousand troops, who had been sent to the southern bank to cover the formation of the line, and who were brought back when this formation was completed. There was no room for them in the line, and they were crowded into the endless multitude behind.

It was a novel experience for Charidemus to watch, as he was compelled to do from his place behind the chariot of Darius, the advance of the Macedonian army. He saw them halted for a brief rest, and watched the men as they took their morning meal. Then again he saw them move forward at a slow pace, preserving an admirable regularity of line. Never before had he had such an opportunity of observing the solidity of their formation; never before had he been so impressed with the conviction of their irresistible strength. Finally, when the front line had come within a bowshot of the river he observed Alexander himself gallop forward on his famous charger, turn with an animated gesture to the line behind him, and advance at a gallop, followed by the cavalry and light-armed foot, while the phalanx moved more slowly on, so as not to disturb the regularity of array on which its strength so much depended.

The terror which this rapid movement caused in the Persian left cannot be described. It was all the more startling because the Macedonian advance had before seemed slow and even hesitating. Nothing less than a panic set in among the troops against whom this sudden attack was delivered. The heavy-armed Asiatics had the equipment and, in a degree, the discipline of European troops, but they wanted their coolness and steadfastness. Before they had felt the thrust of a pike, or the blow of a sword, before even a missile had reached them, they wavered, broke, and turned to fly. The huge multitude behind them caught the infection of panic. So narrow was the space in which they had been crowded together that movement was almost impossible. A scene of frightful terror and confusion followed. The fugitives struggled fiercely with each other—had they shown as much energy in resisting the enemy, they might have changed the fortune of the day. They pushed aside the weak, they trampled pitilessly on the fallen. In less than half an hour from the beginning of the Macedonian charge the whole of the left wing of the Persians was a disorganized, helpless mass. It is true that the rest of the army did not show the same shameful cowardice. The Greeks in the centre stood their ground bravely, and held the division that attacked them in check for some time. Then assailed in the rear by the Macedonian right returning from their own easy victory, they cut their way through the opposing lines and made good their escape. The Persian cavalry on the right wing also behaved with courage, crossing the river, and charging the Thessalian horse on the Macedonian left. But the miserable weakness of the Persian king rendered all their bravery unavailing. When he saw the line of the Asiatic heavy-armed waver and break, and perceived that his own person was in danger, he turned precipitately to flee, and his escort of cavalry followed him, Charidemus being swept away by the rush, without having a chance to extricate himself. Before long the ground became so rough that the chariot had to be abandoned, and the king mounted on horseback, leaving in his hurry his shield and bow behind him. The flight was continued at the fullest speed to which the horses could be put till the king felt sure that for the time at least he was safe from pursuit. He then called a halt, and made his disposition for the future. His own destination was Thapsacus, where there was a ford over the Euphrates, and whence he would make his way to Babylon. The greater part of the escort, of course, accompanied him. The young Persian noble, Artabazus by name, to whose charge Charidemus had been committed, was to make his way to Damascus, with instructions for the officers who had been left there in charge of the treasure and retinue. To the young Macedonian the king addressed a few words of farewell. "Truly," he said, "the Athenian is avenged already. Well; I seem to owe you something for his sake. Take this ring," and he drew, as he spoke, a signet-ring from his finger. "It may help you in need; perhaps, too, you will have the chance of helping some whom I cannot help. My wife and child are, doubtless by this time, in your king's hands, for they can hardly have escaped. I can trust him. But there are others whom you may find at Damascus. When they see this ring it will be proof that they may put faith in you." Then turning to Artabazus, he went on, "Guard this man's life as you would your own."

Damascus

WHETHER Charidemus would have reached his destination in safety in the company of his Persian guardians may well be doubted. Artabazus himself seemed well disposed to him. The young noble had spent some time in Greece, having been attached to more than one embassy sent to that country, spoke the language with ease and fluency, and had at least some outside polish of Hellenic culture. But the troopers were genuine barbarians, exasperated to the last degree by their recent defeat, who would have had little scruple in wreaking their vengeance on unprotected Greeks. Happily for Charidemus, he was not long exposed to the dangers of the journey. Alexander, with his usual energy, had already taken measures to secure Damascus. Parmenio was instructed to push forward to that city, where it was well known that an immense spoil awaited the conquerors. The treasure captured in the Persian camp had not been very large; the bulk had been left in Syria, and it was important to get hold of it without delay.

Parmenio lost no time in executing his commission. His main body would require two or three days' preparation before it could march; but some light horse was sent on at once to cut off any fugitives who might be making their way from the field of Issus to the Syrian capital. It was at one of the fords of the Upper Orontes that this detachment came in sight of Artabazus and his companions. The river had been swollen by a heavy fall of rain among the hills, and was rolling down in a turbid and dangerous-looking stream. The troopers, catching sight of the Macedonian cavalry, as it came in sight over the brow of a neighbouring hill, rushed helter-skelter into the ford, without giving a thought either to their chief or their prisoner. The leader's horse, a young untrained animal, refused to enter the water. Twice, thrice was he brought to the brink, but he could not be induced to go in. Meanwhile the pursuers had come within a stone's-throw of the water. Artabazus saw that escape was hopeless, and he disdained to surrender. He turned his horse from the stream, drew his scymetar from its gilded sheath, and threw himself furiously upon the nearest horseman. The man raised his shield to ward off the blow, but the good Damascus blade sheared off three or four inches of the tough bull's hide, and inflicted a deadly wound on the spot so often fatal, where the lappet of the helmet joined the coat-of-mail. The next moment the Persian's horse was brought to the ground by the thrust of a lance, and the rider, as he lay entangled in its trappings, received a mortal wound from a second blow of the same weapon.

Charidemus, who had been sitting on his horse, a passive spectator of the scene just described, now came forward to report himself to the officer in command. There was no need, he found, to explain who he was, for the officer happened to be an old acquaintance, and warmly congratulated him on his escape. "Many thanks," said Charidemus, "but see whether you cannot save your prisoner there alive. He is of one of the Seven Houses, and should be worth a ransom almost royal."

The officer leapt from his horse, and examined the prostrate man. "He is past all help," was the verdict, after a brief examination, "Not Æsculapius himself could heal him. But he seems to want, to speak to you; I thought I heard him whisper your name."

In a moment Charidemus was on his knees by the dying man's side, and put his ear to his lips. The words that he caught were these: "Damascus—the street of the coppersmiths—Manasseh the Jew." With that his utterance failed; there were a few convulsive gasps for breath, a faint shiver, and then all was over.

It was not a time for much funeral ceremony. A shallow grave was scooped in the sand by the river side, and the body, stripped of armour and weapons, but allowed to retain cloak, tunic, and sandals, was hastily covered over. All the valuables that were found upon the dead were considered to be the booty of the troop; but Charidemus purchased a bracelet, a chain, and a ring. He could not help thinking that the dying man had wished to entrust some commission to him. These articles might at least help to identify him.

After crossing the Orontes, the party halted for the night, and by the bivouac-fire Charidemus told his story, and heard, in his turn, many particulars of the great fight which it had been his strange fortune to see from the side of the vanquished. "We gave you up for lost," said his new companion, who, by the way, was no less distinguished a person than Philotas, son of Parmenio. "A few poor wretches found their way back into the camp; but those brute-like barbarians had shorn off noses, ears, and hands. Many died of loss of blood on the way, and some only just lived long enough to get within the lines. The survivors told us that all the officers had been killed. But, you seem a special favourite of the gods. They must surely be keeping you for something great. And your Theban friend—what of him? I hope that Pylades escaped as well as Orestes."

"Yes, by good luck," said Charidemus, "a Theban exile who was with Darius recognized him, and saved his life. He is, I take it, at Damascus by this time."

"Where we shall soon find him, I hope," returned Philotas. "That is the place we are bound for; and if the stories that the deserters tell us are only half true, we shall have rare sport then. My father is in command of the main body; but we will take care to keep well ahead of the old man, and have the first sight of the good things."

The party had yet more than two hundred miles to ride before reaching their journey's end. Weak as they were—for they did not number in all more than two hundred men—they pushed on in supreme indifference to any possible danger. Danger indeed there was none. The country was stripped of troops, for every available soldier had been swept off by the levies to swell the host that had been gathered only to be scattered to the winds at Issus. A few indeed had found their way back, but these were glad to bury their weapons, and to forget that they had ever wielded them for so unlucky a cause. As for raising them again against these wonderful warriors from the west, before whom the armies of the Great King had melted as snow melts in the sun, that would be madness indeed. Philotas's party met with no opposition; indeed, as far as the Syrian population showed any feeling at all, the new-comers seemed to be welcomed. The Persians had not made themselves beloved, and a change of masters might, it was felt, be a change for the better.

It was about a fortnight after crossing the Orontes that the detachment came in sight of Damascus. They were gazing with delight, as so many travellers have gazed, at the City of Gardens, when a Syrian lad came up to the party, and contrived with some difficulty to make them understand that he had a message to deliver to their chief. Accordingly he was conducted into the presence of Philotas, and put into his hands a small roll of paper. It proved to be a communication from the Persian governor of Damascus. The lad, when further questioned by the help of a peasant who acted as interpreter, said that he had been sent with orders to deliver the letter into the hands of the first Macedonian officer whom he might be able to find. It was thus:—

"Oxathres, Governor of Damascus, to the Lieutenant of the Great and Victorious Alexander, into whose hands this may fall. Seeing that the Gods have so manifestly declared that they adjudge the kingdom of Asia to the great Alexander, it becomes the duty of all their dutiful servants and worshippers to respect their decree. Know, therefore, that great treasures of King Darius, lately deposited by him in this city of Damascus, are now about to be conveyed away by certain disloyal and ill-disposed persons by way of Tadmor."

"We shall have plenty of time to cut them off," remarked Philotas on reading the communication, "for they have the longer distance to travel, and must move slowly. How will they travel, Philip?" he went on, addressing a subofficer, who had been in the country before.

"If they go by way of Tadmor," replied the man, "they must cross the desert, and will use camels; we had best be beforehand with them, before they get far on the way."

Philotas accordingly gave orders to his troop to start immediately. They took an eastward direction, and by sunset had reached a point on the road which would necessarily have to be passed by a caravan journeying from Damascus. The keeper of the inn, one of the shelters for travellers which the Persian Government had provided along the principal roads, informed them that nothing of the kind described had as yet passed.

It was about sunset next day before the caravan appeared. It was accompanied by a small escort of Persian soldiers, who, however, made no attempt to defend their charge. Indeed, they showed so little surprise or alarm at the appearance of the Macedonian troops that Philotas could hardly help suspecting that the whole business had been contrived, the removal of the treasure being only a feint, by means of which the governor of the city hoped to get some credit with his new masters. The packages with which the animals were loaded bore the royal seal. These Philotas thought it best not to disturb. The Persian soldiers were disarmed, and, as it would cause the party inconvenient delay were they to be encumbered with prisoners, dismissed. They gave a promise not to serve again, and as they were all of the unwarlike Syrian race, were very likely to keep it. The caravan was then turned back by the way on which it had come, and Damascus was reached without any further incident.

Philotas had been right when he anticipated that the city would be a prey of extraordinary richness. The camp which had fallen into the hands of the conquerors at Issus had seemed to these simple and frugal soldiers the ne plus ultra of luxury, while Darius and his nobles probably fancied that they had limited what they had brought with them to the very narrowest and most necessary requirements in furniture and followers. It was at Damascus that the invaders discovered in what sort of state the Great King travelled when he was not actually in the face of the enemy. There was a vast amount of gold, though this was small in comparison with what afterwards fell into Alexander's hands; but it was the extraordinary number of ministers to the pleasures of the court that struck the new-corners with astonishment. Parmenio, giving a catalogue of his captures to the king, enumerates the following:

329	Singing-girls.	*("pot-boilers" is the word in the original)*	
46	Male chaplet-makers.		
277	Cooks.	13	Makers of milk puddings.
29	Kitchen-helpers, perhaps turnspits	17	Strainers of wine.
		40	Perfume makers.

And these belonged to the royal establishment alone! The great nobles had establishments, not, indeed, on so large a scale, but still incredibly magnificent and costly. The booty in treasure and slaves that was at the disposal of the conquerors was simply beyond all reckoning.

After an interview with the governor, whom he thanked with perfect gravity for his timely communication, Philotas thought it better to encamp his men outside the city, and there await the arrival of the main body under his father. Some disaster might happen if he allowed his frugal campaigners free access to a place so full of temptations.

Charidemus, who indeed was not strictly under his command, was not prevented from visiting the city. His first inquiries were for Charondas, whom he found in the company of his compatriot, and whose release from the nominal custody in which he had been kept he obtained without difficulty.

He had not, we may be sure, forgotten Barsiné, and, still less, the young Clearista; and he had good reason for believing that they were both in Damascus. Memnon, he remembered, had spoken of sending his wife and his niece to Susa, nominally as hostages, really to remove them as far as possible from the scene of war. Doubtless this had been done. But Darius, he heard, had carried the hostages with him in his train, and when he had resolved to risk a battle, had sent them to Damascus. The difficulty was in finding them. Not only was the city so crowded with the harems of the great Persian nobles that the search would in any case have been difficult, but it was impossible to ask questions. The Persians shut up their wives and daughters with a jealous care, and the Greeks about the Court had adopted their customs. Even intimate friends never spoke to each other about the women of their families. For two young soldiers to go about making inquiries about certain high-born ladies was a thing not to be thought of. If they were so rash as to do it, they certainly would get no answer. The idea of meeting them in public only suggested itself to put aside. At any time it would have been most unlikely. Ladies of high rank never went out but in carriages, and then they were closely veiled. As things were then, with an invading army in possession of the town, it was extremely unlikely that they would go out at all.

Once, indeed, our hero fancied that chance had given him a clue. The two friends had wandered down a lane shaded on either side by the trees that overhung it from two high-walled gardens, and leading down to one of the streams that make Damascus a mass of greenery. A flash of something bright moving amidst the foliage of the trees caught the eye of Charidemus. It disappeared, and then again became visible, to disappear once more as quickly. It was a minute or two before the young man realized that what he saw shining so brightly in the sunshine was the hair of a girl who was swinging between two trees. More he could not see from where he stood, or from any part of the lane, so thick, except in one small spot, was the foliage. Even to climb the wall would not have served him. But the glimpse was enough. Charondas was both incredulous and amused when his friend asserted that this particular tint of auburn was to be found on no head throughout Persia and Greece save on Clearista's alone. They were arguing the point when a huge negro, carrying some gardening tools, issued from a door in the wall of the opposite garden. He made a clumsy salutation to the two young soldiers, but eyed them with an expression of suspicion and dislike. The next time, and that was not later than the following day, that the friends sought to make their way to the same spot, they found the entrance to the lane barred by a quite impracticable gate. That flash of auburn hair in the sunshine might have been a clue; but if so, the clue seemed to have been lost.

Manasseh The Jew

THE two friends had been talking after their supper about the repulse of the morning, and were now musing over the problem before them in a perplexed silence, when Charidemus started up from his seat, and brought down his hand with an emphatic blow upon the table. "I have it," he cried, "Manasseh the Jew!"

Charondas had heard the story of the combat by the ford of the Orontes, and of the confidence, or what, if time had allowed, would have been the confidence, of the dying Persian; but he did not see the connection of the name with the subject of their discussion. "How can the Jew serve you?" he said.

"I am told," answered Charidemus, "that the Jew knows everything. Anyhow I feel that I have got hold of a clue. I am driven to despair by having to climb up what I may call a perfectly blank wall, without a single crevise or crack to put my foot in. Here is something that may give me a hold. This Manasseh is doubtless a man of some importance, one who has dealings with great people. What Artabazus wanted me to do for him, what I am to say to Manasseh, or Manasseh is to say to me, I have not an idea. But still I feel that there is something. There will be some kind of relation between us; he will recognize the chain and bracelet; he will see that Artabazus trusted me. Perhaps I shall be able to help him, and perhaps he will be able to help me. Anyhow I shall go."

"And you had better go alone," suggested Charondas.

"Perhaps so," replied the Macedonian.

It was not difficult to find Manasseh. The Jews had a quarter of their own in Damascus which they had occupied, though not, it may be supposed, without some interruptions, for several centuries. In this quarter Manasseh was one of the leading inhabitants, and Charidemus was at once directed to his dwelling. The exterior of the Damascus houses seldom gave much idea of what the interior was like. You entered by an unpretending door in a mean-looking front, and found something like a palace within. Manasseh's dwelling surprised the visitor in this way. It was built round a spacious quadrangle, in the centre of which a fountain played, surrounded by orange, pomegranate, and myrtle trees. The ground floor of the building was occupied by a colonnade. Above this was the apartment of the family, furnished with a splendour and wealth known only to a few. Chance comers and visitors on business Manasseh the Jew was accustomed to see in a plainly-furnished room close to the gate. The Jews were even then beginning to learn that painful lesson of prudence as regarded the display of their wealth which afterwards they had so many reasons to practise.

Manasseh was civil to his visitor, whom, from a hasty survey of his person, he conjectured to be an impecunious young officer, whose object was to borrow some money, for the Jews had already begun to follow the trade of money-lender. When Charidemus produced the chain and bracelets which had belonged to Artabazus, Manasseh's first impression was that they were articles offered by way of security for an advance. He took them up in a careless way to examine them, but his look and manner changed at a nearer inspection.

"How came you by these?" he asked, and his voice was stern and even menacing.

The Macedonian told the story with which my readers are already acquainted. "What more Artabazus would have told me," he went on to say, "I know not. He had only strength to utter your name, and the place where I might find you. But I felt bound to come. It was clear that for some reason he wished it; and it was the least I could do for him."

"You have done well, sir," said the Jew. "Pardon me if I had harsher thoughts of you. And now, let me think."

Manasseh walked up and down the room several times in an agitation that contrasted strangely enough with the cool and business-like air which he had worn at the beginning of the interview. Then he paused.

"Young man," he said, "you are not, I know, of my faith, and I cannot ask you, as I would ask one of my own race, to swear by the God of Israel. But I have lived long enough among the Gentiles to know that there are oaths which bind them as surely as to swear by the Lord binds a son of Abraham. And I have learnt, too, that there is among them, even as there is among us, that which is stronger than all oaths, the sense of right and truth in the heart. I believe that you are one of those who have this sense; I seem to see it in your face; you have shown it by coming here to-day on this errand. A man who keeps his word to the dead will not break it to the living. I will trust you. And now listen to my story. The dead man whose chain and bracelets you have brought here to-day was, I may say, my friend. Between his race and mine there has been a close tie for many generations. He, indeed, as I dare say you know, was of one of the noblest houses of Persia, and we were of the captivity of Judah. Still my fathers have done some service for his in times past, as, indeed, his have done for mine. You would not care to hear how it was; but, believe me, it was so. We of the house of Israel can sometimes do more than the world would think. But enough of this; let me go on to that which concerns the present. The sister of this Artabazus is Barsiné, who was the wife and is the widow of Memnon the Rhodian."

Charidemus gave an unmistakable start when he heard the name.

"What!" cried the Jew, "you know her?"

Charidemus in as few words as possible related how he had been taken prisoner at Halicarnassus, and had there made the acquaintance of Memnon and his family.

The Jew's face lighted up when he heard it. You make my task easier. I now feel that I can speak to you, not only as to a man of honour, but as to a friend. When Memnon sent his wife and his niece—you saw the niece?"

The young man assented, not without the consciousness of a blush.

"When Memnon sent his wife and niece to court, Artabazus made interest with the king that they should be allowed to reside here in Damascus, rather than at Susa. The climate was better, and there were other reasons. I may tell you, though I dare say you had an opportunity of seeing so much for yourself, that Artabazus, like his sister, had had a Greek bringing up, and that there were some things in Persian ways that did not please him or her. Well, being in high favour with the king, he got his request. Barsiné and the girl were sent to this city, her brother making himself responsible for them. I found a home for them; and I have managed their affairs. A few weeks since the king, as you know, sent all his harem here, all his hostages and guests, in fact, all his establishment of every sort and kind. Then came his defeat at Issus, and now everything belongs to the conquerors. I had hoped that Barsiné and her niece might have lived quietly here till these troubles were passed. If all this crowd of men and women and slaves had been left at Susa it might have been so. But the situation is changed. They too must be included in any list of the prisoners that have come into the possession of your king. I have been think-ing over the matter long and anxiously. Once or twice it has occurred to me to send them away. But whither was I to send them? What place is out of the reach of your arms?"

He paused, overpowered by the perplexities of the situation. "God of Israel," he cried, "what am I to do?"

"What says the Lady Barsiné herself?" interposed the Macedonian. "I judged her, when I was in her company, to be one who could very well think for herself."

"She is so," said Manasseh, "and in any case she must be told of her brother's death. Come to me again, if you will, in two days' time, and come after dark. It is as well to be secret."

Charidemus took his leave, just a little touched in conscience by the Jew's praises. He felt that he had gone on an errand of his own, in which, indeed, he had succeeded beyond all his hopes; and he was ashamed to be praised for a loyalty to the dead which had certainly been quite second in his thoughts.

He did not fail, it may be supposed, to present himself at the appointed time. The Jew greeted him warmly, and said, "The Lady Barsiné wishes to see you. Let us go; but not by the street. It would be well that neither you nor I should be seen."

He led the way into the garden. There was light enough, the moon having now risen, for Charidemus to catch a glimpse of spacious lawns, terraces ornamented with marble urns and balustrades, and trees of a stately growth. His guide conducted him down a long avenue of laurel, and another of myrtle, that ran at right angles with the first. At the end of the second they came to a small door in the wall. This brought them into a lane which the Macedonian seemed to recognize, so far as was possible in so different a light, as that into which he and his companion had strayed three days before. Almost facing the gate by which they had gone out was another in the opposite wall. This opened into another garden, arranged similarly to that which they had just left, but much smaller. The house had no front to the street, but stood pavilionwise in the centre of the enclosure. Manasseh knocked, or rather kicked, at a small postern door. When this had been cautiously opened a few inches, the bolts having been withdrawn but the chain remaining fastened, the Jew gave his name, which was evidently a sufficient password, the chain being immediately withdrawn by the porter.

"The Lady Barsiné awaits you," said the man, and led the way down a richly carpeted passage on which their footsteps fell in perfect silence, to a room which was evidently the library. By the side of the hearth, on which a small fire of cedar-wood was burning, was a chair of ebony richly inlaid with ivory. Close to this stood a citron table, on which was a silver lamp and a roll of manuscript, which a curious eye might have found to be the "Dirges" of Pindar. Book-cases and busts were ranged round the walls, which were hung with embroidery representing the contest of Athena and Poseidon, a design copied from the West Pediment of the Parthenon. One wall of the room, however, was occupied by a replica of Protogenes's great masterpiece, "The Piping Satyr."

The room was empty when the two visitors were shown into it; but in the course of a few minutes Barsiné appeared. Grief had robbed her of the brilliant bloom of her beauty, but had given to her face a new and more spiritual expression. When Charidemus last saw her she might have been a painter's model for Helen, a Helen, that is, who had not learnt to prefer a lover to a husband; now she was the ideal of an Andromaché. She caught hold of Manasseh's hand, and lifted it to her lips, and then turned to greet his companion. She had been prepared for his coming, but the sight of him overcame her self-control. She was not one of the women who sob and cry aloud. Persian though she was—and the Persians were peculiarly vehement in the expression of their grief—she had something of a Spartan fortitude; but she could not keep back the big tears that rolled silently down her cheeks.

"It is a sad pleasure to see you," she said at last, addressing the Macedonian, when she had recovered her voice. "My Memnon liked you well; he often spoke of you after you left us; and now I find that my dear brother liked you and trusted you also. I know you will help me if you can. Have you any counsel to give to the most unhappy of women?"

"Alexander," said the Macedonian, "is the most generous of conquerors. I would say, Appeal to his clemency and compassion. I know that he respected and admired your husband. I have heard him say —for he has often deigned to talk of such things with me—that Memnon was the only adversary that he feared in all Asia. 'Whether or no I am an Achilles'—these, lady, were his very words—'he is certainly a Hector.' Go to him, then, I say—he comes to-morrow or the next day—throw yourself at his feet. Believe me, you will not repent of it."

"Oh, sir," cried the unhappy woman, "that is hard advice for the widow of Memnon and the daughter of Artabazus to follow. To grovel before him on the ground as though I were a slave! It is more than I can bear. Oh! cannot I fly from him to some safe place? Tell me, father," and she caught Manasseh's hand, "you know everything, tell me whither I can go. Should I not be out of his reach in Tyre?"

"Lady," said Manasseh, "I have put this question to myself many times, and have not found an answer. I do not know how you can escape from him. As for Tyre, I am not even sure that it will attempt to stand out against him; but I am sure that if it does it will bitterly repent it. She repented of having stood out against Nebuchadnezzar, and Nebuchadnezzar is to this man as a vulture is to an eagle. And there are words, too, in our sacred books which make me think that an evil time is coming for her. No! I would say, Do not trust yourself to Tyre. And would you gain if you fled to the outer barbarians, to those that dwell by the fountains of the Nile, if you could reach them, or to the Arabs? Would they treat you, think you, better than he, who is at least half a Greek?"

"Let me think," cried Barsiné, "let me have time."

"Yes," said Manasseh, "but not so much time as would rob your supplication of all its grace. Go to him as a suppliant; let him not claim you as a prisoner."

Some little talk on other matters followed; but the conversation languished, and it was not long before the visitors took their leave.

Andromaché

THE next night Manasseh and Charidemus presented themselves at Barsiné's house. Both men were extremely anxious. Further delay, they felt, was impossible. Any hour the unhappy lady might find whatever chance she had irretrievably lost. They did not augur well for her decision that she kept them waiting for nearly an hour after their coming had been announced to her; nor from her first words when at last she appeared.

"The Macedonian has not yet come, has he?" she asked.

"Madam," replied Charidemus, "the king arrived this afternoon."

She wrung her hands in silence.

"And to-morrow the governor of the city will present him with the list of the property and persons left here by King Darius. This will be compared with the list already made by Parmenio."

"But my name may not be in it," she eagerly interposed.

"Madam," said Manasseh, "do not flatter yourself with such a hope. The widow of the man who commanded the Great King's forces is far too important a person to be forgotten. You may depend upon it that there is no one in the whole kingdom, except, it may be, the wife and child of Darius himself, whom the king is more bent on getting into his possession than the widow of Memnon the Rhodian."

"It is so, madam," broke in Charidemus; "nay, I know that your name is in Parmenio's list, for Philotas his son showed it me. I entreat you to act without delay. You should have seen the king on his first arrival. To-night it is impossible. But go to-morrow, as early as may be, before he sees the list—and he begins business betimes—that you may still seem to have given yourself up of your own accord."

Barsiné made no answer, but paced up and down the room in uncontrollable agitation. At last she addressed the Macedonian.

"You know him; you do not speak by hearsay, or as courtiers who flatter a king?"

"Madam," replied Charidemus, "I have seen him at times when men show their real selves—at the banquet and in the battle-field."

"And he is merciful and generous? Strong he is and valiant, I know. My Memnon used to say that he had not his match in the world, and he had seen him fight. But he is one, you say, who can have compassion also, who can pity the suppliant?"

"Madam," said the young man, "I believe from my heart that he is."

"Then I will go to him; I will throw myself at his feet; I will implore his compassion for myself and my children."

"There shall be no need for you to do so, lady," said a voice from the other end of the room.

At the same time the tapestry that covered another door was moved apart, and Alexander himself stood before them. He was unarmed, except for a light cuirass of richly gilded steel and a sword. His head was uncovered; his hair, which he wore long after the fashion of the heroic age, fell in golden curls about his neck. His face, with lustrous deep-blue eyes, features chiselled after the purest Greek type, and fair complexion just now flushed with a delicate rose, was of a beauty singularly attractive.

So unexpected, so startling was the sight that Manasseh and his young companion could only stare in mute astonishment. Charidemus, as became his soldierly instincts and habits, was the first to recover his self-possession. He stood at attention, and saluted. Barsiné covered her face with her hands.

Alexander gazed at the scene with a smile, enjoying, one may believe, with a certain satisfaction the astonishment that his appearance had caused. After a brief silence he spoke again. "I thank you, venerable sir," he began, addressing himself to Manasseh, "for the words of truth that you have uttered, and the admirable advice that you have given to the Lady Barsiné. It is true that there is no one in the whole kingdom of Persia whom Alexander is more anxious to secure than the widow of Memnon the Rhodian. Nor could you have given her better advice than that she should surrender herself to me of her own free will. And you, my young friend," he went on, turning to Charidemus, "you I thank most heartily for the praises that you have bestowed on my clemency. The gods grant that I may always be not less worthy of them than I hope I am this day. And now, lady, after that these gentlemen have spoken, as I trust, so truly of me, let me speak for myself. But, first, will you permit me to be seated?"

Barsiné murmured a half-audible assent, and the king took a chair opposite to the couch on which she was reclining, and signed to the Jew and Charidemus that they should seat themselves. They did so, first respectfully withdrawing to the further end of the room.

The king went on: "Lady; you have never heard of me—save, it may be, from Manasseh and Charidemus here—but as of an enemy, though I trust you have heard no evil; let me now speak as a friend. Your husband fought against me; it was not the will of the gods that he should succeed. Therefore they first blinded the eyes of King Darius so that he could not see the wisdom of his counsel; and then they shortened his days. Had he lived I could not have been here to-day. But would it have been well that he should succeed? He was a Greek, but he fought for Persia. Think you that he wished in his heart that the Persian should triumph over Greece, should be lord of Athens and Sparta, of Delphi and Olympia? I do not forget, lady, that you are Persian by birth. Yes, but you are Greek in soul, and you know in your heart that if one of the two must rule it must be the Greek. But, believe me, I do not come to conquer, I come to unite. Persians and Greeks are brothers, and, if the gods grant me my wish, they shall be one nation of free-men with me for their chief. That your king never could have been, nor, I may say, any Greek before me.

"This is my plan and hope; and now, lady, for the part that you can take in completing and fulfilling it. I shall say it in a word. Be my wife."

Barsiné was silent, and her face was still hidden in her hands; but her neck flushed crimson.

"I am abrupt and hasty," said Alexander, "kings must need be so when they court. It were a happier lot for me, if I were one who could win for himself, if it might be, by such means as lovers use, the heart of one so beautiful and so wise. Still I would have you look on me as one who asks rather than commands. What say you, most beautiful of women?"

"O, my lord," stammered Barsiné, "I am not worthy."

"Let that be my care," said Alexander, "I know of none so worthy. It is only you that have the right to question my choice."

To say that Barsiné was overwhelmed by the situation in which she found herself is to say but a small part of the truth. She had been so much occupied with the thought of whether or no she should appeal to Alexander's compassion, that the idea of what might be the result of her appeal had scarcely crossed her mind. If she had been conscious of any definite hope, it was that she might be allowed to hide herself in some retirement, where she might educate her son. And now what a destiny was put at his feet! To, be the wife of the conqueror of Asia! for who could doubt that he would be this? She was confused, but it was not the confusion of dismay. She was not a broken-hearted widow whose heart was in her husband's grave; and though she had really loved her Memnon, as indeed he was worthy to be loved, life was not over for her. And what a life seemed to be opening before her! And yet it was so sudden! And the wooing was so imperious!

"My lord," she began, "your commands——"

"Said I not," broke in the king, "that I did not command, that I asked? Now, listen to me. You are free; you shall do what you will. If you wish to depart, depart you shall; and I will do my best to provide safely and well for you and yours. But you must think of others. There is your son. Though I come of the race of Neoptolemus, I am not of his temper; I could not hurl a young Scamandrius from the wall, however many the comrades whom his father had slain. Not so; I will deal with him as it is fit that I should deal with Memnon's son. He shall learn to be like his father in my camp. And your niece Clearista" (Alexander, as has been said before, had the faculty of knowing everything), "we must find some more suitable home for her. Perhaps our good friend Manasseh here can think of such. And now, farewell; I shall come again, lady, and ask my answer."

With a deep obeisance to Barsiné he left the room; and Manasseh and Charidemus followed him.

To Jerusalem

THE wooing of kings is commonly successful, and Alexander's courtship was no exception to the rule. It can hardly be said that Barsiné loved him; but then it was not expected that she should. Her first marriage had been, in a great degree, a matter of policy. The most brilliant and able Greek of his day was a husband whom her father had been delighted to secure for her. Even the Great King had exerted himself to further a match which would help to secure so valiant a soldier for the defence of his throne. She had come, to love her Memnon indeed; but this was but an instance of the kindly forgiveness which love often extends to those who break his laws. Her new suitor was not one to be resisted. And, however truly he might profess only to sue, circumstances made his suing a command. If she accepted the liberty that he offered her, whither was she to turn, her father and brother dead, and her country manifestly destined to fall into a conqueror's hand. At the same time the generosity of his offer touched her heart. She might know in her own mind that her choice was not free; but it soothed her woman's pride to be told that it was.

Alexander's feelings in the matter was a curious compound of various sentiments. The woman attracted him; he found her more beautiful even than common report had described her, and according to report she, after the Queen of Darius, was the most lovely of Persian women. Then the idea of making the two nations, Greeks and Persians, into one, was really a powerful motive with him, and he thought it might be furthered by this alliance. But beyond all doubt the master thought in his mind was of a more sentimental kind. As has been said before, it delighted him beyond all things to act Homer. And here was three of the parts ready made to his hand. Memnon was Hector, as long as he lived the chief stay of Persia, Persia being the heir of Troy; Barsiné was Andromaché, and he was Achilles or the son of Achilles. In legend the son of Achilles had taken Andromaché to wife; so would he; only he would play the part in gentler and humaner fashion, as became one who had sat at the feet of the greatest philosopher of the day.

A few days after the marriage had taken place, the king sent for Charidemus to give him some instructions.

"You are to go to Jerusalem," he said. "Manasseh the Jew counsels that Clearista, the queen's niece, should be sent thither. He seems to be in the right. Certainly she cannot go with the army; and I know of no place where she can be more safely bestowed than the city of the Jews. Manasseh, too, has kinsfolk with whom she may sojourn. Of course she must have an escort, and you will take two hundred horsemen with your friend Charondas the Theban as the second in command. Then I have another errand for you. I have a conviction that I shall have trouble with Tyre. The other Phœnician cities, you know, have yielded. The Sidonians actually asked me to choose a king for them, and I did, but I have private information that Tyre means to hold out. If it does, I shall find the Jews very useful. They can send me some soldiers, and their soldiers, I am told, fight very well; but what I shall most want will be provisions. Let them supply my army with these, and they shall not find me ungrateful. This is what I want you to manage. You shall take a letter from me to their High Priest—they have a curious fancy, I understand, for being ruled by priests—which will state what I want. You will have to back it up. Make them understand—and I have been told that they are singularly obstinate— that I shall be better pleased if I can get what I want peaceably, but that I mean to have it somehow."

This commission was, as may be supposed, very much to the young man's taste. Though Jerusalem did not fill as great a space in the mind of a Greek as it does in ours, it was a famous city, and Charidemus was glad to have the chance of seeing it. Then this was his first independent command. And, last not least, there was Clearista, and she was in his charge! It was accordingly in the highest of spirits that he started. It was reckoned to be about a six days' journey if the traveller followed the easiest and most frequented routes; and six happier days the young man had never spent. The care of Manasseh had provided two companions for Clearista. One was an elderly lady, a kinswoman of his own, Mariamne by name, the other one a girl about two years older than the young lady herself, who was to act as her personal attendant. Mariamne was carried in a litter; the two girls rode on donkeys. Two sumpter mules followed with their baggage and effects. Half the escort rode in front under the command of Charondas; of the other half Charidemus took special command, but did not find his duties prevent him from spending a considerable part of his time in the company of his charge. At the end of each day's journey the travellers reached a caravanserai. The soldiers bivouacked in the spacious court-yards of these places; the women had the best of such accommodation as the building could furnish; and Mariamne always invited the two officers in command to share their evening meal. These little entertainments seemed to the guests to come to an end too soon; with so light a gaiety did the talk flow on as they sat round the central brasier in the spacious room of the caravanserai. There was still much of the unconsciousness of childhood in Clearista. Her manner to Charidemus was perfectly frank and sisterly, so unreserved, in fact, that it made it much easier for him to keep his own secret. Still she had developed both in body and mind. Face and form were more commanding, and seemed likely to more than fulfil all their early promise of beauty. And a year of close companionship with a cultured and thoughtful woman in Barsiné had taught her much. Nature had given her a keen intelligence, and she had been now learning with good result how to use it. Every day made Charidemus feel more strongly that the happiness of his life was bound up in this young girl. But he was lover enough to know that her heart was yet to be won. Her gay friendliness, charming as it was, showed that she had not so much as caught a glimpse of what was in his mind.

It could hardly, we may suppose, have been displeasing to the young soldier-lover, if he had had some opportunity of showing his prowess before his lady-love's eyes, even, perhaps, of rescuing her from some imminent peril. Nor indeed was the journey without some chances of this kind. The Arabs of the desert, then as now, thought travellers a lawful source of income, who might fairly be plundered, if they did not pay for protection. These were the regular freebooters of the country, and just then it swarmed with irregulars, fragments of the great host which had been broken to pieces at Issus. Again and again, as the travellers pursued their journey, little bands of suspicious looking horsemen might be seen hovering near. Once, as they were making their way across the fords of Jordan, an attack seemed imminent. A caravan was always most helpless when it was struggling through a ford, and the Arabs knew their opportunity. The vanguard had passed to the western side of the river, and the convoy itself was in mid-stream, while the troopers of the rear-guard were tightening their saddle-girths and generally preparing to enter the water. It was just the moment when, if ever, discipline was relaxed, and the practised eye of the Arab chief who was wont to take toll at that particular spot did not fail to observe it. His horsemen had been lying in ambush in the jungle that skirted the narrow valley of the river. Now they came galloping down, brandishing their spears and uttering wild cries of defiance, till they had come within a bow-shot of the caravan. Had there been the slightest sign of confusion or panic, the feint would have been converted into a real attack. All troops would not have stood firm, for the assailants outnumbered the escort by at least two to one. But the men who had conquered at the Granicus and at Issus were not to be terrified by a horde of marauders. In a moment every man was in his saddle, as cool and as steady as if he had been passing in review under the eyes of his general on a field day. Clearista showed herself a true soldier's daughter, as Charidemus, while doing his part as a leader, found time to observe. Her animal had just entered the water when the charge was made. Instead of urging him on, she turned his head again to the bank, at the same time signalling to her maid to do the same. Many women would have striven in their panic to get as far as possible from the enemy. A braver instinct bade her keep close to her friends. To cross while fighting was going on would have distracted their attention, even had there been no danger in attempting the ford without help.

As a matter of fact not a blow was struck. The Arabs, then as now, loved booty, but seldom cared to fight for it. They certainly did not think of dashing themselves against the iron fence of the Macedonian pikes. At a signal from the chief they checked themselves in full career, and disappeared as suddenly as they had come.

The rest of the journey was accomplished without further adventure. It was just about sunset on the sixth day when the Macedonians reached the northern gate of the city. At the request of Charidemus, the gate-keeper despatched a messenger with a letter for the High Priest with which Manasseh had furnished him. In a short time an official appeared to whom the Macedonian handed over his charges, taking for them a formal receipt. He and his troopers remained for the night outside the walls in quarters specially provided for the accommodation of foreign troops who might approach the Holy City.

The next day he received an intimation that Jaddus the High Priest would receive him. Jaddus had convened the Sanhedrim, or Hebrew Senate, and the demands of Alexander had been considered. The substance of them, it must be understood, was perfectly well known, though they had not yet been formally made. There had been a long and fierce debate upon the matter, but the Persian party, on whose side the High Priest had thrown all the weight of his influence, had prevailed, and the Senate had resolved by a large majority to reject the Macedonian's demands.

The young envoy was introduced into the council chamber, and requested to read the letter which it was understood he had brought from the king. He read it, and it was translated, sentence by sentence into Hebrew by an interpreter. He was then invited to address the Senate if he had anything to urge upon them or to explain. This invitation he declined, briefly remarking that the deeds of his master spoke more emphatically and convincingly of the justice of his demands than any words of his own could do. The question whether the demands of Alexander, King of Macedonia, should or should not be granted was then put. As it had been really decided before, the Senate had agreed to give an unanimous vote; and the envoy, who was not behind the scenes, was not a little surprised at the promptitude and decision with which a negative answer was given.

After announcing the result of the vote the High Priest addressed to the envoy a short speech in justification, the substance of which he was to convey to the Macedonian king.

"Tell your master," he said, "that the children of Abraham desire to be friends with all men, but allies of none. If Alexander has a quarrel with any, let him pursue it with his own arms. The men of Tyre have given us no offence; nay, rather they have been our friends for many generations. When Solomon, son of David, built a house for the Lord, Hiram, King of Tyre, helped him greatly in his work, sending him cedar-wood from Lebanon and diverse other things, and skilful builders and artificers. And when the Chaldæans burned with fire the house that Solomon had set up, and Ezra the priest and Nehemiah the governor under Artaxerxes the king built another in its place, then the men of Tyre helped us again. Therefore it were unjust should we do aught to their prejudice. There is yet another demand to which answer must be made. Your master says, 'Pay me the tribute that you were wont to pay to

Darius.' For the money we care not, but the oath that we have sworn to the king we will not break. So long as he lives, or till he shall himself loose us from it, so long will we be faithful to it."

The envoy received the message in silence, and left the council chamber. A military guard conducted him to the gate, and in the course of a couple of hours he was on his way with his command to join the main army. A week later he was taking part in the investment of Tyre.

Tyre

IT was a formidable task that Alexander had undertaken. Tyre was built upon an island separated from the mainland by a channel half-a-mile broad. Half of this channel was, indeed, shallow, but the other half, that nearest to the city, was as much as twenty feet deep. The island was surrounded by walls of the most solid construction, rising on one side, that fronting the channel, to the enormous height of a hundred and fifty feet. How was a place so strong to be taken, especially when the besiegers had not the command of the sea?

Alexander's fertility of resource did not fail him. A century and a half before Xerxes had undertaken, or rather pretended to undertake, the construction of a mole from the mainland of Attica to the island of Salamis. It was curiously in keeping with Alexander's idea of retaliating upon Persia its own misdoings that he should take one of its cities by accomplishing in earnest what Xerxes had begun in pretence. Accordingly he made preparations for constructing a great mole or embankment, which was to be carried across from the mainland to the island. It was to be seventy yards wide, and so, when completed, would give plenty of space for carrying on against the walls.

Materials in abundance were at hand. The city of Old Tyre was on the mainland. The greater part had been in ruins for many years, in fact, ever since the siege by Nebuchadnezzar, and the rest was now deserted by its inhabitants. From this plenty of stone and brick and rubbish of all kinds could be obtained. Not far off were the forests of Lebanon, contracted, indeed, within narrower limits than they had once been, but still able to supply as much timber as was wanted. Of labour, forced and free, there was no lack. The soldiers worked with a will, and crowds of Syrian peasants were driven in from the neighbourhood to take their part in the labour.

At first the operations were easy enough. The ground was soft so that the piles could be driven in without any difficulty, and the water was so shallow that it did not require much labour to fill up the spaces between them. At the same time the Phœnician fleet did not venture, for fear of running aground, to come near enough to damage or annoy the workmen. It was when the embankment had been carried about half way across the channel, and had touched the deeper water, that the difficulties began. The men worked under showers of missiles, discharged from the ships and even from the walls. The soldiers themselves, accustomed though they were to risk their lives, did not ply their tools as promptly as usual; the unwarlike peasants were simply paralyzed with fear. Though the king himself was everywhere, encouraging, threatening, promising, sometimes even putting his own hand to the work, little progress was made. So far the advantage seemed to rest with the besieged. At the present rate of advance Alexander would be as long making his way into the city as Nebuchadnezzar had been.

The next move was won by the besiegers. Two huge moveable towers were constructed upon the finished portion of the mole. They were made of wood, but the wood was covered with hides, and so made fireproof. Catapults were placed on the top; from these such a fire of javelins, bullets, and stones were kept up that the enemy's ships could not approach. Again the mole began to advance, the towers being moved forwards from time to time so as to protect the newly finished portion.

It was now time for the Tyrians to bestir themselves, and they did so effectually. A huge transport, originally made for carrying horses, was filled with combustibles of every kind, caldrons of pitch and brimstone being attached even to the yardarms of the masts. The stern was heavily weighted with ballast, and the prow thus raised high above water. Taking advantage of a day when the wind blew strongly on to the mole, the Tyrians set light to the contents of this fire-ship, and after towing it part of the way by a small ship on either side, let it drive towards the embankment. It struck between the towers, the elevated prow reaching some way over the top of the mole. The sudden shock, too, broke the masts, and the burning contents of the caldrons were discharged. In a few moments the towers were in a blaze, and all the work of weeks was lost.

It was now clear that without a fleet nothing could be done, and again Alexander's good fortune became conspicuous. Just at the critical time when he most needed help, this help was supplied. The Persian fleet in the Ægean had been broken up. Tyre had summoned back her own ships to aid in her defence, and the other Phœnician cities had also recalled their squadrons. But as these cities had submitted to Alexander their ships were at his disposal. Other small contingents had come in, till he could muster about a hundred men-of-war. Still he was not a match for the Tyrians, the less so as these were by common consent the best of all the Phœnician seamen. It was then that a decisive weight was thrown into his side of the balance. The kings of Cyprus, a country which had no reason to love the Persians, joined him, adding one hundred and twenty more ships to his fleet. He could now meet his adversaries at sea on more than equal terms.

It was necessary indeed before a battle could be ventured on to give some time to discipline and practice. Many of the crews were raw and unskilful, and the various contingents of which the fleet was composed had never learnt to act together. Another great improvement, adding much to the fighting force of the ships, was to put on board each of them a small number of picked soldiers, who took the place of the marines in our own navy. Charidemus and Charondas both found employment in this way, the former being attached to the flag-ship, as it may be called, of the King of Sidon, the latter to that of Androcles, Prince of Amathus in Cyprus.

After eleven days given to practice in manœuvring and general preparation, Alexander sailed out from Sidon, where a rendezvous had been given to the whole naval force. The ships advanced in a crescent formation, the king himself commanding on the right or sea-ward wing, one of the Cyprian princes on the left; the latter skirted the shore as closely as the depth of water permitted. The Tyrians, who now learnt for the first time how great a fleet their enemy had succeeded in getting together, did not venture to fight. They could do nothing more than fortify the entrance to their two harbours, the Sidonian harbour, looking to the north, and the Egyptian, looking to the south. Alexander, on the other hand, established a blockade. The ships from Cyprus were set to watch the northern harbour, those from the submitted Phœnician cities that which looked to the south.

The Tyrians, however, though for the time taken by surprise, were not going to give up without a struggle the command of the sea. They came to the resolution to attack one of the blockading squadrons, and knowing, perhaps, the skill and prowess of their fellow Phœnicians, they determined that this one should be the contingent from Cyprus. Each harbour had been screened from view by sails spread across its mouth. Under cover of these, preparations were actively carried on in that which looked towards the north. The swiftest and strongest of the Tyrian ships, to the number of thirteen, were selected, and manned with the best sailors and soldiers that could be found in the city. Midday, when the Cyprian crews would be taking their noonday meal, and Alexander himself, if he followed his usual practice, would be resting in his tent, was fixed as the time for the attack. At midday, accordingly, the thirteen galleys issued from the harbour mouth, moving in single file and in deep silence, the crews rowing with muffled oars, and the officers giving their orders by gesture. They had come close on the blockading ships without being noticed, when a common signal was given, the crews shouted, and the rowers plied their oars with all the strength that they could muster. Some of the Cyprian ships had been almost deserted by their crews, others lay broadside to; few were in a position to make a vigorous resistance. Just at this moment, and long before his usual time for returning, Alexander came back from his tent, and saw the critical position of affairs. Prompt as ever, he manned a number of the Cyprian ships that were lying at the mole, and sent for help to the other squadron. The mouth of the northern harbour was promptly blockaded, so that no more ships could get out to help the attacking galleys, and these were soon assailed in the rear by a contingent from the blockading squadron on the south side. The fortune of the day was effectually restored, but some loss had already been sustained. Several of the Cyprian ships had been sunk, and their crews either drowned or taken prisoners. This had been the fate of the vessel of Androcles of Amathus. The prince himself was drowned, and Charondas had very nearly shared his fate. Weighed down by his armour, he could only just keep himself afloat by the help of a spar which he had seized. A Tyrian sailor who saw him in this situation was about to finish him with the blow of an oar, when an officer, seeing that the swimmer must be a man of some rank, interfered. The Theban was dragged on board, and, with some thirty or forty others, three of whom were Macedonians or Greeks, carried back into the city.

When the losses of the day were reckoned up the first impression was that Charondas had shared the fate of his captain. Later in the evening the real truth was known. A Cypriote sailor, one of the crew of the lost ship, had seen what had happened. He was supporting himself in the water by holding on to a mass of broken timber, and, luckily for himself, had not been observed. Two or three hours later he had been picked up by a friendly vessel, but in such a state of exhaustion that he could give no account of himself. It was not till late in the night that he recovered his senses. Charidemus, who had refused to give up hope, was called to hear the man's story, and satisfied himself that it was true. But he could not be sure that his friend had not better have been drowned than been taken as a prisoner into Tyre.

His fears were greatly increased by the events of the next day. Alexander, who had a great liking for Charondas, and whose conscience was especially tender whenever anything Theban was concerned, sent a herald early in the morning to negotiate an exchange of prisoners. The man returned without succeeding in his mission. The Tyrians refused the proposal, vouchsafing no other reason for their refusal except that they had other uses for their prisoners.

Charidemus found himself that evening the next neighbour of a young Sidonian noble, at a banquet which the king was giving to some of his Phœnician allies. He asked him what he thought was the real meaning of the somewhat obscure answer which the herald had brought back that morning.

"I hope," said the young man, "that there is no friend of yours among the prisoners."

"Yes, but there is," was the answer. "The very dearest friend that I have is in the city."

The Sidonian—he was the son of the newly-appointed king of that city—looked very grave. "I know something of these Tyrians and of their ways, which indeed are not very different from ours. They mean to sacrifice these prisoners to the gods."

Charidemus uttered an exclamation of horror.

"Yes," said the Sidonian, "it is shocking, but it is not so very long, as I have read, since you Greeks did the same. But let that pass; you are thinking what is to be done. Stop," he went on, for Charidemus started up from his seat, "you can't take Tyre single-handed. And I think I might help you. Let me consider for a few moments."

After a pause he said, "You are ready, I take it, to risk a good deal for your friend."

"Yes," cried the Macedonian, "my life, anything."

"Well; we must get him out. Fortunately there are two or three days to think about it. At least I hope so. There is always a great sacrifice to Melkarth—your Hercules, as, I dare say, you know—on the new moon; and they will probably reserve the principal prisoner for that. The moon is, I know, four days short of being new. So we have time to think. Come with me to my quarters, when we can leave this place, and let us talk the matter over."

It was not long before the two contrived to slip away from their places at the table. When they found themselves alone, the prince began—

"We might get into Tyre, I think, unobserved."

"We," interrupted Charidemus in intense surprise. "Do you think of going with me?"

"Why not?" returned his companion. "I am fond of adventure, and this really seems to promise very well. And I have other reasons, too; but they will do another day when I will tell you my story. Of course you must have some one with you who can speak the language; so that if you are willing to have me for a comrade, I am ready."

The Macedonian could only clasp the prince's hand. His heart was too full to allow him to speak.

"Well," the other went on, "as I said, we might get in unobserved. There is a way of clambering up the wall on the sea side—I lived, you must know, for a year in Tyre, working in one of the dockyards. Or we might swim into one of the harbours at night. But the chances are very much against us; and if we were to be caught, it would be all over with us, and your friend too. And besides, supposing that we did get in, I don't see what we could do. No; we must take a bolder line; we must go openly. We must make some plausible pretext; and then, having got in, we will see what can be done for your friend. Now as for myself, there is no difficulty. I have a good reason. You know we Sidonians took part with your king. It seemed to us that we had no other choice, and that it would have been downright folly to attempt to hold out against him. But these Tyrians, though we are fighting against them, are, after all, of our blood—you see I talk quite frankly to you—and, if things come to the worst with them, as they must come, sooner or later, then we shall do our best to save as many of them as we can. I have really a commission to tell them this, and to warn them that, if the city is stormed, they must make for our ships. But the question is—how are you to go?"

A thought struck Charidemus. He wondered indeed that it had not occurred before. He showed the Sidonian the ring which King Darius had given him. "Perhaps this may help me," he said. The prince was delighted. "It is the very thing," he said. "You need not fear anything, if you have that with you.

86

The Tyrians will respect that, though the prisoners tell us that they are very sore at being left all these months without any help from the king. I should not profess to have any message from him. They have been looking for help, not messages. No; I should recommend you simply to show the ring. It will be a safe-conduct for you. Once in, we shall begin to see our way."

The next morning brought only too convincing a proof that the Sidonian prince was right in his conjecture about the fate destined for the prisoners. Three of these unhappy creatures were brought on to that part of the city wall which faced the mole, and sacrificed as a burnt-offering with all the formalities of Phœnician worship. The besiegers watched the performance of the hideous ceremony with unspeakable rage in their hearts. Their only comfort was to vow vengeance against the ruthless barbarians who perpetrated such atrocities. The three victims, as far as could be made out, were Cypriote sailors belonging to the ships that had been sunk. Charidemus was able to satisfy himself that his friend was not one of them.

It was arranged that the two adventurers should make their way that night to one of the ships of war that guarded the entrance to the Sidonian harbour. They were to put off after dark with every appearance of secrecy, were to be pursued, and as nearly as possible captured, by a Macedonian galley, and so were to present themselves to the besieged as genuine fugitives.

The little drama was acted to perfection. The prince and Charidemus stole out in a little boat from the land. A minute or so afterwards a hue and cry was raised upon the shore, and a galley started in pursuit. The boat was so nearly overtaken that its occupants jumped overboard, and swam to the nearest Tyrian galley. No one who saw the incident could doubt that it was a genuine escape.

The two companions were brought into the presence of Azemilcus, King of Tyre. The king had been in command of the Tyrian squadron in the Ægean fleet, and had seen Charidemus in Memnon's company. By great good fortune he had not happened to inquire in what character he was there. So friendly had Memnon's demeanour been to the young man that no one would have taken him for a prisoner, and Azemilcus had supposed that he was a Greek in the service of Persia, who was assisting Memnon in the capacity of secretary or aide-de-camp. This recollection and the sight of the ring perfectly satisfied him. Nor did he seem to doubt the real friendliness of the Sidonian's message. It seemed to him, as indeed it was, perfectly genuine, and he warmly thanked the two companions for the risk they had run. They frankly explained that they had not really meant to desert from the besieging army. Such a proceeding, indeed, would have seemed suspicious in the critical condition of the city. They had hoped, on the contrary, to come and return unobserved. As it was, having been seen and pursued, they must stay and take their chance with the besieged.

Azemilcus invited the two young men to be his guests at supper. He had lived a good deal with Greeks, and spoke their language fluently, besides having adopted some of their ways of thought. When the conversation happened to turn on the sacrifices to Melkarth, he explained that he had nothing to do with them, though without expressing any particular horror or disgust. "The priests insist upon them, and though I don't like such things, I am not strong enough to resist. You see," he went on to explain, for the benefit of the Greek guests, "we Phœnicians are much more religious than you, and if I were to set myself against an old custom of this kind, it would very likely cost me my throne and my life."

In the course of the conversation it came out that the victims intended for sacrifice were kept in a chamber adjoining the Temple of Melkarth, and that, as the Sidonian prince had supposed, the next great ceremony would take place on the approaching new moon.

The Escape

THE two companions, at the prince's request, shared the same room, and sat up late into the night, considering what was next to be done. The king's palace, where they were quartered, almost adjoined the temple. But, beyond the fact that they were near to the scene of their proposed operations, they could see little light. A hundred plans were started, discussed, and rejected, and they threw themselves down on their beds as dawn began to steal through the windows of their apartment, with a feeling of something like despair. They had come, however, to one conclusion. The Sidonian was to pay a visit to the temple early on the following morning. There would be nothing singular in his doing so. In fact, it would be more remarkable if he did not. If Melkarth was specially worshipped in Tyre, he was, at the same time, not without honour in Sidon; and a prince of the reigning house, the heir, in fact, to the throne, would be expected to pay his respects to the god. Charidemus, on the other hand, it was felt, would do well to stop away. The popular temper was angry and suspicious, and it would be well to avoid anything that might irritate it.

The prince paid his visit accordingly, was present at the morning sacrifice, and propitiated the priests of the temple by an offering of twelve of the gold pieces with which he had prudently filled his pockets. This, however, meant very little. A more hopeful fact, as regarded their chances of success, was the discovery that one of the temple attendants was an old acquaintance of the prince's, like him a Sidonian by birth, who had worked with him in the dock-yards, and had now found a easier place in one of the subordinate offices of the temple. The prince suspected that the man had the charge of the victims, having seen him carry what looked like a basket of provisions into one of the ante-chambers of the temple, but, for fear of arousing suspicion, had not made any inquiries on the subject. He had not even, for the present, discovered himself to his old comrade. The question was, how far the man could be trusted. If he betrayed them, all was lost; on the other hand, could his help be secured, the prospect of escape for themselves and Charondas was most hopeful. And they had large inducements to offer, a handsome sum of money in hand, the promise of his life should the city be taken, and the hope of future advancement in his profession. He might be a fanatic. In that case all would he lost. But the presumption was against the idea. Fanaticism is commonly found in those who worship in a temple rather than in those who serve in it. He might, again, be a coward. That would be equally fatal. But, if he were a man of average temper and courage, who would be willing to rescue a fellow creature from death, if he found himself well paid for doing it, things might go well.

It was finally agreed—indeed no prospect seemed to open out in any other direction—that the prince should discover himself to the man, and sound him. This was done, and with a result that was fairly satisfactory, as far as it went. The man had been much impressed by the new dignity of his former comrade, and still more by his condescension and kindness in seeking him out, and he had been effusively grateful for a present of half-a-score of gold pieces. Asked about his pay and his duties, he had told his questioner that he had charge of the victims destined for sacrifice, and had mentioned that he had several under his care at the moment. He spoke of one in particular with a good deal of feeling. He was a fine young fellow, and he was very sorry for him. It seemed a monstrous thing to butcher him in this fashion. In the course of the conversation it came out that there was a serious difficulty in the case. The care of the victims was divided between two attendants, and the other, according to the Sidonian's account, was a brutal and fanatical fellow, who gloated over the fate of his charges.

After long and anxious consideration a plan was finally decided upon, subject, of course, to such modifications as circumstances might suggest. The prince and Charidemus, the latter being disguised as a slave, were to make their way into the temple, shortly before it was closed for the night. Then, and not till then, the friendly attendant was to be taken into confidence. He seemed a man whom the weight of a secret might very likely so burden as to make him helpless, and who might be best won by large bribes and offers made at the last moment. If the worst came to the worst, he might be overpowered, a course that would certainly have to be taken with his colleague.

There was a private way from the palace into the temple, which was almost in darkness when the companions reached it. Whatever light there was came from a single lamp that hung between the two famous pillars, one of gold, and one, it was said, of emerald, which were the glory of the place and the admiration of travellers. Charidemus had no thoughts for anything but the perilous task that he had in hand, though he carried away from the place a general impression of vast wealth and barbaric splendour.

The friendly attendant came forward to meet the new-comers. The prince caught him by the arm. "Swear," he said, "by Melkarth, to help us, and don't utter another sound, or you die this instant." The man stammered out the oath.

"That is well," said the prince, "we knew that we could trust you. You shall have wealth and honour. When Alexander is master of Tyre, you shall be priest of the temple. Now listen to what we want. We must have this Greek prisoner who is to be sacrificed to the god at the feast of the new moon. He is dear to our king, and must not die."

At this moment the other attendant came up the central avenue of the temple, of course utterly unsuspicious of danger. The prince, a young man of more than usual muscular power, seized him by the throat. He uttered a stifled cry, which, however, there was no one in the temple to hear. The next moment he was gagged, bound hand and foot, and dragged into a small side chapel, the door of which was fastened upon him from the outside. His keys had previously been taken from him.

"Now for the prisoner," said the prince.

The attendant led the way to a door that opened out from the north-east corner of the temple, and this he unlocked. It led into a spacious chamber well lighted by two lamps that hung from the arched ceiling. Charondas was seated on a chair of ebony and ivory; all the belongings of the place were handsome and even costly. Round his waist was a massive chain of gold (the prisoners of the god could not be bound by anything less precious), which was fastened to a staple in the wall. The attendant unlocked it, using—for the lock was double—first his own key, and then one that had been taken from the person of his colleague.

"Explanations afterwards," whispered Charidemus; "now we must act."

The prince looked inquiringly at the attendant. What was to be done after the release of the prisoner was to be left, it had been agreed, to circumstances. What the circumstances really were, no one knew so well as this man.

"I have it," cried the temple servant, meditating for a few moments, and he led the way to a small chamber used for keeping the sacred vestments. He then explained his plan.

"There is a small temple at the mouth of the southern harbour. If we can get there, it will be something; and I think we can. Anyhow it is our best chance."

Charidemus and the prince were disguised as priests. So ample were the robes that the figure of the person wearing them became undistinguishable, while the tall mitre with which the head was covered could be so worn that any slight difference of height would not be observed. The attendant, when he had finished robing them, an operation that of course he performed with a practised skill, pronounced that they made a very good pair of priests. He wore his own official dress, and arrayed the Theban in one that belonged to his comrade.

Thus equipped, the party set out, the pretended priests in front, and the attendants behind, holding a canopy over their superiors. They made their way at the slow and measured pace that befitted their profession to the harbour temple, passed the guard which was set at the land entrance to the port without challenge, and reached the sacred building without any mishap.

They were now close to the water, and could even see the friendly ships of the southern blockading squadron; but the guard ships by which the mouth of the harbour was closed were between them and safety. The question was, how these were to be passed. It was a question that had to be answered without delay, for they could see from a window of the temple which commanded a view of the whole harbour signs of commotion, such as the flashing of torches, which indicated that their escape had been discovered.

This indeed was the case. The king had sent an attendant a little after sunset to summon his guests to the evening meal. He reported their absence to his master, who, however, for a time suspected nothing. But when a second messenger found them still absent, inquiries were made. Some one had heard sounds in the temple, and the temple was searched; after that everything else that had happened could be seen or guessed.

Nothing remained for the fugitives but to strip off their garments and plunge into the water. Unfortunately the temple attendant was an indifferent swimmer. A boat, however, was lying moored some thirty yards from the shore, and this the party managed to reach. But by the time that they had all clambered on board, a thing which it always takes some time to do, the pursuers were within a hundred yards of the harbour-temple.

It must be explained that at each end of the row of ships by which the harbour mouth was protected, was an empty hulk, and that between the hulk and the pier side was a narrow opening only just broad and deep enough for a boat to pass over. This the prince had observed on some former occasion when he had been reconnoitring the defences of the harbour, and he now steered towards it, the rowers tugging at their oars with all their might. The boat had nearly reached the passage when the manœuvre was observed. The crew of the nearest ship hastened to get on board the hulk; but the distance between these two was too great for a leap, and in the darkness the gangway commonly used could not be at once found. At the very moment when it was put into position the boat had cleared the passage. So shallow indeed was the water that the hinder part of the keel had stuck for a few moments, but when the four occupants threw their weight into the bow, which was already in deeper water, it floated over.

Happily the night was very dark. The sky was overcast, and it still wanted a day to the new moon. Nor did the torches with which the whole line of galleys was ablaze, make it easier to distinguish an object outside the range of their light. Still the boat could be dimly seen, and till it was beyond the range of missiles the fugitives could not consider themselves safe. And indeed they did not wholly escape. Both Charidemus and Charondas were struck with bullets that caused somewhat painful contusions, the prince was slightly wounded in the hand, and the attendant more seriously in the arm, which was indeed almost pierced through by an arrow. A few more strokes, however, carried them out of range, and they were safe.

The High Priest

It had only been in sheer despair that Tyre had held out after her fleet lost the command of the sea. Able now to attack the city at any point that he might choose, Alexander abandoned the mole which he had been at such vast pains to construct, and commenced operations on the opposite side of the island, against the wall that fronted the open sea. The battering-rams were put on shipboard, and so brought to bear upon any weak places that had been discovered; and of these the Tyrians, confident of always being able to keep command of the sea, had left not a few. A first attempt failed; a second, made on a perfectly calm day, succeeded, and a considerable length of wall was broken down. A breach having been thus made, the ships that bore the battering-rams were withdrawn, and others carrying pontoons took their places. Two storming parties landed, one commanded by an officer of the name of Admetus, the other by Alexander in person. Admetus, who was the first to scale the wall, was killed by the stroke of a javelin, but his party made good their footing; and the king, landing his guards, was equally successful. The defenders of the wall abandoned it, but renewed the fight in the streets of the city. The battle raged most fiercely in the precincts of the Chapel of Agenor, the legendary founder of Tyre. The building had been strongly fortified, but it was taken at last, and the garrison was put to the sword. Before nightfall all Tyre was in the hands of Alexander. The king exacted a frightful penalty for the obstinate resistance which had baffled him for nearly a year. But he respected the Temple of Melkarth, where Azemilcus and a few of the Tyrian nobles had taken sanctuary, and the Sidonian prince had the satisfaction of saving more than a thousand victims from slavery or death. They took refuge in the galleys that were under his command, and Alexander either did not know of their escape, or, as is more probably the case, did not care to inquire about it. Hundreds of the principal citizens were executed; the remainder, numbering, it is said, thirty thousand, were sold as slaves.

Melkarth, whose city had been thus depopulated, was then honoured with a splendid sacrifice. All the soldiers, in full armour, marched round the temple; games, including a torch race, were held in the precincts; while the battering-ram that had made the first breach in the wall, and the galley that had first broken the boom guarding the harbour, were deposited within the temple itself.

"And now," said the king, at the banquet with which the great festival of Melkarth was concluded, "we will settle with that insolent priest who would not help us against these Tyrian rebels."

"Sir," said Hephaestion, "it is said that the god whom these Hebrews worship is mighty." And he went on to relate some of the marvels of Jewish history of which he had lately been hearing.

The king, who had something of a Roman's respect for foreign religions, listened with attention. "Have you heard anything of this kind?" he went on, addressing Charidemus. "Did your friend Manasseh tell you anything like this?"

Charidemus, as it happened, had been greatly impressed by his conversations with the Jew. The story of the end of Belshazzar, and of the mysterious hand that came out upon the palace wall, as the impious king sat with his nobles, drinking out of the sacred vessels of the temple, and that wrote his doom in letters of fire, had particularly struck him, and he now repeated it. Alexander heard it in silence, sternly checking some scoff on which one of his younger courtiers ventured when it was finished.

His resolve, however, to visit the seat of this formidable Deity was strengthened rather than weakened; and on the following day he set out with a select body of troops and a numerous retinue of native princes, leaving the main body of the army in charge of Parmenio, to follow the road which led to Egypt—which country he proposed next to deal with—over the Maritime Plain of Palestine. The distance between Tyre and Jerusalem was somewhat under a hundred miles, and was traversed in about six days. It was the evening of the seventh when he reached the hill-top, now known by the name of Scopus, or the Outlook, which is the northern spur of the ridge of Olivet. Fronting him stood the Hill of Sion, crowned with the Temple buildings, not yet, indeed, grown to the majestic strength which they attained in later days, but still not wanting in impressiveness and dignity. Below were the walls, now restored to their old strength, which had withstood more than one conqueror in his march, and the city, which, during more than a century of prosperity and peace, had more than repaired the desolation of the last siege. Just then it was made singularly picturesque by the greenery of the booths of branches, under the shade of which the people were keeping the Feast of Tabernacles, and which crowded every open space in the city.

But the attention of the visitors was arrested by a remarkable procession that met them as they reached the crest of the hill. At the head of it walked the High Priest, in all the magnificence of his robes of office. He wore a long garment or tunic of blue, made of the finest linen, that reached to below his knees. Below this were drawers of white linen, while the feet were protected by sandals. The upper part of his person was covered by the vestment known as the ephod, the tunic above described being "the robe of the ephod." The ephod was a mixture of gold, blue, purple, and scarlet, and was richly embroidered. On each shoulder was a large onyx, while the breast was covered with the splendid "Breastplate of Judgment," with its twelve precious stones, and round the waist was the "girdle dyed of many hues with gold interwoven with it." Round the bottom of the robe of the ephod were pomegranates wrought in blue, purple, and scarlet, and golden bells. Behind this gorgeous figure came the priests in their robes of spotless white, and behind these again a crowd of citizens in holiday attire.

The king stepped out from the ranks, and saluted the High Priest. So full of respect was his gesture that his attendants expressed, or at least looked, their surprise.

"I adore," said the king, "not the priest, but the God whom he serves. And this very man, clothed in these very robes, I now remember myself to have seen in a dream before I crossed into Asia. I had been considering with myself how I might best win the dominion over these lands, and he exhorted me boldly to cross over, for he would himself conduct my army and give me his blessing. Seeing him therefore this day I both thank the God whose servant he is for that which I have already attained, and beseech Him that I may attain yet more, even the fulfillment of all that is in my heart."

A solemn entry into the Temple, a sacrifice conducted by the king according to the High Priest's directions, and the offering of some splendid gifts to the treasury followed, and the king did not fail to enforce his compliments by conferring on his new subjects substantial privileges. The Jews were henceforth to live under their own laws; every seventh year, as they reaped no harvests, they were to pay no tribute; the same immunity was to be extended to all of Jewish race that might be found within the borders of the Persian kingdom. The High Priest, on the other hand, engaged to furnish a contingent from his nation for the Macedonian army. He only stipulated, and the king readily agreed, that the recruits should not be required to do anything that might be at variance with the law which they were bound to observe.

These matters concluded, Charidemus was summoned to the royal presence.

"Are you bent," asked the king, "on going with me into Egypt?"

"To tell you the truth, my lord," answered the young man, "I had not thought of it one way or the other."

"Well," said Alexander, "I have something for you to do here. First, you will take charge of the queen, who does not wish to travel just now. Then I want you to recruit and drill some of these sturdy Jews for me. They look like fine stuff for soldiers; and, if they are anything like their fathers, they should fight well. The High Priest thinks that you will do best in the Galilee country, where the people are not quite so stiff about their law. But you can settle these matters with Hephaestion, who knows my mind."

Queen Barsiné, who was expecting shortly to become a mother, had made interest with the king to have the young Macedonian put in charge of her establishment, partly because she had great confidence in him, partly because she had a kindly interest in his attachment to her niece, a feeling which, of course, had not escaped her quick woman's eyes.

The eight months that followed were, perhaps, the happiest that our hero ever enjoyed. A little walled town on the western shore of the Sea of Galilee had been chosen for Barsiné's residence during her husband's absence in Egypt, and Charidemus was appointed its governor. He was in command of a garrison of some hundred and fifty men, and had a couple of light galleys at his disposal, His duties were of the lightest. Two or three veterans, who had grown a little too old to carry the pike, drilled under his superintendence a couple of thousand sturdy Galilæan peasants, who had eagerly answered the summons to enlist under the great conqueror's banners. This work finished, he had the rest of his time at his own disposal. The more of it he could contrive to spend with Clearista, the happier of course he was. As long as the summer lasted, and, indeed, far into the autumn, there were frequent excursions on the lake, Clearista being accompanied by her gouvernante, the daughter of a Laconian farmer, who had been with her from her infancy. The waters then as now abounded with fish, and Charidemus was delighted to teach his fair companion some of the secrets of the angler's craft. As the year advanced there was plenty of game to be found in the forests of the eastern shore. The young Macedonian was a skilful archer, and could bring down a running deer without risk of injuring the choice portions of the flesh by an ill-aimed shaft. He found a keener delight in pursuing the fiercer creatures that haunted the oak glades of Bashan, and many were the trophies, won from wild boar and wolf and bear, that, to the mingled terror and delight of Clearista, he used to bring back from his hunting excursions. Nor were books wholly forgotten. Charidemus had always had some of a student's taste, and Barsiné had imparted to her niece some of her own love of culture. The young soldier even began—so potent an inspirer is love—to have literary ambitions. He wrote, but was too shy to exhibit, poems about his lady's virtues and beauty. He even conceived a scheme of celebrating the victories of Alexander in an heroic poem, and carried it out to the extent of composing some five or six hundred hexameters which he read to the admiring Clearista. Unfortunately they have been lost along with other treasures of antiquity, and I am unable to give my readers a specimen.

Meanwhile little or nothing in which he would have cared to have a part had been happening elsewhere. Alexander's march through Egypt was not a campaign, but a triumphal procession. The Persian satrap had made no attempt at resistance, and the population gladly welcomed their new masters. They hated the Persians, who scorned and insulted their religion, and eagerly turned to the more tolerant Greek. So the country was annexed without a blow being struck. Grand functions of sacrifice, in which Alexander was careful to do especial honour to Egyptian deities, with splendid receptions and banquets, fully occupied the time; and then there was the more useful labour of beginning a work which has been the most permanent monument of the conqueror's greatness, the foundation of the city of Alexandria. Charondas, who was attached to the king's personal suite, kept his friend informed of events by letters which reached him with fair regularity. I shall give an extract from one of these because it records the most important incident of the sojourn in Egypt.

"Charondas to Charidemus, greeting.

"I have just returned safe—thanks to the gods—from a journey which I thought more than once likely to be my last. Know that the king conceived a desire to visit the Temple of Zeus Ammon, where there is an oracle famous for being the most truth-speaking in the world. Not even the Pythia at Delphi—so it is said—more clearly foresees the future, and a more important matter, it must be confessed, more plainly expounds what she foresees. The king took with him some five thousand men, many more, in my judgment, than it was expedient to take, seeing that the enemy most to be dreaded in such an expedition, to wit, thirst, is one more easily to be encountered by a few than by a multitude. At the first we marched westwards, keeping close to the sea, through a region that is desolate indeed, and void of inhabitants, but rather because it has been neglected by men than because it refuses to receive them. There are streams, some of which, it is said, do not fail even when the summer is hottest, and in some places grass, and in many shrubs. Thus we journeyed without difficulty for a distance of about 1,600 stadia. Then we turned southward; and here began our difficulties and dangers. The difficulty always is to find the right way, for such a track as there is will often be altogether hidden in a very short space of time; and so it was with us. The danger is lest the traveller, so wandering from the way, should perish of hunger and thirst, for it is not possible that he should carry much provision with him. How, then, you will ask, did we escape? Truly I cannot answer except by saying that it was through the good fortune of Alexander, not without the intervention of some Divine power. Many marvellous things were told me about the means by which we were guided on our way. Some averred that two serpents, of monstrous size, went before the army, uttering cries not unlike to human speech. Of these I can only aver that I neither saw nor heard them, and that I have had no speech with any that did see or hear, although not a few have borne witness to them second-hand, affirming that they had heard the story from those that had been eye-witnesses. The same I am constrained to say concerning the ravens which some declared to have been guides to the army. I saw them not, nor know any that did see them. But I had some converse with a native of these parts who was hired to be our guide. This man, I found, trusted neither to serpents, whether dumb or not, nor to ravens, but to the stars. And I noticed that he was much perplexed and troubled by what seemed a matter of rejoicing to the rest of us, namely, that the sky became overcast with clouds. We were rejoiced by the rain which assured us that we should not perish of thirst; but he complained that his guides were taken from him. Nevertheless, as the clouds were sometimes broken, he was not wholly deprived of the help in which he trusted.

"Let it suffice, then, to say that we got safely to our journey's end, not without assistance from the gods. No more beautiful place have I seen, though doubtless my pleasure in seeing it was the greater by reason of the desolation of the region through which we had passed. It is, as it were, an island in the sand, nowhere more than forty stadia across, covered with olives and palms, and watered by a spring, the marvels of which, unlike the serpents and the ravens, I can affirm of my own knowledge. That it is coldest at noonday and hottest at midnight, I have myself found by touching it. Or was this, you will perhaps say, by contrast only, because my own body was subject to exactly the opposite disposition? It may be so; nevertheless in such matters common tradition and belief are not wholly without value.

"You will ask, What said the Oracle? To the king it said that without doubt he was the son of Ammon; to others that they would do well, if they reverenced him as being such. Whether more be intended by this than what Homer says of Achilles and other great heroes that they were Zeus-descended I cannot say. Many take it to be so, and some are not a little displeased. Last night I heard two soldiers talking together on this matter. 'Comrade,' said one to the other, 'if I had King Philip for my father, I should be content, nor seek another.' 'Aye,' returned the other, 'thou sayest true. If Alexander be the chicken, truly Philip was the egg.' 'But now,' the first speaker went on, 'but now they say that the king's father was this Ammon. Didst ever see such a god? It is like a Pan with the goat-part uppermost. And who ever heard talk of a hero that had Pan for his father? Nay, nay, I would liefer have a plain honest Macedonian for my father, so he had head and legs like a man, than all the Ammons in the world.' So many talk in the camp, though there are some who are ready to say and do anything that may bring advancement. But these are dangerous matters to trust even to paper. We will talk of them, if need be, when we meet. Till then, farewell!"

From Tyre to The Tigris

THE pleasant sojourn on the shores of the Sea of Galilee came to an end in the early summer of the following year. Charidemus was summoned to meet the king at Tyre, where he was intending to complete his plans for his next campaign, a campaign that would, he hoped, be decisive. And it was arranged that the young man's charges should accompany him. Alexander had fixed on another residence for his wife and child. (Barsiné, it should be said, had given birth to a son in the early part of the winter.) His choice had fallen on Pergamos, one of the strongest fortresses in his dominions. The fact is that schemes of conquest were opening up before him which he felt would occupy him for many years. The next campaign would complete the conquest of Persia proper, but the eastern provinces would remain to be subdued, and after these, India, and after India the rest, it might be said, of the habitable world, for nothing less would satisfy his vast ambition. In Barsiné's son he had an heir, possibly not the heir who would succeed him, but still one who might be called to do so. To place him in safety was a desirable thing, and Pergamos, which was not far from the coast of the Ægean, with its almost impregnable citadel, seemed an eligible spot.

Charidemus's instructions were to make the best of his way with his charges to Pergamos, and to rejoin the army with all speed, a fast-sailing Sidonian vessel being assigned for the service. Both voyages were accomplished with unusual speed. But it is probable that in any case the first, made in such delightful company, would have seemed too short; the second, with a decisive and exciting campaign in view, too long.

It was early in May when Charidemus left Tyre, and the end of July, when, having accomplished his mission, he landed again at Sidon. Here he was met by an invitation to the palace, where he had the pleasure of meeting Charondas. The young man had been left behind when Alexander set out, to complete his recovery from an attack of illness. King Abdalonymus hospitably pressed the friends to prolong their stay with him for some days. Charondas, he said, would be better for a little more rest, while Charidemus wanted refreshment after his double voyage. At any other time the offer would have been gladly accepted, for Abdalonymus was a very striking personage. He had been little more than a day labourer when he was suddenly raised to the throne; but power had done nothing to spoil him. He was as frugal and temperate as ever; and he kept, rarest of possessions in a palace, his common sense. The two friends, however, were eager to set out. The army had already had ten days' start of them, and the bare idea of any decisive battle being fought before they had come up with it was intolerable.

They were on horseback at dawn the next morning. Their road was up the valley of the Leontes, and then, turning eastward, between the ranges of Lebanon and Anti-Lebanon. So far as the great ford over the Euphrates at Thapsacus there could be no question as to their route. Practically there was only one way, and that was the one which the army had taken. Arrived at the ford they found that they had gained three days. A week still remained to be made up, and this it seemed easy enough to do at the cost of some extra labour and, possibly, a little risk. Darius, it was known, had gathered a vast host more numerous even than that which had been routed at Issus, and was going to make a final struggle for his throne. His whereabouts was not exactly known, but it was certainly somewhere to the eastward of the Tigris, which river would probably be made his first line of defence. Anxious to make his march as little exhausting as possible to his men, Alexander had taken a somewhat circuitous line, turning first to the north, in the direction of the Armenian mountains, then striking eastward, and touching the Tigris at its lowest ford, some thirty miles above Nineveh. To go straight from Thapsacus to this point would be to save no little time if it could be done. The two friends resolved to make the experiment.

The first day passed without adventure. The travelers did not see a human creature from morning to evening, and had to spend the night under a terebinth, with no more refreshment than the food which they had had the fore-thought to carry with them, and a scanty draught of very muddy water. Their halting-place on the second day seemed to promise much better entertainment. As they drew rein beside an inviting looking clump of trees they were accosted by a venerable stranger, who, in broken but intelligible Greek, of-fered them hospitality for the night. Their host showed them a small tent where they would sleep, and made them understand that he should be glad of their company at his own evening meal. Half-an-hour afterwards they sat down to a fairly well-dressed supper, a lamb which had been killed in their honour, barley cakes baked on the embers, and palm-wine. There was not much conversation, for the old sheikh's stock of phrases did not go very far, and the two somewhat sullen looking youths who made up the company, seemed not to know a word of any language but their own. When the host found that the strangers declined his offer to try another skin of palm-wine, he smilingly wished them good-night. One of the silent young men showed them to their tent, and they were left to repose.

The hour was still early, and the friends did not feel inclined for sleep. Both had a good deal to say to each other. Besides personal topics they had to talk about the prospects of the war, and that a war which seemed to prom-ise adventures of the most exciting kind. It must have been about an hour short of midnight when, just as they were thinking of lying down for the night, their attention was attracted by a slight noise at the tent door. Charon-das going, lamp in hand, to see what it meant started back in horror at the sight that met his eyes. A dwarfish looking man stood, or rather crouched before him. His figure was bent almost double by bodily infirmity, it would seem, rather than by age. The long black hair streaked with grey, that fell on his shoulders was rough and unkempt, his dress was ragged and filthy. But the horror of the poor wretch's appearance was in the mutilation which had been practised upon him. His ears had been cut off; his nostrils had been cropped as close as the knife could shear them, his right arm had been cut short at the elbow, and his left leg at the knee.

"Let me speak with you," said the stranger, "if you can bear awhile with a sight so hideous."

He spoke in pure Greek, and with the accent of an educated man.

"Speak on," said Charidemus, "we feel nothing but pity for a countryman who has been unhappy;" and he took the sufferer's hand in his own, and pressed it with a friendly grasp.

"I am come to warn you," said the visitor, "but if I do not first tell you my story you will scarce believe me."

He paused overcome with emotion.

"I am a native of Crotona, and belonged to a family of physicians. We reck-oned among our ancestors the great Democedes, whom the first Darius, as you may remember, honoured and enriched. Some political troubles with which I need not weary you compelled me to leave my country, and I settled at Ephesus. There I did well enough, till in an evil hour I was sent for to pre-scribe for the satrap of Phrygia. I had acquired, I may say, some reputation for myself, but my name—it is the same as that of my great ancestor—did far more for me. It has made, indeed, the fortune of many a physician of our na-tion. Well, I cured the satrap, who indeed had nothing worse the matter with him than too much meat and drink. He was very grateful, and bribed me by the promise of a great salary—three hundred minas, if you will believe me, gentlemen," explained the poor wretch with a lingering feeling of pride in his professional success, "he bribed me, I say, to go with him when he returned to court. For a time all went well; then a favourite slave fell ill. The poor lad was in a consumption; not Æsculapius himself could have cured him; and I could do nothing for him, but make his end easy. Masistius—that was my employer's name—was in a furious rage. He maimed me in the cruel way you see, and sold me for a slave."

"What! you a free-born Greek," exclaimed the young men with one voice.

"Yes," replied the man, "and 'tis no uncommon experience, as you will find when you get further into the country. Yes; there are hundreds of Greeks who have suffered the same horrors as you see in me. Well; he sold me as a slave to the villain whose meat you have been eating to-night."

"Do you call him villain?" said Charidemus in surprise. "He seemed kind and hospitable enough."

"Aye, he seems," replied the man, "that is part of his craft. But for all his amiable looks, he is a robber and a murderer. He makes it his business to do away with guests whom he entertains as he has entertained you. Commonly he plies them with his accursed palm-wine till they fall into a drunken sleep. When that fails, they are stabbed or strangled. One or two I have contrived to warn; but they generally prevent me from coming near the poor wretches."

"That is brave of you," said one of the young men.

"Oh!" was the answer, "I deserve no credit, I am weary of my life, and should be thankful if they would put an end to it, though a sort of hope pre-vents me from doing it myself. And yet what hope!" he went on in a lower tone, "what can a mutilated wretch such as I am hope for but to escape from the sight of my fellow men? But they leave me alone; I am too valuable to them to be injured. The wretches are never ill themselves, but they set me to cure their cattle and sheep, and I save them a great deal more than the mis-erable pittance of food and drink which they give me. But now for what con-cerns yourselves. The wretch will send his assassins—those two brutal-looking sons mostly do his work for him—about the end of the third watch when a man commonly sleeps his soundest. So you have two hours and more before you. Your horses are picketed at the other end of the grove from that by which you entered, not where you saw them fastened, that was only done to deceive you. It is just where you see the moon showing itself above the trees. Get to them as quietly as you can, and then ride for your lives. But mind, go westward, that is, back along the way you came. In about an hour's time turn sharp to the north. Another hour will bring you to a little stream; cross that, and after you have gone some thousand paces you will come to another clump of trees very like this. Another Sheikh has his encampment there; I am not sure but that he does a little robbery and murder on his own account; but just now he has the merit of being at daggers drawn with his neighbour here. And he has a kindness for me, for I cured his favourite horse; and if you mention my name to him, I am sure that he will treat you well. And now, farewell!"

"What can we do for you?" said Charidemus, "we are on our way to join the great Alexander; it is such wrongs as yours that he has come to redress."

"Do for me!" cried the unhappy man, in a tone of inexpressible bitterness; "forget that you have ever seen me. I should be sorry that any but you should know that Democedes has suffered such wrongs, and yet has been willing to live. But stay—I would gladly see that villain Masistius crucified, if he is still alive, as indeed I trust he is; and you will remember your kind and venerable host of to-night. And now, again, farewell!"

The two friends lost no time in making their way to the spot whence they were to find their horses. A man had been set to watch the animals. Happily for the fugitives he had fallen asleep. It went against the grain with them, generous young fellows as they were, to kill him in his slumber; but, unless they were to alarm the encampment, they had no alternative. His employment, too, showed that he was in the plot. It was not in their owners' interest that he had been set to watch the horses. With half-averted face Charondas dealt him the fatal blow, and he died without a struggle or a groan. A short time was spent, for the advantage seemed worth the delay, in muffling the horses' hoofs. That done, they rode back, quietly at first and then at full speed, by the road by which they had come, till it was time, as they judged, for them to turn off. The day had dawned when they reached the other encampment. The name of Democedes proved as good an introduction to the chief as they could wish. When he further learnt that his guests were officers on their way to join the army of the great Alexander, he was profuse in his offers of help and entertainment. They accepted an escort of horsemen who should see them well out of the reach of their treacherous host, and under their protection and guidance reached a district where no further danger was to be apprehended. It was with no small pleasure that at the very moment when the Tigris came in sight their eyes caught the glitter of arms in the distance. The vanguard of the Macedonian army was filing down the slopes that led to the ford.

Arbela

"THESE Persians must be either very much frightened or very bold, if they have nothing to say to us at such a place as this."

Such in substance was what every one in the Macedonian army was saying or thinking as they struggled through the dangerous and difficult ford of the Tigris. It was indeed a crossing which even a few resolute men posted on the opposite shore would have made disastrous, if not impossible, to the advancing army. The stream was at its lowest—the time was about two-thirds through the month of September—but the rapid current fully justified the name of the "Arrow," for such is the meaning of the word Tigris. The cavalry, keeping as steady a line as they could across the upper part of the ford, did their best to break the force of the stream, but did not save the infantry from a vast amount of labour and some loss. In their lances and armour, not to speak of other accoutrements, the men had to carry an enormous weight; they trod on a river-bed of shifting stones, and the water was nearly up to their necks. If a man stumbled it was very difficult for him to recover his footing, and it was only the exceptionally strong who could do anything to help a comrade in difficulties. It was already dark when the last lines painfully struggled up the slippery bank on the eastern side of the river. The depression of spirits caused by fatigue and discomfort were aggravated by the portent of an eclipse. The soldiers saw with dismay the brilliant moon, for whose help in arranging their bivouac they had been so thankful, swallowed up, as it seemed, by an advancing darkness, and they drew the gloomiest omens from the sight. But Alexander was equal to the occasion. A disciple of Aristotle, the greatest natural philosopher of the ancient world, he knew the cause of the phenomenon, but as a practical man, whose business it was to understand the natures with which he had to deal, he knew also that a scientific explanation of that cause would be useless. Aristander the soothsayer was directed to reassure the terrified multitude with something more adapted to their wants; and he did not fail to produce it. "The moon," he said, "was the special patron of Persia, as the sun is of Greece. It is to the Persian now as more than once before that the eclipsed moon portends defeat." This reassuring explanation was eagerly listened to, and when, after the sacrifices of the next day, sacrifices with which Alexander impartially honoured sun, moon, and earth, Aristander confidently declared that the appearance of the victims indicated certain, speedy, and complete victory, he was readily believed. "Before the new moon shall be visible," he boldly predicted, "the kingdom of Persia shall have fallen."

That the final struggle was at hand was soon put beyond a doubt. Towards the close of the sixth day after the passage of the Tigris—two days out of the six had been allowed for repose some Persian troopers were espied in the distance. The king himself at once started in pursuit, taking the best mounted squadron of his cavalry with him. Most of the enemy escaped, but some were taken, perhaps allowed themselves to be taken, for Darius's disastrous cowardice at Issus had weakened his hold on the fidelity of his subjects. From these men Alexander learnt all that he wanted to know. Darius had collected a host far larger even than that which had fought at Issus. The contingents of which it was composed came indeed chiefly from the remoter east. Western Asia had passed out of the Great King's power and was added to the resources of the invader; but the eastern provinces from the Caspian to the Persian Gulf and even to the Indus were still faithful to him. The town of Arbela had been named as the rendezvous of the army, and there the magazines and baggage had been located; but the place chosen as the battle-field, where Darius would meet his enemy on ground selected by himself, was Gaugamela, a village some ten miles east of Nineveh, and situated on a wide and treeless plain, on which the Persian engineers had levelled even such slopes as there were. At Issus they had fought in a defile where their vastly superior numbers could not be utilized; on the vast level of the Babylonian plains every man, horse, and chariot could be brought into action.

Alexander saw that he must fight the enemy on their own ground, and took his measures accordingly. Daring as he was—he knew that he had to deal with Asiatics—he threw away no chance, and neglected no precaution. On hearing what the prisoners had to say about the force and position of the enemy, he called a halt, and ordered the construction of an entrenched camp. Here the soldiers had four days' repose. After sunset on the fourth day he gave the signal to advance. His intention was to attack the enemy at daybreak, but the ground over which he had to pass presented so many difficulties that when the day dawned he was still three miles distant from the hostile lines.

The sight of them made him hesitate and reconsider his plans. Though he did not doubt of victory, he saw that victory was not to be won by a haphazard attack. And indeed it was a formidable array that stretched itself before him, as far as the eye could reach, or at least as far as the eye could distinguish anything with clearness. On the extreme right were the Syrians, the Medes, once the ruling people of Western Asia and still mindful of their old renown, the Parthian cavalry, and the sturdy mountaineers of the Caucasus; on the opposite wing were the Bactrians, hill men for the most part, and famous for fierceness and activity, and the native Persians, horse and foot in alternate formation. But it was in the centre of the line, round the person of Darius, where he stood conspicuous on his royal chariot, that the choicest troops of the empire were congregated. Here were ranged the Persian Horseguards, a force levied from the noblest families of the dominant people, and distinguished by the proud title of the "Kinsmen of the King;" and the Footguards, also a corps d'élite, who carried golden apples at the butt end of their pikes. Next to these stood the Carians, men of a race which had shown itself more apt than any other Asiatic tribe to learn Greek discipline and rival Greek valour; and next to these again, the Greek mercenaries themselves.

In front of the line were the scythed chariots, numbering two hundred in all, each with its sharp-pointed sides projecting far beyond the horses, and its sword-blades and scythes stretching from the yoke and from the naves of the wheels. Behind the line, again, was a huge mixed multitude, drawn from every tribe that owned the Great King's sway.

So formidable was the host, and so strong its position that Alexander halted to take counsel with his generals how the attack might be most advantageously delivered. A new entrenched camp was constructed, and the rest of the day was spent in carefully reconnoitring the enemy's forces. Some of the most experienced officers—Parmenio among them—suggested a night attack. Alexander rejected the proposal with scorn. Raising his voice that he might be heard by the soldiers, who were crowding round the tent where the council was held, he cried, "This might suit thieves and robbers, but it does not suit me. I will not tarnish my fame by such stratagems, for I prefer defeat with honour to a victory so won. Besides I know that such an attack would fail. The barbarians keep a regular watch; and they have their men under arms. It is we, not they, who would be thrown into confusion. I am for open war."

And this, of course, was the last word.

The next morning the Macedonian king drew out his order of battle. As usual he put himself at the head of the right wing. This was made up of the Companion Cavalry, under the immediate command of Philotas, son of Parmenio, with next to them the light infantry, and three of the six divisions of the Phalanx. The three other divisions, with a strong body of cavalry from the allied Greek states, formed the left wing, commanded as usual by Parmenio.

But behind the first line of the army stood another in reserve. Frequent reinforcements had not only enabled the king to supply all losses, but had also largely increased his numbers. The thirty thousand infantry which had been brought into action at the Granicus had now grown to forty thousand, the four thousand five hundred cavalry to seven thousand. It was thus easier to have a reserve, while the nature of the battle-field made it more necessary, for attacks on the flanks and rear of the main line might probably have to be repelled. This second line consisted of the light cavalry, the Macedonian archers, contingents from some of the half-barbarian tribes which bordered on Macedonia, some veteran Greek mercenaries, and other miscellaneous troops. Some Thracian infantry were detached to guard the camp and the baggage.

The Persians, with their vastly superior numbers, were of course extended far beyond the Macedonian line. Left to make the attack, they might have easily turned the flanks and even the rear of their opponents. Alexander seeing this, and following the tactics which had twice proved so successful, assumed the offensive. He put himself at the head of the Companion Cavalry on the extreme right of his army, and led them forward in person, still keeping more and more to the right, and thus threatening the enemy with the very movement which he had himself reason to dread. He thus not only avoided the iron spikes which, as a deserter had warned him, had been set to injure the Macedonian cavalry, but almost got beyond the ground which the Persians had caused to be levelled for the operations of their chariots. Fearful at once of being outflanked and of finding his chariots made useless, Darius launched some Bactrian and Scythian cavalry against the advancing enemy. Alexander, on his part, detached some cavalry of his own to charge the Bactrians and the action began.

The Bactrians commenced with a success, driving in the Greek horsemen. These fell back on their supports, and advancing again in increased force threw the Bactrians into confusion. Squadron after squadron joined the fray till a considerable part of the Macedonian right wing and of the Persian left were engaged. The Persians were beginning to give way, when Darius saw, as he thought, the time for bringing his scythed chariots into action, and gave the word for them to charge, and for his main line to advance behind them. The charge was made, but failed, almost entirely, of its effect. The Macedonian archers and javelin throwers wounded many of the horses; some agile skirmishers even contrived to seize the reins, and pull down the drivers from their places. Other chariots got as far as the Macedonian line, but recoiled from the pikes; and the few whose drivers were lucky enough or bold enough to break their way through all the hindrances were allowed to pass between the Macedonian lines, without being able to inflict any damage. As a whole, the charge failed.

Then Alexander delivered his counter attack. He ceased his movement to the right. Then, wheeling half round, his Companion Cavalry dashed into the Persian line at the spot where the Bactrians, by their advance, had broken its order. At the same time, his own main line raised the battle cry, and moved forward. Once within the enemy's ranks he pushed straight for the point where, as he knew, the battle would be decided, the chariot of the king. The first defence of that all-important position was the Persian cavalry. Better at skirmishing than at hand-to-hand fighting, it broke before his onslaught. Still there remained troops to be reckoned with who might have made the fortune of the day doubtful, the flower of the Persian foot and the veteran Greeks. For a short time these men stood their ground; they might have stood it longer, but for the same disastrous cause that had brought about the defeat of Issus, the cowardice of King Darius. He had been dismayed to see his chariots fail, and his cavalry broken by the charge of the Companions, and he lost heart altogether when the dreaded Phalanx itself with its bristling array of pikes seemed to be forcing his infantry apart, and coming nearer to himself. He turned his chariot and fled; the first, when he should have been the last, to leave his post.

The flight of the king was the signal for a general rout, as far, at least, as the left wing and centre of the Persian host were concerned. It was no longer a battle; it was a massacre. Alexander pressed furiously on, eager to capture the fugitive Darius. But the very completeness of his victory, it may be said, hindered him. So headlong was the flight that the dust, which, after months of burning summer heat, lay thick upon the plain, rose like the smoke of some vast conflagration. The darkness was as the darkness of night. Nothing could be heard but cries of fury or despair, the jingling of the chariot reins, and the sound of the whips which the terrified charioteers plied with all their might.

Nor, indeed, was Alexander permitted to continue the pursuit as long as he could have wished. Though the precipitate flight of Darius had brought the conflict on the Persian left to a speedy end, the right had fought with better fortune. Mazæus, who was, perhaps, the ablest of the Persian generals, was in command, and knew how to employ his superiority of numbers. While the sturdy Median infantry engaged Parmenio's front line, Mazæus put himself at the head of the Parthian horse and charged his flank. Parmenio was so hard pressed that he sent an orderly to the king with an urgent demand for help. Alexander was greatly vexed at receiving it, feeling that any chance that remained of capturing the person of Darius, a most important matter in his eyes, was now hopelessly lost. But he knew his business as a general too well—being as cautious when the occasion demanded as he was bold when boldness was expedient—to neglect the demand of so experienced an officer as Parmenio. He at once called back his troops from the pursuit, and led them to the relief of the left wing. Parmenio had sent the same message to the left division of the phalanx, which, though under his command, had actually taken part in the advance made by the right division. These, too, prepared to come to his assistance.

Before, however, the help thus demanded could be given, the need for it had almost ceased to exist. On the one hand, the Thessalian cavalry had proved themselves worthy of their old reputation as the best horsemen in Greece. Held during the earlier part of the engagement in reserve, they had made a brilliant charge on the Parthians, and more than restored the fortune of the day. And then, on the other hand, Mazæus and his men had felt the same infection of fear which the flight of Darius had communicated to the rest of the army. The conspicuous figure which was the centre of all their hopes had disappeared, and they had nothing to fight for. Parmenio felt the vigour of the enemy's attack languish, though he did not know the cause, and he had had the satisfaction of recovering and more than recovering his ground before any reinforcements reached him.

Strangely enough it was in the very last hour of the battle, when nothing could have changed the issue of the fight, that the fiercest conflict of the whole day occurred. The cavalry, mainly Parthian, as has been said, but with some squadrons of Indian and Persian horse among them, which had won a partial victory over Parmenio's division, encountered in their retreat across the field of battle, Alexander himself and the Companions. Their only hope of escape was to cut their way through the advancing force. It was no time for the usual cavalry tactics. Every man was fighting for his life, and he fought with a fury that made him a match even for Macedonian discipline and valour. And they had among them also some of the most expert swordsmen in the world. Anyhow, the Companions suffered more severely than they did in any other engagement of the war. As many as sixty were slain in the course of a few minutes; three of the principal officers, Hephaestion being one of them, were wounded; and Alexander himself was more than once in serious danger. It is not easy to say what might have been the result if the chief thought of the Persians had not been to cut their way through and save themselves. Those who succeeded in doing this did not think of turning to renew the fight, but galloped off as hard as they could.

Yet another success was achieved by the Persians in the extreme rear of the Macedonian army. The wheeling movement of the left companies of the phalanx to help Parmenio had left a gap in the line. A brigade of Indian and Persian horse plunged through this gap, and attacked the camp. The Thracians who had been left to guard it were probably not very reliable troops, and they were hampered by the number of prisoners over whom they had to keep watch. Many of these prisoners contrived to free themselves. The chief object of the attack was to liberate the mother of Darius (the king's wife had died a few weeks before, worn out with grief and fatigue). This object might have been attained but for the unwillingness of the lady herself. Whether she was afraid to trust herself to her deliverers, or despaired of making her escape, or was unwilling to leave Alexander, it is certain that she refused to go. Meanwhile, some troops from the second line had come to the rescue of the camp, and the assailants had to save themselves as best they could.

Alexander, his fierce struggle with the retreating cavalry over, was free to renew his pursuit of Darius. The Persian king had reached the Lycus, a river about ten miles from the battle-field. His attendants strongly urged him to have the bridge which spanned the stream broken down, and so delay the conqueror's pursuit. But, though his courage had failed him at the near sight of the Macedonian spears, he was not altogether base. He thought of the multitudes whom the breaking of the bridge would doom to certain death, and determined to leave it standing. It was dark before Alexander reached the river, and the cavalry was by that time so wearied that a few hours' rest was a necessity. Accordingly he called a halt, and it was not till midnight that he resumed the pursuit. Even then many had to be left behind, their horses being wholly unfit for service. With the rest the king pushed on to Arbela, where he thought it possible that he might capture Darius. In this he was disappointed. Darius had halted in the town only so long as to change his chariot for a horse. The chariot with the royal robe and bow fell into Alexander's hands, but Darius himself, safe, at least for the present, was on his way to the Median Highlands.

At Babylon

THE victory of Arbela was decisive. Alexander of Macedon was now, beyond all question, the Great King. All of the hundred and twenty-seven

provinces out of which Cyrus and his successors had built up the huge structure of the Persian Empire were not indeed yet subdued, and the person of
Darius had still to be captured; but the title was practically undisputed. The
first consequence of the victory was that Babylon and Susa the two capitals,
as they may be called, were at once surrendered by the satraps that gov-
erned them. Mazæus was in command at Babylon. He had done his best, as
we have seen, on the fatal day of Arbela; but he had seen that all was lost, and
that nothing remained but to make such terms as was possible with the conqueror. He met the Macedonian king as he approached the city, and offered
him the keys; and Susa, at the same time, was surrendered to the lieutenant
who was sent to take possession of it and its treasures.

It was indeed rather as a Deliverer than as a Conqueror that Alexander
was received by the inhabitants of Babylon. The Persians had never been
more than a garrison, and had made themselves as hated there as they had
elsewhere. Hence it was with genuine delight that the population flocked out
to meet their new master. Sacrifices over which the priests prayed for his
welfare were offered on altars built by the wayside, and enthusiastic crowds
spread flowers under his feet.

Among those who came out to pay their respects to the king was a deputation from the great Jewish colony which had long existed in the city, and
which, indeed, continued to inhabit it, till almost the day of its final abandonment. Alexander greeted them with especial kindness, and promised that
they should have his favour and protection. Charidemus had been furnished
by Manasseh of Damascus with a general letter of introduction to the heads
of the dispersed Hebrew communities. This he lost no time in presenting,
and he found that he had made a most interesting acquaintance.

Eleazar of Babylon was indeed a remarkable personage, His family, which
was distantly connected with the royal house of David, had been settled in
the city for more than two centuries, tracing itself back to a certain Gemariah
who had been one of the notables removed from Jerusalem by Nebuchadnezzar in the first Captivity. He was now in extreme old age, having completed
his ninety-second year, and he had for some time ceased to leave his apartments. But his intellectual faculties retained their full vigour. He still held the
chief control of a vast business which had grown up under his care. The Jews
had already begun to show their genius for finance, and Eleazar surpassed
predecessors and contemporaries in the boldness and skill of his combina-
tions. The Persian kings were far too wealthy to need the help which modern
rulers are often glad to get from bankers and capitalists; but their subjects of
every rank often stood in want of it. A satrap, about to start for his province,
would require a loan for his outfit, and would be able to repay it, with liberal
interest, if he could hold power for a year. A courtier, anxious to make a present to some queen of the harem, a merchant buying goods which he would
sell at more than cent. per cent. profit to the tribes of the remote east; in fact,
every one who wanted money either for business or for pleasure was sure to

find it, if only he had security to offer, with Eleazar of Babylon, or with one of his correspondents. The old man had able agents and lieutenants, but no single transaction was completed without his final approval. Even the little that Charidemus and his friend could see, as outsiders, of the magnitude of his affairs, struck them with wonder. Greek commerce was but a petty affair compared to a system which seemed to take in the whole world. But there was something in Eleazar far more interesting than any distinction which he might have as the head of a great mercantile house. He was, so to speak, a mine of notable memories, both national and personal.

Among the worthies with whom his family claimed relationship was the remarkable man who had held high office under three successive dynasties of Babylonian rulers—Nebuchadnezzar, the conqueror of Jerusalem; Astyages the Mede; and Cyrus the Persian. One of Eleazar's most precious possessions was a book of manuscript, written, it was believed, by the great statesman's own hand, which recorded the story of himself and his companions. Eleazar, when he found that his young guests were something better than mere soldiers of fortune, thinking of nothing but fighting and prize money, and had a sympathetic interest in great deeds and great men, would read from this precious volume its stirring stories of heroism, translating them as he went on from the original Hebrew or Aramaic into Greek, a language which he spoke with ease and correctness. The narrative stirred the two friends to an extraordinary degree, and indeed may be said to have influenced their whole lives. They admired the temperate self-restraint of the young captives who preferred their pulse and water to the dainties from the royal tables, sumptuous but unclean, which their keepers would have forced upon them.

"Why," cried Charondas, when the story was finished, "the young fellows might have won a prize at Olympia. 'Tis in the training, I believe, that more than half of the men break down."

The young man blushed hot as soon as the words had escaped him. It was, he remembered, a painful subject, and he could have bitten his tongue out in his self-reproach for mentioning it. The smile on Charidemus's face soon reassured him. Larger interests and hopes had made the young Macedonian entirely forget what he had once considered to be an unpardonable and irremediable wrong.

With still more profound interest did the friends listen to the tale of how the dauntless three chose rather to be thrust into the burning fiery furnace than to bow down to the golden image which the king had set up.

"Marked you that?" cried Charidemus to his friend, when the reader, to whom they had listened with breathless eagerness, brought the narrative to an end; "Marked you that? If it be so, our God whom we serve is able to deliver us out from the burning fiery furnace, and He will deliver us out of thine hand, O king. But if not, be it known unto thee, O king, that we will not serve thy gods. How splendid! If not—I can understand a man walking up to what looks like certain death, if he feels quite sure that Apollo, or Poseidon, or Aphrodité, is going to carry him off in a cloud; and I can understand—for of course we see it every day—a man taking his life in his hand, from duty, or for a prize, or, it may be, from sheer liking for danger; but this passes my comprehension. Just to bow down to an image, which every one else is doing, and they won't do it. Their God, they feel sure, will save them; but in any case they will stand firm. Yes, that if not is one of the grandest things I ever heard."

Old Eleazar heard with delight the young man's enthusiastic words. He had no passion for making proselytes, and, indeed, believed that they were best made without direct effort; but he could not help saying, "Ah! my young friends, is not that a God worth serving? It is something to be sure as these Three were sure, that He will save you; but it is still more to feel, that whether He save you or no, anything is better than to do Him any wrong."

Eleazar had also recollections of his own which keenly interested the young men.

"Your king's success," he said one day, "has not surprised me. In fact, I have been expecting it for these last sixty years and more. When I was a young man I saw something of events of which, of course, you have heard, when the younger Cyrus brought up some ten thousand of your soldiers to help him in pulling down his brother from the Persian throne, and setting himself upon it. Mind you, I never loved the young prince; if he had got his way, no one but himself and his soldiers would have been a whit better for it. Indeed, I did all that I could to help the king against him. We Jews have a good deal to say to the making of war, even when we don't carry swords ourselves; gold and silver, you may easily understand, are often far more powerful than steel. Well; I was present at the battle, and though I did not wish well to your countrymen's purpose, I could not help seeing how very near they came to accomplishing it. I saw the pick of the Persian army fly absolutely without striking a blow when the Greek phalanx charged it. Nor could there have been a shadow of doubt that what the Greeks did with the left of the king's army they would have done with his centre and his right, if they only had had the chance. It was only the foolish fury of the young prince that saved the king. If Cyrus had only kept his head, the day was his. Well, what I saw then, and what I heard afterwards of the marvellous way in which these men, without a general, and almost without stores, made their way home, convinced me that what has happened now was only a matter of time. For sixty years or more, I say, I have been waiting for it to come to pass. Time after time it seemed likely; but something always hindered it. The right man never came, or if he came, some accident cut him off just as he was setting to work. But now he has come, and the work is done."

The friends spent with their venerable host all the time that was not required for their military duties; and these, indeed, were of the very slightest kind. The fact was that his society was very much more to their taste than that of their comrades. Alexander's army had been campaigning for more than three years with very little change or relaxation. If they were not actually engaged in some laborious service, they had some such services in near prospect; and what time was given them for rest had to be strictly spent in preparation. Never, indeed, before, had the whole force been quartered in a city; and a month in Babylon, one of the most luxurious places in the world—not to use any worse epithet—was a curious change from the hardships of the bivouac and the battle-field. And then the soldiers found themselves in possession of an unusual sum of money. An enormous treasure had fallen into Alexander's hand, and he had dispensed it with characteristic liberality, giving to each private soldier sums varying from thirty to ten pounds, according to the corps in which he served, and to the officers in proportion. Such opportunities for revelry were not neglected, and the city presented a scene of license and uproar from which Charidemus and his friend were very glad to escape.

For Charondas the household of Eleazar possessed a particular attraction in the person of his great-grand-daughter Miriam. He had chanced, before his introduction to the family, to do the girl and her attendant the service of checking the unwelcome attentions of some half-tipsy soldiers. The young Miriam began by being grateful, and ended by feeling a warmer interest in her gallant and handsome protector. So the time passed only too quickly by. There was no need to go for exercise or recreation beyond the spacious pleasure grounds which were attached to Eleazar's dwelling. They included, indeed, part of the famous "hanging-garden" which the greatest of the Babylonian kings had constructed for his queen, to reproduce for her among the level plains of the Euphrates the wooded hills, her native Median uplands, over which she had once delighted to wander. The elaborate structure—terrace rising above terrace till they overtopped the city walls—had been permitted to fall into decay; but the wildness of the spot, left as it had been to nature, more than compensated, to some tastes at least, the absence of more regular beauty. In another part of the garden was a small lake, supplied by a canal which was connected with the Euphrates. This was a specially favoured resort of the young people. Water-lilies, white, yellow, and olive, half covered its surface with their gorgeous flowers; and its depths were tenanted by swarms of gold fish. A light shallop floated on its waters, and Miriam often watched with delight the speed with which the friends could propel it through the water, though she could never be induced to trust herself to it. Days so spent and evenings employed in the readings described above, and the talk which grew out of them, made a delightful change from the realities of campaigning, realities which, for all the excitements of danger and glory, were often prosaic and revolting.

A Glimpse into The Future

"CHARIDEMUS," said the Theban to his friend one morning, when, the order to march having been given, the two friends were busy with their preparations, "Charidemus, we have been more than a month in Babylon, and yet have never seen its greatest wonder."

"What do you mean?" returned the other. "The place seems to me full of wonders, and I should be greatly puzzled to say which is the greatest."

"I mean the magic, of course. Everybody says that the Babylonian magicians are the most famous in the world. I don't think we ought to go away without finding out something about them."

"I cannot say that I feel particularly disposed that way. Do you think that people have ever got any real good from oracles and soothsaying and auguries and such things? It seems to me that when they do get any knowledge of the future, it is a sort of half-knowledge, that is much more likely to lead them astray than to guide. However, if you are very curious about these magicians, I don't mind coming with you."

"Who will tell us the best man to go to? Do you think that Eleazar would be likely to know? "

"He may know, as he seems to know everything. But I don't think that we had better ask him. I feel sure that he hates the whole race. Don't you remember when he was reading out of that book his explaining that the 'wise men' of Babylon were the magicians, and saying that whatever in their art was not imposture was wickedness?"

"Yes; and he wondered why Daniel, when he came to have the king's ear, did not have the whole race exterminated. As you say, Eleazar is not likely to help us."

The two friends, however, easily found the information that they wanted. There could be no doubt who was the man they should consult. All agreed that the prince of the magicians was Arioch. "If you want to know what the stars can tell you," explained a seller of sword blades with whom they had had some dealings, and whom they consulted, "you must go to Zaidu. He is the most learned of the star-gazers, of the astrologers. Or, if you want to learn what can be found out from the entrails of beasts, and the flight or notes of birds, you must go to Zirbulla. The best interpreter of dreams, again, is Lagamar. But if you want a magician, then Arioch is your man. And if you want my advice, young gentlemen," went on the sword-dealer, who seemed indeed to have thought a good deal about the subject, "I should say, Go to a magician. You see the stars are very much above us; they may have something to say in great matters—wars, and such like—but I don't see how they can concern themselves with you and me. Then the birds and beasts are below us. And as for dreams, what are they but our own thoughts? Don't understand me, gentlemen," he exclaimed, "to say that I don't believe in stars and dreams and the other things; but, after all, magic, I take it, is the best way of looking into the future."

"Why?" asked the two friends, to whom much of this distinguishing between different kinds of divination was new.

"Because the magicians have to do with spirits, with demons," said their informant, his voice sinking to an awe-stricken whisper; "and the demons are not above us like the stars, nor below us like the beasts. They are with us, they are like us. Some of them have been men, and now that they are free from the body they see what we cannot see. But Arioch will tell you more about these things than I can. I am only in the outside court; he is in the shrine."

Arioch's house was in the best quarter of the city, and was so sumptuous a dwelling, both within and without, as to show clearly enough that magic was a lucrative art. The magician himself was not the sort of man whom the friends had expected to see. He was no venerable sage, pale with fasting and exhausted with midnight vigils, but a man of middle-age, whose handsome face was ruddy with health and brown with exercise, and who, with his carefully curled hair and beard and fashionable clothing, seemed more like a courtier than a sorcerer.

Arioch received his guests with elaborate politeness. He clapped his hands, and a slave appeared, carrying three jewelled cups, full of Libyan wine, a rare vintage, commonly reserved, as the young men happened to know, for royal tables. He clapped his hands again, but this time twice, and a little girl, with yellow hair and a complexion of exquisite fairness, came in with a tray of sweetmeats. She had been bought, he explained, from a Celtic tribe in the far West, and he hinted that the cost of her purchase had been enormous. A conversation followed on general topics, brought round gradually and without effort, as it seemed, to the object of the visit.

"So your want to have a look into the future?" he asked.

The two friends admitted that they did.

"Perhaps I can help you," said the magician. "But you know, I do not doubt, that one does not look into the future as easily as one reads a calendar or a tablet."

For a short time he seemed to be considering, and then went on, "I must think the matter over; and if the thing can be done there are some preparations which I must make. Meanwhile my secretary shall show you some things which may be worth your looking at."

He touched a silver hand-bell which stood on a table—a slab of citron wood on a silver pedestal—which stood by his side. A young man, who was apparently of Egyptian extraction, entered the room. Arioch gave him his directions.

"Show these gentlemen the library and anything else that they may care to see."

The library was indeed a curious sight. To the Greeks five centuries consti-tuted antiquity. Legends, it is true, went back to a far remoter past, but there was nothing actually to be seen or handled of which they could be certain that it was much older than this. But here they stood in the presence of ages, compared to which even their own legends were new.

"This," said their guide, pointing to an earthen jar, "contains the founda-tion cylinder of the Sun Temple, written by the hand of Naramsin himself. Nabonidus, whom you call Labynetus, found it more than two hundred years ago, and it was then at least three thousand years old. These again," and he pointed as he spoke to several rows of bricks covered with wedge-shaped characters, "are the Calendar of Sargon. They are quite modern. They can be scarcely two thousand years old. This roll," he went on, "was part of a library which King Nebuchadnezzar brought back from Egypt. He gave it to an an-cestor of my master. It is the story of the king whom you call Sesostris, I think."

These were some of the curiosities of the collection. But it contained a number of more modern works, and was especially rich, as might be ex-pected, in works dealing with the possessor's art. "There was no book of im-portance on this subject," the secretary was sure, "that his master did not possess." He pointed to the most recent acquisition, which had come, he said, from Carthage.

"It is almost the first book," he remarked, "that has been written in that city; not worth very much, I fancy; but, then, my master likes to have every-thing, and there must be bad as well as good."

There were other things in the library which some visitors might have thought more interesting than books. The heavy iron doors of a cupboard in the wall were thrown back, and showed a splendid collection of gold and sil-ver cups and chargers, some of them exact models, the secretary said, of the sacred vessels from Jerusalem. The originals had been all scrupulously re-stored by Cyrus and his successors. A drawer was opened, and found to be full of precious stones, conspicuous among which were some emeralds and sapphires of unusual size. "Presents," exclaimed the secretary, "from distin-guished persons who have received benefit from my master's skill."

The visitors were politely given to understand that they, too, would be expected to contribute something to this lavish display of wealth.

"It is usual," said the secretary, "for those who consult the future to make some little offering. This part of the business has been put under my man-agement. The master never touches coin; he must go into the presence of the spirits with clean hands. Touched with dross, they might raise the wrath of the Unseen Ones."

The two friends thought the scruple a little fine-drawn, but said nothing.

"My master," the secretary went on, "is unwilling that any one should be shut out from the sight of that which might profit him for lack of means, and has fixed the fee at five darics. There are rich men who force upon him, so to speak, much more costly gifts."

The friends, who happened to have their pockets full of prize-money, produced the ten darics, not without a misgiving that what they were to hear would scarcely be worth the money. But the adventure, if followed so far, would have to be followed to the end. To grumble would be useless, and if there was anything to be learnt, might injure the chance of learning it.

The gold duly handed over, the inquirers were taken back, not to the chamber in which Arioch had received them, but to one of a far more imposing kind. It was a lofty vaulted room, pervaded with a dim green light coming from an invisible source, as there were neither lamps nor any window or skylight to be seen. The tessellated floor had strange devices, hideous figures of the demons which were the life-long terror of the superstitious Babylonians. On a brazen altar in the centre of the room some embers were smouldering. These, as the visitors entered, were fanned by some unseen agency to a white heat. A moment afterwards Arioch threw some handfuls of incense on them, and the room was soon filled with fumes of a most stupefying fragrance. The magician himself was certainly changed from the worldly-looking personage whom the friends had seen an hour before. His face wore a look of exaltation; while the dim green light had changed its healthy hue to a ghastly paleness. His secular attire had been changed for priestly robes of white, bound round the waist by a girdle which looked like a serpent, and surmounted by a mitre in the top of which a curious red light was seen to burn. The young men, though half-contemptuous of what they could not help thinking to be artificial terrors, yet felt a certain awe creeping over them as they gazed.

"You desire," said the magician in a voice which his visitors could hardly recognize as that in which he had before accosted them, "you desire to hear from the spirits what they have to tell you of the future."

"We do," said Charidemus.

"There are spirits and spirits," continued Arioch, "spirits which come in visible shape, and with which you can talk face to face, and spirits whose voices only can be discerned by mortal senses. The first are terrible to look upon and dangerous to deal with."

"We do not fear," said the young men.

"But I fear," returned the magician, "if not for you, yet for myself. What would your king say if two of his officers, traced to my house, should be missing, or—I have seen such things—should be found strangled? Not all my art—and I know something I assure you—would save me. And then I dread the spirits, if I call them up unprepared, even more than I dread your king. No, my young friends, I dare not call up the strongest spirits that I know. But, believe me, you shall not repent of having come, or think your time wasted."

"Do as you think best," said Charidemus. "We shall be content; it is your art, not ours."

Arioch commenced a low chant which gradually grew louder and louder till the roof rang again with the volume of sound. The listeners could not understand the words. They were in the tongue of the Accadian tribes whom the Babylonian Semites had long before dispossessed; but they could distinguish some frequently recurring names, always pronounced with a peculiar intonation, which they imagined, to be the names of the spirits whom the magician was invoking.

The chant reached the highest pitch to which the voice could be raised, and then suddenly ceased.

"Be sure," said Arioch, in his usual voice, "that you stand within the circle, and do not speak."

The circle was the region that was protected by incantations from the intrusion of spirits, that of the more powerful and malignant kind being excepted, as the magician had explained.

"These strangers seek to know the future," said Arioch, with the same strained voice and in the same tongue which he had used in his invocation. He interpreted his words in Greek, as he also interpreted the answers. These answers seemed to come from a distance; the language used was the same, as far as the hearers could judge of words which they did not understand; the voice had a very different sound.

"They were foes and they are friends. Dear to the immortal gods is he that can forgive, and dear is he who can bear to be forgiven. The years shall divide them, and the years shall bring them together. They shall travel by diverse ways, and the path shall be smooth to the one and rough to the other, but the end shall be peace, if only they be wise. The tree that was a sapling yesterday to-morrow shall cover the whole earth. But it shall be stricken from above, and great will be its fall. Many will perish in that day. Happy is he who shall be content to stand afar and watch."

The voice ceased, and a moment afterwards the strange light of the chamber changed to that of the ordinary day. "The spirit will speak no more," said Arioch. "Come with me." And he led them out of the chamber. When they had got back to the room into which they had been ushered at first, he said, "These things are for your own ears; I leave it to your discretion to determine when you will speak of them. At least let it not be for years to come. For yourselves, I see nothing but light in the future; but for one who is greater than you, there is darkness in the sky. But be silent. It is dangerous to prophecy evil to the mighty. Yet, if the occasion should come, say to your master, 'Beware of the city whose fortifications were built by the potters.' "

"Was this worth our ten darics, think you?" said the Theban, as they walked to their own quarters, through streets filled with the bustle of preparation, for the army was getting ready to march. "Surely one might get good luck told to one, and good advice given for less. But he seemed to know something about us."

The two friends were never able quite to make up their minds, whether the magician's words were a happy guess, or a genuine prediction. As they came to know more of the marvels of Eastern sorcery they thought less of the outside marvels of the scene which they had witnessed. They made acquaintance, for instance, with ventriloquism, a curious gift scarcely known in the West, but frequently used for purposes of religious imposture by some of the Asiatic peoples. And they could make a shrewd guess that persons in Arioch's position made it their business to gather all the knowledge that they could about the past history of those who consulted them. But there was always an unexplained remainder. This, as most of my readers will probably allow, was not an uncommon experience. There is plenty of carefully gathered knowledge of the past, plenty of shrewd guessing at the future, and plenty, it cannot be doubted, of imposture—but something more.

Vengeance

TWO days after the interview with the magician the army marched out of Babylon. Its destination was, in the first place, Susa, where a large reinforcement was awaiting it. There had been some losses in battle, and many times more from sickness. The month spent amongst the luxuries of Babylon had been at least as fatal as three months of campaigning. But all vacancies were more than made up by the fifteen thousand men from Macedonia, Thrace, and Greece, who now joined the standards. As for money, it was in such abundance as never had been witnessed before, or has been witnessed since. The treasure found at Babylon had sufficed, as we have seen, to furnish a liberal present to the troops; but the treasures of Susa were far greater. Fifty thousand talents is said to have been the total, and there remained more than double the sum yet to be acquired at Persepolis. This was the next point to be reached. It lay in the rugged mountain region from which the conquering Persian race had emerged some two centuries before, to found an empire which has scarcely a parallel in history for the rapidity of its growth and its decay.

The army had halted for the night at the end of the fifth day's march, when a company of rudely clad strangers presented themselves at one of the gates of the camp, and demanded an audience of the king. They were admitted to his presence, and proceeded by their interpreter to make their demands. These were couched in language, which, softened though it was by the tact of the interpreter, still had a very peremptory sound.

"Powerful Stranger," they began (the "powerful" was interpolated in the process of translation) "we are come to demand the tribute customarily paid by all who would traverse the country of the Uxii. The Great King, from the days of Cyrus himself, has always paid it, as will you also, we doubt not, who claim to be his successor. If you refuse, we shut our pass against you, as we would have shut it against him."

A flush of rage at this unceremonious address rose to the face of the king, but he mastered himself. "It is strange," said he, after a moment, "to be thus addressed. There is no one, from the Western Sea to this spot, who has been able to stay my advance. On what strength of your arms, or on what favour of the gods do you depend, that you talk so boldly? Yet I would not refuse aught that you have a right to ask. On the third day, as I calculate, I shall reach that pass of which you speak. Be there, and you shall receive that which is your due."

Thoroughly mystified by this answer, the Uxians returned to their native hills, and having collected a force which was held sufficient to garrison the pass against any assailant, they awaited the arrival of their new tributary. But to their astonishment he approached them from behind. His eagle eye had discovered a track, known, of course, to the mountaineers, but certainly unknown to his guide. A few wreaths of smoke rising into the clear air, far up the heights of the hills, caught his eye as early one morning he surveyed the mountain range over which he had to make his way. At the same time he traced the line of a slight depression in the hills. "Where there is a dwelling there is probably a path," said the king to Parmenio, who accompanied him in his reconnoitring expedition, "and we shall doubtless find it near a watercourse."

The watercourse was discovered, and with it the path. Greedy as ever of personal adventure, Alexander himself led the light troops whom he selected as the most suitable force for this service. Starting at midnight he came just before dawn on one of the Uxian villages. The surprise was complete. Not a man escaped. By the time the next village was reached some of the inhabitants had gone about their work in the fields and contrived to get away. But they only spread the alarm among their tribesmen. As there was not a fortress in the whole country, there was nothing left for the humbled mountaineers but absolute submission. Even this would not have saved the tribe from extermination, the penalty which the enraged Alexander had decreed against them, but for the intercession of the mother of Darius.

"My son," she said, "be merciful. My own race came two generations back from these same mountaineers. I ask their lives as a favour to myself. If they are haughty, it is the Persian kings in the past who by their weakness have taught them to be so. Now that they have learnt your strength, you will find them subjects worth ruling."

"Mother," said Alexander, "whatever you are pleased to ask, I am more than pleased to give."

And the shepherds were saved.

Another pass yet remained to be won, the famous Susian gates, and then Persepolis was his. But it was not won without an effort. One of the sturdiest of the Persian nobles held it with a body of picked troops, and the first assault, delivered the very morning after his arrival, was repulsed with loss. The next, directed both against the front and against the flank, always a weak point with Asiatic troops, was successful, and the way to Persepolis was open.

The king had invited Charidemus to ride with him as the army made its last day's march to Persepolis, and the young Macedonian had related to him the adventure which he and his friend had encountered on their way from the fords of Euphrates to join the army, and had dwelt with some emotion on the story of the unhappy man who had been the means of their escape. A turn of the road brought them face to face with a pitiable spectacle for which his tale had been an appropriate preparation. This was a company of unhappy creatures—it was afterwards ascertained that there were as many as eight hundred of them—who had suffered mutilation at the hands of their brutal Persian masters. Some had lost hands, some feet; several of the poor creatures had been deprived of both, and were wheeled along in little cars by some comrades who had been less cruelly treated. On the faces of many of them had been branded insulting words, sometimes in Persian and sometimes—a yet more intolerable grievance—in Greek characters. "Not men but strange spectres of men"; they greeted the king with a Greek cry of welcome. Their voices seemed the only human thing about them.

When the king saw this deplorable array, and understood who and what they were, he leapt from his horse, and went among the ranks of the sufferers. So manifest was his sympathy that they could not but welcome him, and yet they could not help shrinking with a keen sense of humiliation from the gaze of a countryman. Bodily deformity was such a calamity to the Greek with his keen love for physical beauty, that such an affliction as that from which they were suffering seemed the very heaviest burden that could be laid upon humanity. Yet there were none who were not touched by the king's gracious kindness. He went from one to another with words of sympathy and consolation, inquired into their stories, and promised them such help as they might require. A strange collection of stories they were that the king heard. Some doubtless were exaggerated; in others there was some suppression of truth; but the whole formed a record of pitiless and often unprovoked cruelty. Many of the unhappy men were persons of education: tutors who had been induced to take charge of young Persian nobles and had chanced to offend either employer or pupil; unlucky or unskilful physicians, such as he whom Charidemus had encountered; architects where buildings had proved unsightly or unstable. Mercenary soldiers who had been convicted or suspected of unfaithfulness were a numerous class. A few, it could hardly be doubted, had been really guilty of criminal acts.

So moved was Alexander by the horror of what he saw and heard that he burst into tears. "And after all," Charidemus heard him murmur to himself, "I cannot heal the sorrows of one of these poor creatures. O gods, how helpless have ye made the race of mortal men!"

Still, if he could not heal their sorrows, he could alleviate them. The sufferers were given to understand that they should have their choice of returning to their homes in Greece, or of remaining where they were. In either case, their means of livelihood in the future would be assured. They were to deliberate among themselves, and let him know their decision in the morning.

The question was debated, we are told, with some heat.

"Such sorrows as ours," said the spokesman of one party, "are best borne where they are borne unseen. Shall we exhibit them as a nine-days' wonder to Greece? True it is our country; but wretches such as we are have no country, and no hope but in being forgotten. Our friends will pity us, I doubt not; but nothing dries sooner than a tear. Our wives—will they welcome in these mangled carcasses the bridegrooms of their youth; our children—will they reverence such parents? We have wives and children here, who have been the sole solace of our unhappy lot. Shall we leave them for the uncertain affection of those who may well wish, when the first emotion of pity is spent, that we had never returned?"

It was an Athenian who represented the opposite views. "Such thoughts as you have heard," he said, are an insult to humanity. Only a hard-hearted man can believe that other men's hearts are so hard. The gods are offering us today what we never could have ventured to ask—our country, our wives, our children, all that is worth living or dying for. To refuse it were baseness indeed; only the slaves who have learnt to hug their chains can do it."

The counsels of the first speaker prevailed; and indeed many of the exiles were old and feeble and could hardly hope to survive the fatigues of the homeward journey. A deputation waited on Alexander to announce their decision. He seems to have expected another result, promising all that they wanted for their journey and a comfortable subsistence at home. The offer was heard in silence, and then the king learnt the truth. It touched him inexpressibly that men could be so wretched that they were unwilling to return to their country. His first thought was to secure the exiles a liberal provision in the place where they had elected to stay. Each man had a handsome present in money, and suitable clothing, besides a well-stocked farm, the rent of which he would receive from some native cultivator. The second thought was to carry into execution a resolve which the sight of these victims of Persian cruelty had suggested. He would visit these brutal barbarians with a vengeance that should make the world ring again.

A council of generals was hastily called, and Alexander announced his intentions.

"We have come," he said, "to the mother-city of the Persian race. It is from this that these barbarians, the most pitiless and savage that the world has ever seen, came forth to ravage the lands of the Greek. Up till to-day we have abstained from vengeance; and indeed it would have been unjust to punish the subjects for the wickedness of their masters. But now we have the home of these masters in our power, and the day of our revenge is come. When the

120

royal treasure has been removed I shall give over Persepolis to fire and sword."

Only one of the assembly ventured to oppose this decision, though there were many, doubtless, who questioned its wisdom.

"You will do ill, sire, in my opinion," said Parmenio, the oldest of his generals, "to carry out this resolve. It is not the wealth of the enemy, it is your own wealth that you are giving up to plunder; it is your own subjects—for enemies who have submitted themselves to the conquerors are subjects—whom you are about to slaughter."

"Your advice, Parmenio," retorted the king, "becomes you, but it does not become me. I do not make war as a huckster, to make profit of my victories, nor even as King of Macedon, but as the avenger of Greece. Two hundred years of wrong from the day when the Persians enslaved our brethren in Asia cry for vengeance. The gods have called me to the task, and this, I feel, is the hour."

After this nothing more was said. The royal treasure was removed, loading, it is said, ten thousand carts each drawn by a pair of mules, and five thousand camels. Then the city was given up to plunder and massacre, and, when it had been stripped of everything valuable, burnt to the ground, the king himself leading the way torch in hand. In a few hours a few smoking ruins were all that remained of the ancient capital of the Persian race. We may wish that Alexander had shown himself more magnanimous; but it must be remembered that this savage act only expressed the common sentiment of his age. For the most part he was a clement and generous conqueror; but "vengeance on Persia" he could not entirely forget.

Darius

ALEXANDER'S most pressing care was now the capture of Darius himself. As long as the Great King was at liberty he might become the centre of a dangerous opposition. If he was once taken Persia was practically conquered. He had fled to Ecbatana, the ancient capital of the Medes, from the field of Arbela; and now he had left Ecbatana to find refuge in the wilds of Bactria, the most rugged and inaccessible of all the provinces of the empire. But he was not far in advance; Alexander was only eight days behind him at Ecbatana, and eight days would not, he thought, be difficult to make up, when his own rate of marching was compared with that of the fugitive. Affairs that could not be neglected kept him some days at Ecbatana. These disposed of, he started in pursuit, hoping to overtake the flying king before he could reach the Caspian Gates, a difficult mountain-pass on the southern side of the range which now bears the name of Elburz. He pressed on in hot haste, but found that he was too late. He was still fifty miles from the Gates, when he heard that Darius had passed them. And for the present it was impossible to continue the chase. So worn out were the troops that he had to allow them five days for rest. After this the fifty miles that still separated him from the Gates were traversed in two days. At the first halting place on the other side he heard news that made him curse the delays that had hindered his movements.

Toilsome as this rapid march had been, Queen Sisygambis, the mother of Darius, had, at her own earnest request, accompanied it. Alexander had just finished his evening meal on the evening of the first day after passing the Gates, when he received a message from the queen's mother, requesting an interview on matters of urgent importance. He obeyed the summons at once, and repaired to the tent.

The queen, usually calm and self-possessed, was overwhelmed with grief. "Speak, and tell your story," she said, addressing the elder of two men who stood by wearing the dress of Bactrian peasants. The man stepped forward.

"Stay," cried Alexander, "first tell me who you are, for, unless my eyes deceive me, you are not what you seem."

"It is true, sire," replied the man. "We have disguised ourselves that we might have the better chance of bringing you tidings which it greatly concerns both you and the queen to know. My companion and I are Persian nobles. We have been faithful to King Darius. Till three days ago we followed him, and it is our duty to him that brings us here."

"What do you mean?" cried Alexander. "Where is he? How does he fare?"

"Sire," said Bagistanes, for that was the Persian's name, "he is king no longer."

"And who has presumed to depose him?" said Alexander, flushing with rage. "Who is it that gives and takes away kingdoms at his pleasure?"

"Sire," replied Bagistanes, "since the day when King Darius fled from the field of Arbela—"

The speaker paused, and looked doubtfully at the queen. It was impossible to tell the truth without implying blame of the king, who had in so cowardly a fashion betrayed his army.

"Speak on," said Sisygambis. "I have learnt to bear it."

"Since that day, then," resumed Bagistanes, "the king has had enemies who would have taken from him the Crown of Persia. Bessus, Satrap of Bactria, conspired with other nobles against their master. They consulted whether they should not deliver him to you, and had done so, but that they doubted whether you were one that rewarded traitors. Then they resolved to take him with them in their flight eastward, and in his name to renew the war."

"But had he no friends?" asked the king.

"Yes, he had friends, but they were too weak to resist, nor would the king trust himself to them. Patron, who commanded the Greeks that are still left to him, warned him of his danger, but to no purpose. 'If my own people desert me,' he said, 'I will not be defended by foreigners.' And Patron, who indeed had but fifteen hundred men with him—for only so many are left out of the fifty thousand Greeks who received the king's pay four years ago—Patron

122

could do nothing. Then Artabazus tried what he could do. 'If you do not trust these men because they are foreigners, yet I am a Persian of the Persians. Will you not listen to me?' The king bade him speak, and Artabazus gave him the same advice that Patron had given. 'Come with us, for there are some who are still faithful to you, into the Greek camp. That is your only hope.' The king refused. 'I stay with my own people,' he said. That same day Patron and his Greeks marched off, and Artabazus went with him. My companion and I thought that we could better serve our master by remaining, and we stayed. That night Bessus surrounded the king's tent with soldiers—some Bactrian savages, who know no master but the man who pays them—and laid hands on him, bound him with chains of gold, and carried him off in a covered chariot, closely guarded by Bactrians. We could not get speech with him; but we went a day's journey with the traitors, in order to find out what direction they were going to take. We halted that night at a village, the headman of which I knew to be a faithful fellow—in fact, he is my foster-brother. He gave us these disguises, and we got off very soon after it was dark. Probably we were not pursued; the start was too great. This is what we have come to tell you."

"You will save him, my son," said Sisygambis to Alexander.

"I will, mother," replied the king, "if it can be done by man, and the gods do not forbid."

Within an hour a picked body of troops was ready to continue the pursuit. Two small squadrons, one of the Companion Cavalry, the other of Macedonian light horse—the Thessalians had gone home from Ecbatana—and a company of infantry, selected for their strength and endurance, formed the van of the pursuing force. Alexander, of course, took the command himself. Charidemus, who was beginning to have a reputation for good luck, a gift scarcely less highly esteemed even by the wise than prudence and courage, received orders to accompany him. No man carried anything beyond his arms and provisions for two days, the king himself being as slenderly equipped as his companions. The main body of the army was to follow with the baggage at a more leisurely pace.

It was about the beginning of the first watch when the flying column started. It made a forced march of two nights and a day, making only a few brief halts for food, and taking a somewhat longer rest when the sun was at its hottest. When the second day began to dawn, the camp from which Bagistanes had escaped to bring his information could be descried. Bessus was now three days in advance. Another forced march, this time for twenty-four hours, broken only by one brief siesta, for the men ate in their saddles, materially decreased the distance. The column reached a village which Bessus and his prisoner had left only the day before. Still the prospect was discouraging. The headman was brought before Alexander, and questioned by means of an interpreter. The man had plenty to tell, for it was only the day before that he had been similarly questioned by Bessus. From what had fallen from the satrap, the headman had concluded that it was the intention of the fugitives to push on night and day without halting.

"Can we overtake them?" asked the king. "Tell me how I may do it and you shall have a hundred gold coins for yourself, and your village shall be free of tribute for ever."

"You cannot overtake them by following them; but you can cut them off."

The man then described the route which would have to be followed. It lay across a desert; it was fairly level and not unusually rough, but it was absolutely without water. Sometimes used in winter, it was never traversed between the spring and the autumn equinox. But the distance saved was very large indeed.

Alexander's resolution was at once taken. He was one of the men to whom nothing is impossible, and this waterless desert was only one of the obstacles which it was his delight to overcome. But, if his idea was audacious, he had also a consummate readiness of resource, and a most careful and sagacious faculty of adapting means to ends. He began by selecting from the cavalry force which accompanied him the best horses and the best men. All the infantry were left behind. The riding weight of the chosen horsemen was reduced to the lowest possibility, even the ornaments of the horses being left behind. Then he gave them a long rest, so long that there was no little wonder among them at what seemed a strange waste of time. But the king knew what he was doing. He was going to make one supreme effort, and everything must be done to avoid a breakdown.

The start was made at nightfall, but the moon was fortunately full, and the riders had no difficulty in keeping the track. By an hour after sunrise on the following day they had completed nearly fifty miles, and their task was all but accomplished.

They had, in fact, cut the Persians off. The two bodies of men were marching on converging lines, which, had they been followed, would have actually brought them together. Unluckily some quick-sighted Bactrian had caught a glimpse of the Macedonians, and had given the alarm to his commander. Bessus and his column were already in flight when they, somewhat later, became visible to the Macedonians.

The best mounted of the troopers started at once in pursuit. They recognized the figure of the satrap, and took it for granted that Darius would be with him. The chase would in any case have been fruitless, for the Bactrians had not been pushing their horses during the night, and easily distanced the wearied pursuers. But, as a matter of fact, Darius was not there, and it was Charidemus who, by mingled sagacity and good luck, won the prize of the day. His eye had been caught by an object in the Persian line of march which he soon discovered to be a covered chariot, surrounded by troops. He saw it become the centre of a lively movement and then observed that it was left standing alone. He also observed that before the soldiers left it they killed the animals which were drawing it. It at once occurred to him that it was here that Darius would be found. He looked round for the king, intending to make his conjecture known to him. But Alexander was a long way behind. His horse, not the famous Bucephalus, which was indeed too old for such work, but a young charger which he was riding for the first time, had broken down. No time was to be lost, and Charidemus galloped up to the chariot.

His guess had been right. Darius was there, but he was dying. The story told afterwards by the slave who, hidden himself, had witnessed the last scene, was this: Bessus and the other leaders, as soon as they discovered that the Macedonians had overtaken them, had urged the king to leave the chariot and mount a horse. He refused. "You will fall," cried Bessus, "into the hands of Alexander." "I care not," answered Darius. "At least he is not a traitor." Without further parley they hurled their javelins at him and fled, not even turning to see whether the wounds were mortal.

The king was near his end when Charidemus entered. The slave had come out of his hiding-place, and was endeavouring in vain to stanch the flow of blood. Darius roused a little as the strange figure came in sight.

"Who are you?" he asked.

"Charidemus, my lord," was the answer.

"What?" murmured the dying man, "do his furies haunt me still?"

"My lord," said the young man, "I have only kindness to remember."

Darius recognized his voice. "Ah! I recollect," he said, "you were at Issus. But where is your king?"

"He is behind; he is coming; but his horse failed him."

"He will be too late, if indeed he wished to see me alive. But it matters not: Darius, alive or dead, is nothing now. But give him my thanks, and say that I commend my mother to him and all of my kindred that may fall into his hands. He is a generous foe, and worthier than I of the sceptre of Cyrus. But let him beware. He is too great; and the gods are envious."

Here his voice failed him. A shudder passed over his limbs; he drew a few deep breaths, and the last of the Persian kings was gone.

About half an hour afterwards Alexander arrived, having obtained a horse from one of his troopers. For some minutes he stood looking at the dead man in silence. Then calling some of his men, who by this time had collected in considerable numbers, he bade them pay the last duties to the dead. The corpse was conveyed to the nearest town, and there roughly embalmed. In due time it received honourable burial in the royal tomb at Pasargadæ.

Invalided

THE extraordinary fatigues which Charidemus had undergone, together with continual exposure to the burning summer heat, resulted in a long and dangerous illness. He had strength enough to make his way along with a number of other invalided men to Ecbatana; but immediately after his arrival in that city the fever which had been lurking in his system declared itself in an acute form. For many days he hovered between life and death, and his recovery was long and tedious, and interrupted by more than one dangerous relapse. All this time the outer world was nothing to him. First came days of delirium in which he raved of battles and sieges, with now and then a softer note in his voice contrasting strangely with the ringing tone of the words of command. These were followed by weeks of indifference, during which the patient took no care for anything but the routine of the sick-room. When his thoughts once more returned to the business and interests of life it was already autumn. Almost the first news from the world without that penetrated the retirement of his sick-room was the story of a terrible tragedy that had happened almost within sight and hearing.

Parmenio, the oldest, the most trusted of the lieutenants of Alexander, was dead, treacherously slain by his master's orders; and Philotas his son, the most brilliant cavalry leader in the army, had been put to death on a charge of treason. Whether that charge was true or false no one knew for certain, as no one has been able to discover since. But there were many who believed that both men had been shamefully murdered. The accusation was certainly improbable—for what had Parmenio and his son, both as high in command as they could hope to be, to gain? And it rested on the weakest evidence, the testimony of a worthless boy and a still more worthless woman.

All Charidemus's feelings were prepossessed in favour of the king; but the story came upon him as an awful shock. With Parmenio he had had no personal acquaintance, but Philotas had been in a way his friend. Haughty and overbearing in his general demeanour, he had treated Charidemus with especial kindness. The first effect of the news was to throw him back in his recovery. For a time, indeed, he was again dangerously ill. He ceased to care for life, and life almost slipped from his grasp.

He was slowly struggling back to health, much exercised all the time by doubts about his future, when a letter from the king was put into his hands. It ran thus:—

"Alexander the king to Charidemus, greeting.
"I hear with pleasure that the gods have preserved you to us. But you must not tempt the Fates again. You have had four years of warfare; let it suffice you for the present. It so happens that at this moment of writing I have before me the demand of Amyntas, son of Craterus, to be relieved of his command. He is, as you know, Governor of Pergamos, and he wishes to take part in the warfare which I purpose to carry on in the further East. This command, therefore, of which he is not unreasonably weary, you may not unreasonably welcome. Herewith is the order that appoints you to it. My keeper of the treasure at Ecbatana will pay you two hundred talents. Consider this as your present share of prize-money. You will also find herewith letters that you will deliver with your own hand. If you have other friends in Pergamos, greet them from me, and say that I wish well

both to them and to you. Be sure that if hereafter I shall need you I shall send for you. Farewell."

This communication solved at least one of the problems over which the young man had been puzzling. The physician had told him most emphatically that for a year or more all campaigning was out of the question. Here was a post which, as far as its duties were concerned, was practically equal to retirement. If he had had his choice he could not have picked out anything more suitable to his circumstances. A doubt indeed occurred whether, after what had happened, he could take anything from Alexander's hands. But the State, he reflected, must be served. Pergamos must have its garrison, if for no other reason, at least because the child who was at present the king's only heir was there, and the garrison must have its commander. And besides— who was he that he should judge the king? It would be painful, he acknowledged to himself, to be in daily contact with a man whose hands were red with the blood of a friend. That pain he would be spared. But it was another thing to refuse office at his hand. That would be to pronounce sentence in a case which he had no means of deciding. It was only after conscientiously weighing the matter by the weights of duty that the young man suffered himself to consult his private feelings. Here at least there was not a shadow of doubt in his mind. It was a grief to the ambitious young soldier to be checked in his active career. The campaign which the king was meditating in the further East promised to be full of adventure and interest, but if he was, for the future, to hear only of these glories, where could he do so with greater content than in the daily companionship of Clearista?

The westward journey was begun the next week. It was accomplished far more easily and speedily than would have been the case a short time before. The traffic between the coast and Upper Asia was now constant; the passage of invalided soldiers homeward, and of fresh troops to join the army, went on without intermission, and consequently the service of transport had been effectively organized. In about eight weeks Charidemus reported himself at Pergamos, and took possession of his new command.

Barsiné welcomed him with the liveliest delight, and was never wearied of his stories of the campaigns through which he had passed. Clearista, now grown from a girl into a woman—it was nearly four years since the two first met in the citadel of Halicarnassus—had exchanged the frank demeanour of childhood for a maidenly reserve. The young soldier, who had had little experience of women's ways, was at first disappointed and disheartened by what seemed her coldness. He knew nothing, of course, of the intense eagerness with which she had looked out for tidings of him during these years of absence, of the delight with which she had heard of his probable return, of the day-dreams of which he was ever the principal figure. She treated him as a casual acquaintance, but he was her hero, and not the less so, because, while he was full of striking reminiscences of the war, it was very difficult to get from him any account of personal adventure.

127

Greek courtships were not conducted, as my readers are probably aware, after English fashion, a fashion which is probably singular, whether we compare it with the ways of ancient or of modern life. Certainly a Greek treatise on the subject of "How Men Propose" would have had to be very brief, for lack of variety. Men proposed, it may be said, invariably to the parents or guardian of the lady. But it must not be supposed that then, any more than now, among people where marriage arrangements seem most rigorously to exclude any notion of choice, there was no previous understanding between the young people. Cramp and confine it as you will, human nature is pretty much the same in all times and places.

Charidemus made his suit in due form and to the person whom he was bound by custom to address, to Barsiné. But he did not make it till he had satisfied himself, as far as that could be done without actual words, that the suit would be welcome to the party chiefly interested. Reserve, however carefully maintained, is not always on its guard; a look or a word sometimes betrayed a deeper interest than the girl chose to acknowledge; in short, Charidemus felt hopeful of the result when he opened his heart to Barsiné, and he was not disappointed.

The marriage was solemnized on the fifth anniversary of the day on which Alexander had crossed over from Europe into Asia.

News from The East

THE six years that followed were years of quiet, uneventful happiness for Charidemus and his wife. The governorship of Pergamos was not exactly a sinecure, but it was not laborious. The garrison duty was of the slightest. The place was practically safe from attack, even if there had been any enemies to attack it. The governor's chief duty was the charge of a depôt, for which the town had been found a convenient situation. New troops were trained at it; troops who were invalided, or who had passed their time, were sent there to receive their formal discharge. These veterans had much to tell of what the army was doing. Of course plenty of fable was mixed with the fact, the more so as much of the news came at second or third hand and from very remote regions indeed. A more regular and reliable source of information were the letters which Charondas, who had been attached to headquarters, continued to send to his friend. The two had contrived a system of cypher, and so the Theban was able to express himself with a freedom which he would not otherwise have been able to use. Some extracts from these letters I shall give:

"...So Bessus the murderer has met with his deserts. We crossed the Oxus, the most rapid and difficult river that we have yet come to. We got over on skins, and lost, I am afraid, a good many men and horses. I myself was carried down full half a mile before I could get to land, and thought more than once

128

that it was all over with me. If Bessus had tried to stop us there must have been disaster; but we heard afterwards that he had been deserted by his men. Very soon after we had crossed the river he was taken. I have no pity for the villain; but I could wish that the king had not punished him as he did. He had his nostrils and ears cut off. You remember how Alexander was moved when he saw those poor mutilated wretches at Persepolis, what horror he expressed. And now he does the same things himself! But truly he grows more and more barbarian in his ways. Listen again to this. We came a few days since on our march to a little town that seemed somewhat differently built from the others in this country. The people came out to greet us." Their dress was partly Greek, partly foreign; their tongue Greek but mixed with barbarisms, yet not so much but that we readily understood them. Nothing could be more liberal than their offers; they were willing to give us all they had. The king inquired who they were. They were descended, he found—indeed they told the story themselves without any hesitation—from the families of the priests of Apollo at Branchidæ. These priests had told the secret of where their treasures were kept to King Xerxes after his return from Greece, and he to reward them, and also we may suppose, to save them from the vengeance of their countrymen, had planted them in this remote spot, where they had preserved their customs and language as well as they could. Now who could have imagined that the king should do what he did? He must avenge forsooth the honour of Apollo on these remote descendants of the men who caused his shrine to be robbed! He drove the poor creatures back into their town, drew a cordon of soldiers round it, and then sent in a company with orders to massacre every man, woman, and child in it. He gave me the command of these executioners. I refused it. 'It is against my vows, my lord,' I said. I thought that he would have struck me down where I stood. But he held his hand. He is always tender with me, for reasons that he has; and since he has been as friendly as ever. But what a monstrous deed! Again I say, the barbarian rather than the Greek.

"Another awful deed! O my friend, I often wish that I were with you in your peaceful retirement. In war the king is as magnificent as ever, but at home he becomes daily less and less master of himself. Truly he is then as formidable to his friends, as he is at other times to his enemies. What I write now I saw and heard with my own eyes. At Maracanda there was a great banquet—I dread these banquets a hundred-fold more than I dread a battle—to which I was invited with some hundred other officers. It was in honour of Cleitus, who had been appointed that day to the government of Bactria. When the cup had gone round pretty often, some of those wretched creatures who make it their business to flatter the king—it pains me to see how he swallows the flatteries of the very grossest with greediness—began to magnify his achievements. He was greater than Dionysus, greater than Hercules; no mortal could have done such things; it was only to be hoped that the gods would not take him till his work was done. If I was sickened to hear such talk, what think you I felt when Alexander himself began to talk in the same strain. Nothing would satisfy him but that he must run down his own father Philip. 'It was I,' he said, 'who really won the victory of Chæronea, though Philip would never own it. And, after all, what petty things that and all his victories are compared to what I have done!' On this I heard Cleitus whisper to his neighbour some lines from Euripides:

" 'When armies build their trophies o'er the foe,
Not they who bear the burden of the day,
But he who leads them reaps alone the praise.'

" 'What did he say?' said the king, who guessed that this certainly was no flattery. No one answered. Then Cleitus spoke out. He, too, had drunk deeply. (What a curse this wine is! Do you remember that we heard of people among the Jews who never will taste it. Really I sometimes think that they are in the right.) He magnified Philip. 'Whoever may have won the day at Chæronea,' he said, 'anyhow it was a finer thing than the burning of Thebes.' I saw the king wince at this as if some one had struck him. Then turning directly to Alexander, Cleitus said, 'Sir, we are all ready to die for you; but it is hard that when you are distributing the prizes of victory, you keep the best for those who pass the worst insults on the memory of your father.' Then he went on to declare that Parmenio and Philotas were innocent—in fact, I do not know what he said. He was fairly beyond himself. The king certainly bore it very well for a long time. At last, when Cleitus scoffed at the oracle of Ammon—'I tell you the truth better than your father Ammon did,' were his words—the king's patience came to an end. He jumped from his couch, caught hold of a spear, and would have run Cleitus through on the spot had not Ptolemy and Perdiccas caught him round the waist and held him back, while Lysimachus took away the lance from him. This made him more furious than ever. 'Help, men,' he cried to the soldiers on guard. 'They are treating me as they treated Darius.' At that they let go their hold. It would have been dangerous to touch him. He ran out into the porch and caught a spear from a sentinel. Just then Cleitus came out. 'Who goes there?' he said. Cleitus gave his name. 'Go to your dear Philip and your dear Parmenio!' shouted the king, and drove the spear into his heart.

"The king is better again, but he has suffered frightfully. Again and again he offered to kill himself. For three days and nights he lay upon the ground, and would neither eat nor drink. At last his bodyguard fairly forced him to do so. One curious reason for the king's madness I heard. The fatal feast was held in honour of the Twin Brethren, and it was one of the sacred days of Bacchus! Hence the wrath of the neglected god. It is certainly strange how this wrath, be it fact or fancy, continues to haunt him.

"Thank the gods we are in the field, and Alexander is himself again. Nay, he is more than himself. Sometimes I scarcely wonder at the flatterers who say that he is more than man. There never was such energy, such skill, so much courage joined to so much prudence. His men will follow him anywhere; when he heads them they think nothing impossible. Since I last wrote he has done what no man has ever done before; he has tamed the Scythians. The great Cyrus, you know, met his end at their hands; Darius narrowly escaped with his life. And now this marvellous man first conquers them and then makes friends of them. A week ago he took in a couple of days a place which every one pronounced to be impregnable: the 'Sogdian Rock,' they called it. Never before had man entered it except with the good will of those who held it. It was a rock some two hundred cubits high, rising almost sheer on every side, though, of course, when one looked closely at it, there were ledges and jutting points on which an expert climber could put his foot. The king summoned the barbarians to surrender. If they would, he said, they should go away unharmed, and carry all their property with them. They laughed at him. 'If you have any soldiers with wings, you should send them,' they said, 'we are not afraid of any others.' The same day the king called an assembly of the soldiers. 'You see that rock,' he said, 'we must have it. The man who first climbs to the top shall have twelve talents, the second eleven, the third ten, and so on. I give twelve prizes; twelve will be enough.' That night three hundred men started for this strange race. They took their iron tent-pegs with them, to drive into the ice or the ground, as it might be, and ropes to haul themselves up by. Thirty fell and were killed. The rest reached the top, the barbarians not having the least idea that the attempt was being made. At dawn Alexander sent the herald again. 'Alexander,' he said, 'has sent his soldiers with wings, and bids you surrender.' They looked round, and the men were standing on the top. They did not so much as strike a single blow for themselves. It is true that others did this for the king. But this is the marvel of him. Not only does he achieve the impossible himself, but he makes other achieve it for him.

"We have fought and won a great battle, greater by far than Granicus, or Issus, or Arbela. We had crossed the Indus—I talk, you see, familiarly of rivers of which a year or two ago scarcely any one had ever heard the name— and had come to the Hydaspes. There a certain Porus, king of the region that lies to the eastward of that river, was encamped on the opposite bank. Our Indian allies—happily the tribes here have the fiercest feuds among themselves—said that he was by far the most powerful prince in the whole country. And indeed when we came to deal with his army we found it a most formidable force, not a few good troops with an enormous multitude of helpless creatures who did nothing but block up the way, but really well-armed, well-disciplined soldiers. The first thing was to get across the river. It was quite clear that Porus was not going to let us get over at our own time and in our own way, as Darius let us get across the Euphrates and the Tigris. You would have admired the magnificent strategy by which Alexander managed it. First, he put the enemy off their guard by a number of false alarms. Day after day he made feints of attempting the passage, till Porus did not think it worth while to take any notice of them. Then he gave out that he should not really attempt it till the river became fordable, that is, quite late in the summer. Meanwhile he was making preparations secretly. The place that he pitched upon was about seventeen miles above Porus's camp. The river divides there, flowing round a thickly-wooded island. To get to this island—a thing which could be done without any trouble—was to get, you see, half across the river. We had had a number of large boats for the crossing of the Indus. These were taken to pieces, carried across the country, and then put together again. Besides these there was a vast quantity of bladders. Craterus was left with about a third of the army opposite to Porus's camp. He was to make a feint of crossing, and convert it into a real attempt if he saw a chance of making good his landing. You see the real difficulty was in the enemy's elephants. Horses will not face elephants. If Porus moved his elephants away, then Craterus was to make the attempt in earnest. Some other troops were posted half way between the camp and the island. These were to make another feint. The king himself was going to force a passage at all hazards. Then came in his good luck, which is really almost as astonishing as his skill. There was a violent thunderstorm in the night. In the midst of this, while there was so much noise from the thunder and the torrents of rain that nothing could be heard on the opposite bank, the king's force got across to the island. Then, by another stroke of good fortune, the rain ceased, and the rest of the crossing was finished without having to strike a blow.

"Meanwhile Porus had heard that something was going on higher up the river, and sent a detachment of cavalry under one of his sons to defend the bank. It was too late. If they had come while we were crossing, they might have made the work very difficult. As it was, they were simply crushed by our cavalry.

"Then we marched on—I had crossed, I should have told you, with the king—and about half way to Porus's camp, found him with his army drawn up. Very formidable it looked, I assure you. In front of the centre were the elephants. We had never met elephants before. Some of our men had never even seen them. I think now, after trial of them, that they look a great deal worse than they are; but at the time they alarmed me very much. How our lines could stand firm against such monsters I could not think. On the wings were the chariots, with four horses all of them. Each chariot had six men in it, two heavily-armed, two archers, and two drivers. The cavalry were posted behind the chariots, and the infantry behind the elephants.

"Alexander began by sending the mounted archers into action, by way of clearing the way for himself and his cavalry. The archers sent a shower of arrows on the chariots in front of the left wing. These were closely packed together, and made an excellent mark. Some of the arrows, I observed, fell among the cavalry behind them. Meanwhile Alexander, with the élite of the cavalry, had gained one of their flanks, while Cœnus threatened the other.

They tried to form a double front. While they were making the change, the king fell upon them like a thunderbolt. They held their own for a short time; but our cavalry was too heavy for them. They fell back upon the elephants.

"Here there was a check. At one time I thought there was going to be more than a check. Our horses could not be brought to face the great brutes; the horses of the Indians were used to them, and moved in and out among them freely. Nor could the phalanx stand against them. The long spears were simply brushed aside like so many straws when an elephant moved up against the line. If their drivers could have kept them under control, it must have gone hard with us. But they could not. There are thin places in the animal's skin where it can be easily wounded; and when it is wounded it is at least as dangerous to friends as to enemies. Only a few of the creatures were killed, but many became quite unmanageable. At last, as if by common consent—and this was one of the most curious things I had ever seen—such as were still serviceable, turned and left the field. They seemed to know that they were beaten. Indeed, I have since been told that their sagacity is wonderful.

"Porus was mounted on the largest elephant, and, I suppose, the bravest, for it was the last to turn. The king had been wounded in several places, and was faint with loss of blood. The driver of his elephant was afraid that he would fall, and made his beast kneel. Just then Alexander came up; and thinking that the king was dead ordered his body to be stripped of the arms, which were of very fine workmanship, I may tell you. The elephant, when it saw this, caught up its master with its trunk, and lifted him to its back, and then began to lay about it furiously. It was soon killed, but not till it had done great deal of mischief. King Porus was carried to our camp by Alexander's orders, and attended to by the physicians with the greatest care. When he was recovered of his wounds, and this it did not take him long to do, for these Indians are amazingly healthy people, he was brought before the king. I was there, and a more splendidly handsome man, I never saw. 'How would you have me treat you?' asked Alexander. 'As a king should treat a king,' was the answer. And so, I hear, it is to be. Porus is to be restored to his throne, and a large tract of country is to be added to his dominions.

"We have had a great festival of Bacchus. The god himself was represented riding on a tiger, which, by the way, was very well made up. After the procession there was a competition in drinking wine. What marvellous amounts these Indians drank! One swallowed twenty-three pints and got the prize. He lived only four days afterwards.

"At last we have turned back. We came to a river called the Hyphasis, beyond which, our guide told us, there lived Indians bigger and stronger than any that we had hitherto seen. All this, as you may suppose, fired the king's fancy, and made him more anxious than ever to go on. But the soldiers began to murmur. 'They had gone far enough,' they said. 'Was there ever to be an end? Were they ever to see their country again?' Then Alexander called the men together, and expounded his great scheme. I cannot pretend to give you his geography, for I did not understand it. But I remember he told us that if we went on far enough we should come out somewhere by the Pillars of Hercules. His promises were magnificent; and indeed if we were to conquer the world, they could not be too big. His speech ended, he asked our opinion. Any one that differed from him was to express his views freely. This is just what we have been learning not to do. In fact, he is less and less able to bear free speech. There was a long silence. 'Speak out,' the king said again and again; but no one rose. At last Cœnus, the oldest, you know of the generals, came forward. The substance of what he said was this: 'The more you have done, the more bound you are to consider whether you have not done enough. How few remain of those who set out with you, you know. Let those few enjoy the fruits of their toils and dangers. Splendid those fruits are; we were poor, and we are wealthy; we were obscure, and we are famous throughout the world. Let us enjoy our wealth and our honours at home. And you, sire, are wanted elsewhere, in your own kingdom which you left ten years ago, and in Greece which your absence has made unquiet. If you wish henceforth to lead a new army, to conquer Carthage and the lands that border on the Ocean, you will find volunteers in abundance to follow you, all the more easily when they shall see us return to enjoy in peace all that you have given us.' The king was greatly troubled—that was evident in his face—but he said nothing, and dismissed us. The next day he called us together again, and briefly said that he should carry out his purpose; we might do as we pleased. Then he shut himself up in his tent two days. He hoped, I fancy, that the men would yield. As there was no sign of any change in their feelings, he gave way, but in his own fashion. He ordered sacrifice to be offered as usual. The soothsayer reported that the signs were adverse. Then we were called together a third time. "The will of the gods," he said, "seems to favour you, not me. Let it be so. We will turn back.' You should have heard the shout that the men sent up! Having yielded the king did everything with the best grace, behaving as if he were as glad to go back as the rest of us."

Along with this letter Charidemus received a despatch from the king requiring his presence at Babylon in a year and a half's time from the date of writing.

The End

CHARIDEMUS arrived at Babylon punctually at the time appointed, reaching it at a date which may be put in our reckoning as early in January, 323. Alexander had not arrived, but was on his way from Susa.

A week after his arrival he had the pleasure of meeting his Theban friend, who had been sent on in advance to superintend the final arrangements for a ceremony which occupied most of the king's thoughts at this time, the funeral of Hephaestion. For Hephaestion was dead, killed by a fever, not very serious in itself, but aggravated by the patient's folly and intemperance, and Al-

134

exander was resolved to honour him with obsequies more splendid than had ever before been bestowed on mortal man. The outlay had already reached ten thousand talents, and at least two thousand more would have to be spent before the whole scheme was carried out. And then there were chapels to be built and priesthoods endowed, for the oracle of Ammon had declared that the dead man might be lawfully worshipped as a hero, though it had forbidden the divine honours which it was asked to sanction.

In April the king reached Babylon. The soothsayers had warned him not to enter the city. He might have heeded their advice but for the advice of his counsellor, the Greek sophist Anaxarchus, who had permanently secured his favour by his extravagant flatteries. "The priests of Belus," he suggested, "have been embezzling the revenues of the temple, and they don't want to have you looking into their affairs." His stay was brief; the funeral preparations were not complete, and he started for a voyage of some weeks among the marshes of the Euphrates, an expedition which probably did not benefit his health.

In June he returned, and, all being then ready, celebrated the funeral of his friend with all the pomp and solemnity with which it was possible to surround it. The beasts offered in sacrifice were enough to furnish ample meals for the whole army. Every soldier also received a large allowance of wine. The banquet given to the principal officers was one of extraordinary magnificence and prolonged even beyond what was usual with the king.

Two or three days afterwards the two friends were talking over the disquieting rumours about the king's health which were beginning to circulate through the city. They could not fail to remember the curious prediction which they had heard years before from the lips of Arioch, or to compare with it the recent warnings of the Babylonian soothsayers. Charondas, too, had a strange story to tell of Calanus, an Indian sage, who had accompanied the conqueror in his return from that country. Weary of life the man had deliberately burnt himself on a funeral pile raised by his own hands. Before mounting it he had bidden farewell to all his friends. The king alone he left without any salutation. "My friend," he had said, "I shall soon see you again."

When the friends reached their quarters they found Philip, the Acarnanian, waiting for them. The physician looked pale and anxious.

"Is the king ill?" they asked with one voice. "Seriously so," said Philip, "if what I hear be true."

"And have you prescribed for him?"

"He has not called me in; nor would he see me if I were to present myself. He has ceased to believe in physicians; soothsayers, prophets, quacks of every kind, have his confidence. Gladly would I go to him, though indeed a physician carries his life in his hand, if he seeks to cure our king or his friend. Poor Glaucias did his best for Hephaestion. But what can be expected when a patient in a fever eats a fowl and drinks a gallon of wine? Æsculapius himself

135

could not have saved his life. And then poor Glaucias is crucified because Hephaestion dies.

And, mark my words, the king will go the same way, unless he changes his manners. What with his own folly and the folly of his friends, there is no chance for him. You saw what he drank at the funeral banquet. Well, he had the sense to feel that he had had enough, and was going home, when Medius must induce him to sup with him, and he drinks as much more. Then comes a day of heavy sleep and then another supper, at which, I am told, he tried to drain the great cup of Hercules, and fell back senseless on his couch. The next morning he could not rise; and to-day, too, he has kept his bed. But he saw his generals in the afternoon and talked to them about his plans. I understood from Perdiccas that he seemed weak, but was as clear in mind as ever. And now, my friends, I should recommend you not to leave Babylon till this matter is settled one way or another. If Alexander should die—which the gods forbid–there is no knowing what may happen; and there is a proverb which I, and I dare say you, have often found to be true, that the absent always have the worst of it."

In obedience to this suggestion the two friends remained in Babylon, waiting anxiously for the development of events. On the second day after the conversation with Philip, recorded above, Charidemus met the admiral Nearchus, as he was returning from an interview with the king. "How is he?" he asked. "I can hardly say," replied the admiral. "To look at him, one would say that things were going very badly with him. But his energy is enormous. He had a long talk with me about the fleet. He knew everything; he foresaw everything. Sometimes his voice was so low that I could hardly hear him speak, but he never hesitated for a name or a fact. I believe that he knows the crew and the armament, and the stores of every ship in the fleet. And he seems to count on going. We are to start on the day after to-morrow. But it seems impossible."

Three days more passed in the same way. The councils of war were still held, and the king showed the same lively interest in all preparations, and still talked as if he were intending to take a part himself in the expedition. Then came a change for the worse. It could no longer be doubted that the end was near, and the dying man was asked to whom he bequeathed his kingdom. "To the strongest," he answered, and a faint smile played upon his lips as he said it. Afterwards an attendant heard him muttering to himself, "They will give me fine funeral games." The following day the generals came as usual; he knew them, but could not speak.

And now, human aid being despaired of, a final effort was made to get help from other powers. The desperately sick were sometimes brought into the temple of Serapis, the pleasure of the god having been first ascertained by a deputation of friends who spent the night in the temple. Accordingly seven of the chief officers of the army inquired of the deity whether he would that Alexander should be brought into the shrine. "Let him remain where he is," was the answer given in some mysterious way; and the king was left to die in peace.

One thing, however, still remained to be done. The news of the king's dangerous illness had spread through the army, and the men came thronging in tumultuous crowds about the gates of the palace. It was, too, impossible to quiet them. They would see him; they would know for themselves how he fared; if he was to be concealed, how could they be sure that some foul play was not being practised. The murmurs were too loud and angry, and the murmurers too powerful to be disregarded with impunity. The officers and a certain number of the soldiers, selected by their comrades, were to be admitted within the gates and into the sick chamber itself. It was a strange and pathetic sight. The dying king sat propped up with pillows on his couch. He had not, indeed, worn and wasted as were his features, the aspect of death. The fever had given a brilliance to his eyes and a flush to his cheek that seemed full of life. And he knew his visitors. He had a truly royal memory for faces, and there was not one among the long lines of veterans, weeping most of them with all the abandonment of grief which southern nations permit themselves, whom he did not recognize. Speak he could not, though now and then his lips were seen to move, as though there were something that he was eager to say. When Charondas passed him he seemed to be specially moved. He bent his head slightly—for he could not beckon with his hands, long since become powerless—as if he would speak with him. The Theban bent down and listened intently. He could never afterwards feel sure whether he had heard a sound or guessed the word from the movements of the lips, but he always retained an absolute conviction that the king uttered, or at least formed in his breath, the word "Dionysus." He had walked all his days in fear of the anger of the god. Now it had fallen upon him to the uttermost. Thebes was avenged by Babylon.

That evening the great conqueror died.

"There was some truth after all in what Arioch told us," said Charidemus to his friend, about a week after the death of the king, "though I have always felt sure that the spirit which he pretended to consult was a fraud. But was there not something which concerned ourselves?"

"Yes," replied Charondas, "I remember the words well. 'Happy are they who stand afar off and watch.' And indeed it scarcely needs a soothsayer to tell us that."

"You have heard, I dare say," said Charidemus, "of what Alexander was heard to whisper to himself. 'They will give me fine funeral games.' Have you a mind to take part in these same games?"

"Not I," replied his friend; "two or three of the big men will win great prizes, I doubt not; but little folk such as you and me will run great risk of being tripped up. But what are we to do?"

The Macedonian paused a few moments, "I have thought the matter over many times, and talked it over too with my wife, who has, if you will believe me, as sound a judgment as any of us. You see that standing out of the tumult, as I have been doing for the last five years and more, I have had, perhaps, better opportunities for seeing the matter on all sides. I always felt that if the king died young—and there was always too much reason to fear, quite apart from the chances of war, that he would—there would be a terrible struggle for the succession. No man living, I am sure, could take up the burden that he bore. Many a year will pass before the world sees another Alexander; but there will be kingdoms to be carved out of the empire. That I saw; and then I put to myself the question, what I should do. It seemed to me that there would be no really safe resting-place where a man might enjoy his life in peace and quietness in either Macedonia or Greece. I sometimes thought that there would be no such place anywhere. And then I recollected a delightful spot where I spent some of the happiest months of my life, while you were with the king in Egypt, that inland sea in the country of the Jews. If there is to be a haven of rest anywhere, it will be there. What say you? are you willing to leave the world and spend the rest of your days there?"

"Yes," said the Theban, "on conditions."

"And what are these conditions?"

"They do not depend upon you, though you may possibly help me to obtain them."

The conditions, as my readers may guess, were the consent of Miriam, the great-grand-daughter of Eleazar of Babylon, to share this retirement, and the approbation of her kinsfolk. These, not to prolong my story now that its main interest is over, were obtained without much difficulty. Eleazar was dead. Had he been alive, it is likely that he would have refused his consent, for he kept with no little strictness to the exclusive traditions of his race. His grandson and successor was more liberal, or, perhaps we should say, more latitudinarian in his views. Charondas bore a high reputation as a gallant and honourable man; and he had acquired a large fortune, as any high officer in Alexander's army could hardly fail to do, if he was gifted with ordinary prudence. A bag of jewels which he had brought back from India, and which were estimated as worth four hundred talents at the least, was one of the things, though it is only fair to say, not the chief thing that impressed the younger Eleazar in his favour. Miriam's consent had virtually been given long before.

Charidemus and his wife had a painful parting with Barsiné. She recognized the wisdom of their choice; but she refused to share their retirement. "I must keep my son," she said, "where his father placed him. Some day he may be called to succeed him, and his subjects must know where to find him."

In the spring of the following year the two households were happily established in two charming dwellings at the southern end of the Lake of Galilee. Though the friends never formally adopted the Jewish faith, they regarded it with such respect that they and their families became "Proselytes of the gate." It is needless to tell the story of their after lives. Let it suffice to say that these were singularly uneventful and singularly happy.